# The Mullah From Kashmir

*By the same author:*

DRUMS ALONG THE KHYBER
LIEUTENANT OF THE LINE
SADHU ON THE MOUNTAIN PEAK
THE GATES OF KUNARJA
THE RED DANIEL
SUBALTERN'S CHOICE
BY COMMAND OF THE VICEROY

# The Mullah From Kashmir

*An 'Ogilvie' novel*

by

## Duncan MacNeil

**HODDER AND STOUGHTON**
LONDON SYDNEY AUCKLAND TORONTO

# 1

THE MAN, SILENT as any cat intent upon a mouse, was no more than a momentary reflection of the moon on oiled naked skin as he scaled the perimeter fence and then dropped into a crouch, listening, waiting. Few sounds broke the night's stillness: the distant cry of a bird, the barking of a dog spasmodically, the crunch of a sentry's boots as he marched his post by the main gate into the Royal Strathpeys' cantonment. Having as it were assimilated these sounds, and having observed the otherwise silent aspect in the vicinity of the Officers' Mess, the man stole forward, sliding into the shadows in the lee of the cantonment buildings, where once again he remained for a while concealed. Moving on again, he gained the verandah: this, away from the direct moonlight, stood in shadow. The native seemed as light as a feather: as he moved across the boards of the verandah, there was not the smallest creak of woodwork. Against the wall of the building now, he reached out towards the shutters of a window and gently opened them. Throwing one leg across the sill, he went in. Carefully he pulled the shutters to behind him before approaching the officer lying sweat-soaked on the bed. It was no sound that brought James Ogilvie awake: it was some sixth sense, some awareness that he was not alone, some almost premonitive penetration of sleep that owed its being to a hard experience of Indian frontier life.

Remaining still, Ogilvie opened his eyes fractionally: the native was three paces from the bed. Ogilvie saw him only as a shadow deeper than the surrounding dark; he reached down and brought up his revolver from its place beside his bed on the floor, and like lightning squirmed clear of the single sheet that covered him, then fired. He had aimed to scare and not to hit: the bullet smashed into woodwork, the noise of the explosion was shattering. Ogilvie saw the shutters fly open and a body go through. He followed, calling out to the night sentry on the officers' quarters: the man was already doubling along the verandah from the right. Ogilvie snapped, "A native—that way. Get him! You can explain in the morning how he got past you." He raised his voice towards the guardroom by the main gate. "Sergeant of the Guard!"

"Sir!"

"Turn out the guard, man!"

"Turning out now, sir."

Orders were shouted into the night: men ran across, their rifles at the ready. Quickly the stand-by company was roused out, streamed half dressed to throw a too-late cordon around the perimeter: the native had already faded back to whence he came, unseen, unknown. By now the cantonment had come alive with men: as a crash of boots slammed the ground behind him, Ogilvie turned.

"Sar'nt Major—"

"Sir!"

Bosom Cunningham's hand quivered at the salute: two o'clock in the morning, and he was turned out as if for parade, his pace-stick beneath his left arm. "I'm told you were the intended victim. What did the man want, Captain Ogilvie, sir?"

Ogilvie shrugged. "I'm damned if I know! I know one thing, though: I'm having Private Drumblane on a charge for letting the fellow through. See to that, if you please, Sar'nt Major."

"Aye, sir, I'll do that. I've no doubt he was having a smoke—"

"The last he'll have for a while, then," Ogilvie said. "Where's the *chaudikah*?"

"I'll check, sir. And I'll muster the go-down too." The Regimental Sergeant-Major turned away, as angry as Ogilvie: it was unforgivable that anyone should penetrate living accommodation and the *chaudikah*, the night-watchman who should have been patrolling the compound for the express purpose of keeping off sneak-thieves and other marauders, would feel the full weight of his boot upon a cringing backside. Here on the North-West Frontier of India, close to the Khyber Pass and the warring Pathans who spilled over from Afghanistan to raid and plunder and kill, even the Peshawar cantonment was not secure, and

6

offered no excuse for a shameful lack of alertness. As Mr Cunningham sent a party of men under a colour-sergeant to rouse out and call the roll of the lowly inhabitants of the go-down, the large, white-walled enclosure occupied by the sweepers, Ogilvie turned again upon hearing his name spoken.

"James, what's all this about?" Andrew Black, Adjutant, smelling sourly of stale whisky, stared around the parade-ground with more than a touch of malevolence. Ogilvie explained, was given the impression he was being held in some way to blame for the intrusion and the disturbance of regimental sleep. Black said, "Well, the man appears to have made good his escape, does he not?"

"From the cantonment, yes. I presume you'll inform Brigade, and have a wider search made?"

"In the morning. I doubt if his intrusion is of much importance." Black pulled at his moustache. "Some petty thief—you say there was no personal attack?"

"No attack," Ogilvie agreed, "but I rather think my own reaction guaranteed that, Andrew! You're right it has the hallmarks of petty thievery, but the man should be caught, and taught a lesson."

\*         \*         \*

The man, as it happened, was found shortly after: at least, a discovery was made of a native body with a knife sticking from between the shoulder-blades. This discovery was made within a stone's throw of the Royal Strathspeys' cantonment; and Surgeon-Major Corton gave it as his opinion that death had occurred within the last hour. James Ogilvie, summoned by the Adjutant, was unable to give any positive identification but noted the fresh graze of a bullet on the left upper arm; and was intrigued to be told by the doctor that the body had had its tongue cut out.

"Recently?" he asked.

"As a matter of fact, yes. Very recently. In my judgement, after he paid you his visit—assuming it's the same man, that is."

"I think he is—that bullet graze." Ogilvie caught the eye of Colour-Sergeant MacTrease, who had been in charge of the detail that had found the body, scaring off some men who were probably the killers, men who had vanished rapidly into the night. "What d'you think, Colour MacTrease?"

"It's him, sir. The body's oiled as you can see, sir. That says

7

the bugger was up to no good, sir. And he was close to the barrack area too. And then there's the cutting-out of the tongue, sir. That says something also."

"Says what?"

"It looks to me, sir, very much like the native way of dealing with persons who've said—or are thought to have said—something out of turn, sir."

"What d'you mean by that, precisely?"

MacTrease shrugged. "I don't know, sir. This is India, sir. They're all as artful as bloody monkeys, sir. That's all I can say."

Ogilvie frowned. The removal of the tongue was not, in fact, the only strange circumstance in connection with the body. Ogilvie suspected, and suspected strongly, a religious connotation. The body was that of a young man, dressed in nothing but a loin-cloth, with thick oiled hair lank about the face rather than piled turban-wise upon the head, and it bore the caste mark of the Sundra, lowest of Hinduism's four main casts—and the man had been killed, for a certainty, by a Muslim: on the body had been irreverently deposited flesh from a cow, murdered flesh of sacred cow that no Hindu would have touched, be he Brahmin or degraded Sudra, offspring of the lowly feet of Brahma. Pondering on all this, Ogilvie went back to his bed but found no sleep: he was still pondering when Reveille brought the cantonment to life and the voices of the drill-sergeants began raucously to disturb the early-morning peace. At this moment, religion was very much in the air for British India, and Ogilvie fancied that the night's intruder could perhaps have come for more than petty thievery: in India where the impossible was often the commonplace and the unlikely was a part of life, the events of the night could conceivably impinge upon forthcoming and momentous movements of high personages that, casting their shadows before, had already disturbed the brooding peace of Lieutenant-General Francis Fettleworth's Divisional Headquarters in Nowshera...

\*     \*     \*

The Colonel, it seemed, was of similar mind. Ogilvie, about to carry out an after-breakfast inspection of company rifles, was approached by Lord Dornoch's runner.

"Captain Ogilvie, sir."

"Yes?"

8

"The Colonel's compliments, sir. He would like to see you at once."

"Thank you, MacKechnie." Ogilvie returned the man's salute and told off his senior subaltern to make the rifle inspection in his place. He marched across the parade-ground to the battalion office, smartly, returning the salutes of the drill sergeants on the way. In his office, Lord Dornoch was seated at his desk: the Adjutant was in attendance, standing moodily by the window and looking out across the dust of the parade-ground, dust thrown up by the busy marching feet as the Scots companies stamped and wheeled to the stentorian shouts of the NCOs. Dornoch looked up from his reading of a despatch.

"Ah, James—sit down if you please."

"Thank you, Colonel." Ogilvie sttod at ease, removed his Wolseley helmet, and relaxed into a basketwork chair before the Colonel's desk.

"This business during the night. More to it than meets the eye. The tongue-cutting, the defilement—all the circumstances. D'you follow me?"

"I think so, Colonel. I've had similar thoughts."

"Along the lines of religion?"

Ogilvie nodded. Thoughtfully, Dornoch filled his pipe from a silver tobacco-case. Within the last week intelligence had come through from Simla where His Excellency the Viceroy, forsaking Calcutta as usual during the monsoon season, was still in residence if only for a matter of a few weeks longer now that October was approaching with the end of the rains. Lord Elgin had conceived the notion that before returning east to Calcutta he would visit the Northern Army's First Division in Peshawar and Nowshera, paying thereby an immense compliment to Bloody Francis Fettleworth, Divisional Commander. The Commander-in-Chief in India, Sir George White, would be in waiting upon His Excellency: the pomp and ceremony would be tremendous and was looked forward to with mixed feelings by the officers of the garrison: when the rank-and-file were informed, the air would be blue. There was, however, another connected matter that was currently in the mind of James Ogilvie and also, it seemed, of Lord Dornoch: the reason for the state visit of His Excellency was not merely to gratify Bloody Francis, to whom pomp and circumstance was very heaven, but more importantly in the interest of affairs of state. His Excellency intended to make the long journey on from Peshawar to Srinagar and pay his respects, in the name of the Queen-Empress, to His Highness Pertab Singh, Maharajah of Jammu and Kashmir—who was of course a Hindu. It would be the state visit to end all state visits, for at this moment there was another visitor on his way to Peshawar and thence to Srinagar: Pertab Singh's distant-brother in religion, Sir Krishna-rajah Wadyar Bahadur IV, Maharajah of Mysore, being escorted north along the interminable miles of the sub-continent by his cavalry and infantry and elephants...

The Colonel's impatient voice broke into Ogilvie's thoughts: "Well, James?"

"An opportunity for someone to make trouble, Colonel—"

Dornoch slammed a fist into his palm. "Exactly! If the frontier tribes wish to stir things up in the most striking manner possible, they could scarcely do better than make their mark whilst two maharajahs are in conclave with a viceroy!"

"Then in last night's visitation, Colonel, you—"

"I suspect a link, James. The man who died was a Hindu—and after considering all the reports I've come to the conclusion that he was most probably the same man as came to your quarters." Dornoch paused. "Further—I believe it's quite possible he was seeking to make contact with a British officer."

"For what purpose, Colonel?"

Dornoch shrugged. "We don't know, do we? I've an idea we might have learned more if his killers had been taken—a great pity they were not! He may have had information to pass on, mayn't he?"

"It's possible, Colonel. But why choose me?"

"Perhaps he didn't—that could have been the sheerest chance, James. On the other hand, we could make out a case, I think, for his choosing you with intent. Consider the facts: you've worked for the Political Service on secondment—some time ago admittedly, but the fact remains. There will be people who remember. And there's another aspect that musn't be overlooked."

"Colonel?"

"Your father!"

"My father?"

"I mean," Dornoch said, holding a lighted match over the bowl of his pipe, "that you are the son of the General Officer Commanding, Northern Army! Now—d'you suppose that is germane, or not?"

Ogilvie stared. "An indirect contact with my father?"

"It's a suggestion. How does it strike you?"

"Knowing India . . . not entirely impossible." Glancing towards Andrew Black, Ogilvie noticed the sardonic look on the Adjutant's face: even in such a situation as this one, Black's nostrils were as ever aflare to catch the smell of nepotism. "It's an interesting theory, Colonel! Do you suppose it worth reporting to Brigade?"

Dornoch nodded, smiling slightly. "I believe the Political Officer might very well find it interesting as you say. Yes, I'll pass it on, James." He paused. "In the meantime, what do you know of Dasara?"

"Dasara . . . it's some sort of religious festival, isn't it, in the Hindu faith?"

Dornoch laughed: there was a sycophantic smirk from the Adjutant. Dornoch said, "An understatement! Dasara's a very big event—goes on for nine days and involves all manner of high ceremonial. But I gather it's not general to the whole of Hinduism —it's in fact particular to Mysore and to a goddess known as Chamundi. Chamundi had her origins a devil of a long time ago, but she's still there—in silver, sitting on a hilltop outside Mysore. Now do you see a connection?"

"I think so, Colonel. The Maharajah—"

"Is on his way here to Peshawar—precisely! And, by God, James, I'm now told he's bringing Dasara with him! He's due to make his entry in October, as you know—and October is the month of Dasara. Normally, the Maharajah wouldn't be on his travels during Dasara—he's supposed to be confined to his palace until the tenth day, when he goes in procession to Chamundi Hill and all manner of things take place. This year, an exception's being made and it's not being taken lightly. What does that suggest?"

"The importance of the meeting with the Maharajah of Jammu and Kashmir, Colonel?"

"Yes. And don't forget His Excellency! Nothing's been said specifically, but I have a feeling, and it's this: something important is brewing for British India. I'm highly suspicious of your nocturnal visitor, and I suggest you keep your eyes and ears open from now on. We don't want anything to go wrong in this command while His Excellency and Their Highnesses are within our protection."

11

"You mean whilst in Peshawar, Colonel? They won't—"

"Whilst in Peshawar, of course, but also inside Kashmir. Additional orders have reached me this morning, from General Fettleworth. As well as taking our part in the welcoming ceremonies and the parade and march-past of the garrison, we are ordered to join the Maharajah's escort into Kashmir, which journey will commence before the start of Dasara and will be accompanied by His Excellency and his retinue. It's a high honour...but by God, it's a big responsibility as well!"

\* \* \*

In the Sergeants' Mess, the Regimental Sergeant-Major stood with his back against the bar, temporarily closed and bereft of its native servants. In his hand, Cunningham carried a sheaf of notes; before him were assembled all the battalion's NCOs down to and including the lance-corporals.

Standing straight and square, minus helmet and Sam Browne belt, the RSM cleared his throat and began. "Dasara," he announced. "I am about to instruct you, gentlemen, in the meaning and ceremonies of Dasara, which is an affair of considerable *seriousness* to the Hindus and in particular to His Highness Sir Krishnaraja Wadyar Bahadur, Maharaja of Mysore." As concisely as possible, Cunningham outlined the concept of Dasara: in the days of very long ago, a tyrant with the head of a bull buffalo, named Maheshashur, a monster immune from human attack, had roamed southern India. To cut a long story short, said Cunningham, the destruction of this beast had been encompassed by Parvati, wife of the great god Siva, Destroyer of Life, who after attaining success in her task, and having also destroyed two more unpleasant spirits, had thereupon become a goddess in her own right and as such was worshipped.

"As to the ceremonies," the RSM went on loudly, "the Maharajah spends the nine days of what you might call the anniversary of the lady's battle inside his palace, *contemplating*. Also searching for the truth, et cetera. On that point, the bull from Division is not too precise and I will pass it over." He shuffled his papers. "During these nine days, which on this occasion will be spent not in his palace but in his howdah, Sir Krishnaraja Wadyar Bahadur does not wash nor have his clothing attended to. During the nine days, he is untouched by human hand.

12

Notwithstanding this, His Highness, during his confinement, will frequently be shriven and blessed. This will take place daily. During the shriving, there will no doubt be much coming and going of priests and whatnot. The full muster will be approximately seventy such priests. There will be no *laughing*. That is an order, and you will all see that it is obeyed. Laughing will entail a charge, gentlemen, and Captain Black has promised severity. He asks me to remind you that you'd not appreciate laughter at the kirk in Scotland. You will also remember that His Highness the Maharajah is a child, a wee boy of eleven, no more. Though he is no doubt acclimatised so to speak, it will be a strain for him such as you'd not inflict on your own bairns." The RSM studied his notes afresh. "There is much about jollity whilst His Highness is contemplating...wrestling, cavalry rides, dancing...waving of silk banners, and umbrellas with tassels, and yaks' tails...God bless my soul, it's a lot for a bairn to put up with!" There was a good deal more background, and the RSM proceeded patiently to the end of his instructions. Then, dismissing the corporals and lance-corporals, he ordered the re-opening of the bar and retired gratefully to a chair beneath a punkah with a glass of whisky. Yawning, he riffled again through Division's interpretation of Dasara: a religious man himself, Cunningham was appreciative of any man's worship, though he had a deep mistrust of a faith that involved so many gods when every Christian knew there was but one...and he had a feeling that on this occasion Dasara would prove somewhat abortive to His Highness of Mysore: normally the proceedings terminated at Chamundi Hill. This time, it would have to be done by proxy. His thoughts echoed those of his Colonel: there was something mighty big in the air. Take God—the God of the Scottish kirk: if you wanted to make a pilgrimage to Bethlehem, you didn't go to Birmingham...the RSM finished his whisky and called a bearer to refill his glass. He was a fighting soldier, not a minister, and the religious side must take its course. For his part he would see to it that every man in the battalion was ready for whatever might be coming.

\*     \*     \*

Next morning James Ogilvie was summoned to the office of the Political Officer attached to Division at Nowshera, whence he proceeded by the train. Major Blaise-Willoughby he had met

13

before: a portly man late of Skinner's Horse, accompanied wherever he went by a pet monkey named Wolseley. This morning Wolseley, innocent of any knowledge that he had been named after the Commander-in-Chief of the British Army, sat on Blaise-Willoughby's right shoulder, grinning and shelling a nut: fragments cascaded down the Political Officer's lapel; he seemed not to notice. He was too busy: his desk was piled with papers, an untidy mess. His clothing was rumpled as though he had slept fully clad; an unprepossessing sight to any regimental officer. He greeted Ogilvie perfunctorily, waved him to a chair which had first to be cleared of yet more paperwork, and then lost no time.

"That native, Ogilvie." He paused to fondle Wolseley. "I've had your Colonel's report."

"Yes?"

"I take it seriously, though I can't begin to see an actual link. We must not take risks, you'll realise that. I say I can't see a link, and I can't. But I have imagination or I wouldn't be a Political, would I? What I have in mind is this: you, your father, your regiment."

"Why my regiment?"

"Because, my dear chap, the 114th are detailed for the princely escort to Srinagar!" Blaise-Willoughby waved a hand, slightly dislodging Wolseley, who chattered angrily but went on eating. "It's far from precise, of course, but there may be something there." He leaned forward. "I'd like you to find out, Ogilvie. I have a plan."

Ogilvie said, "Go on, then."

"You've worked for the Political side before, so it won't come entirely strange. You speak Pushtu. You've plenty of experience of the Frontier and its peoples, you know the Pathan mind as well as anyone of your rank and service. And you've been contacted— or you may have been. At all events I intend to make that assumption until we know different." He paused, scanning Ogilvie's face "I want you to return the compliment."

"But—how, Major? What are you suggesting?"

"Make yourself available for a further contact."

"By doing what? I'm available now—aren't I?"

Blaise-Willoughby shook his head impatiently. "Far from it. An attempt has failed, a man has died—and been degraded into the bargain. They may not try again if you remain encased in regimentals and behind quarter-guards. You must mingle,

Ogilvie: you must go out into the alleys and the bazaars—and *attract* a contact!"

"D'you mean act as a spy?"

"I dislike the word," Blaise-Willoughby said, "I dislike it intensely, but it'll serve. You will go out as a native, Ogilvie, a Pathan—and see what you will see, find out what you will find out. We shall—"

"And my regiment, and the Colonel?"

Blaise-Willoughby glanced at a clock on the wall to Ogilvie's left. "By now I rather think Lord Dornoch will have had orders regarding your movements—"

"Orders from whom, Major?"

The Political Officer chuckled. "Word from our heavenly summit: Bloody Francis himself. He sets great store by Intelligence—and he's practically glued to his thunderbox with anxieties about being responsible for His Excellency! He expects great things from you, my dear fellow...."

# 2

TO A LARGE extent the British private soldier in India brought Britain with him to cantonments: his British possessions included his prejudices and his sense of humour; and not least among the indigenous things at which he poked fun were the various religions of the sub-continent. The beliefs, the objects of reverence, the sacred cows, the ringing of bells, the processions and the decorations and the physical postures of the faithful at prayer were his natural butts. Set alongside the dour, respectable ministers of Kirk and Church all the Indian religions—Mohammedan, Hindu, Parsi, Buddhist, Sikh, Jain—had their incongruous aspect and the barrack-rooms of the British Army seized upon them gleefully, but good-humouredly rather than viciously. In the Royal Strathspeys' cantonment, the Regimental Sergeant-Major's talk to the assembled NCOs was quickly made common property and loudly commented upon. The jokes were perhaps to be expected: the nine-day-long abstinence from washing on the part of His Highness of Mysore would lead to problems of hygiene that would perhaps be inflicted more upon the unfortunate officers of the escort than upon the common rank-and-file; the period of—in the RSM's words—His Highness' confinement to his howdah was capable of a double interpretation within the bawdy terms of reference of any barrack-room; and many were the mock words of command facetiously bellowed in the stentorian voices of the privates, urging the falling-in at the double of the shriving and blessing details and the mustering of the cooks at the field-kitchens to prepare food untouched, in accordance with the strict requirements of Dasara, by human hand. It was to be expected: and James Ogilvie, hearing some of the loud laughter and ribald comment from the barrack-rooms, grinned and passed on his way. Not so Captain Black before dinner in the anteroom of the Officers' Mess, drinking a *chota peg*. He was moved to break the 'no shop' rule.

"The company commanders must have a care," he said moodily. "A word in the ears of the colour-sergeants, I think. D'you hear me, James?"

Ogilvie nodded. "I hear you, Andrew, but I wouldn't take it too seriously."

"You would not?" The Adjutant gave a harsh laugh, and called for another *chota peg*. "Nevertheless, you'll do as I say. We must risk no upsets, no hurt susceptibilities that could lead to bloodshed—"

"Oh, they'll all be careful enough once they're in company with the natives, Andrew," Ogilvie broke in with a touch of impatience. Black glowered but said no more, clutching at the whisky glass when it was brought by a mess servant, throwing back the contents in a single gulp. Going in to dinner a few minutes after, Ogilvie looked at the scene through the eyes of a man to whom this night's formalities would be the last for some while at least: he was well enough aware of the dangers of the lonely mission that would start after midnight. Familiar as danger was to any man serving on the North West Frontier where life was held as cheap as dirt, Ogilvie found that his thoughts, projecting ahead to midnight, made the ordered brilliance of the Mess strike home that evening more sharply than usual. The gleam of the regimental silver down the table's centre reflected the lamp-light as it struck down from the branched candlesticks; from the great loving-cup, supported by four intricately-worked silver Highlanders, that, filled with port, was by regimental tradition passed from hand to hand on guest nights after the drinking of the toast to the Sovereign; from the MacIndall snuff-box presented to the mess by the regiment's last survivor of Corunna—every piece telling of the fighting history of the 114th Highlanders, The Queen's Own Royal Strathspeys. As the officers assembled for dinner, Ogilvie watched the play of yellow lamplight on starched white shirt-fronts, on the scarlet mess jackets and the tartan waistcoats, on the gilded stars and crowns of rank, on the subdued colours of the dress kilts and the hafts of the *skean dhus* pushed to regulation depth into the stockings, on the shining, spotless white of the tunic of the corporal of mess servants and the white gloves of the

17

native bearers standing ready to serve the meal. He looked along towards the Colonel at the head of the long table: in that chair two Ogilvies had sat before Lord Dornoch—Ogilvie's father and grandfather, before moving on to command brigades and subsequently larger army formations. The name of Ogilvie of Corriecraig was as much a part of the history of the Royal Strathspeys as was the mess silver, as were the Queen's and regimental colours with their battle honours and the proud badge of the 114th. Nor was Ogilvie the only name to recur through the generations: the Earls of Dornoch had a tradition of service; so had the MacKinlays and the Stuarts, while in the Sergeants' Mess and in the barrack-rooms were many sons and grandsons of those who had served in the past. The regiment was a family: the exception was its Adjutant, Andrew Black, a man of small Scots blood but much Sassenach money from his mother's side, a man efficient enough but humourless and seldom understanding of the independent ways of Scots soldiers. Ogilvie gave a somewhat grim smile to himself as he looked across the white tablecloth towards Black's dour, sallow face, long and thin like the man himself, cut into by a thin, dark moustache: if anybody should upset His Highness the Maharajah of Mysore, then that man was more than likely to be Captain Black!

Nevertheless, Ogilvie, before going early to his room after dinner, took his senior subaltern aside for a moment. "A word of shop if you don't mind, Neil, since you'll be taking over the company from midnight. Andrew's worried about religious matters!"

Neil Baird laughed. "Tell me more!"

"It's not a joke to our Adjutant." Ogilvie explained. "You'd better warn Colour MacTrease. I don't want to find you all in irons when I get back!"

"I'll see to it." Baird held out a hand. "Good luck, James. Look after yourself."

They shook hands. Ogilvie turned away to snatch a couple of hours' sleep before midnight. Taking off his uniform he stretched out on the *charpoy* beneath the mosquito netting, a towel around his middle. No sleep came, and he was wide awake when his bearer called him.

"Captain Ogilvie Sahib, it is—"

"All right, Kasim, thank you."

"Is there anything you require, Sahib?"

"Only the Farrier-Sergeant Sahib. Tell him I'm ready."

"Yes, Sahib. The Farrier-Sergeant Sahib waits now, Sahib." The bearer went out onto the verandah; a moment later the Farrier-Sergeant knocked and entered, carrying a canvas hold-all and a Gladstone bag. He was grinning all over his face.

"What's the joke, Sar'nt Burnie?"

"Sir, I'm thinking the joke's going to be you, when you're done up—"

"All right, all right! It's no joke to me, Burnie. What have you got there?"

Sergeant Burnie tipped out the contents of the hold-all and the Gladstone bag. Oddly perhaps for his rank of farrier-sergeant, Burnie was a master of disguise and over the years in India had performed miracles for soldiers' concert-parties, giving the Royal Strathspeys an unusual reputation for authenticity in performing characters of both sexes. Out of the containers came dark, sober clothing and a flat-shaped black hat; also grease-paints and other materials for altering facial appearance and darkening hair. With no time lost the Farrier-Sergeant got to work on Ogilvie: a look in the mirror when he had finished showed the perfect priest, dog-collared and with a black drooping moustache in place of Ogilvie's own fair, tightly-clipped one, now shaven. His skin looked as sallow as that of the Adjutant, and lines of age and a long if vicarious experience of sin drove clefts from his nose to the corners of his mouth.

He studied the reflection critically. "Beautifully done, Sar'nt!"

"Aye, sir, you're a credit to me." Burnie wiped the back of a hand across his face. "Is there anything else you want, Captain Ogilvie, sir? Bibles, hassocks and cassocks—"

"Don't let's overdo it."

"—Church Hymnals, communion sets, chalices, confetti, candles, bishops' rings—"

"Oh, put a sock in it, Sar'nt Burnie! All I want is my horse—and a tight shut mouth from you."

"That's understood, of course, sir." Burnie added, "Your horse is waiting, sir." Ogilvie nodded and went out onto the verandah. There was a high moon silvering the parade ground, and the air was very still. The footfalls of the gate sentry could be heard clearly as Ogilvie took over his horse from a waiting *syce*, mounted, and walked the animal across the sandy space towards the quarter-guard. As he drew level, the guard sergeant, who had

19

been warned that a priest would be riding out, saluted. Ogilvie stopped his return salute in time, and managed instead to remove his black hat with a flourish. Moving through the gateway out of the cantonment he headed towards the city, and after covering the two miles to Peshawar began to pass through the mean alleys with their bundles of humanity lying in their huddled, filthy rags in the shadows of the clustered shacks, the stench of the open drains sharp and foul in his nostrils: scenes and smells with which he would shortly need to become rather more familiar. Coming out into open country on Peshawar's north-eastern perimeter he headed on towards Nowshera.

\*     \*     \*

Some five miles short of Nowshera, with the moon now going down the sky against the far distant backcloth of Himalaya's foothills, Ogilvie came to the remnant of a deserted village, a native village that some while previously had been burned down as a reprisal for the murderous attacks of its inhabitants upon British patrols. The place had been left in too great a state of ruination for any attempt at re-emergence: and few of the villagers had in any case been left alive by the punitive expedition. The survivors were believed to have taken to the hills. Approaching this stricken place, Ogilvie caught the brief glimmer of a lantern from behind a half demolished wall. He rode on, slowing his horse to a walk. As he moved along he heard the sharp clatter of a flung stone that descended into some rubble beside his horse.

He reined his mount in, and looked around. Once more the lantern's flicker was seen. Ogilvie remained motionless, silhouetted in the moonlight, waiting. There was the sound of footsteps, of dislodged rubble, an eerie sound in the otherwise deserted village: a figure came into view—Blaise-Willoughby from Division, emerging with his lantern from the lee of the broken wall. Inevitably on his shoulder sat Wolseley, chattering anxiously.

Blaise-Willoughby approached. "Well done, Ogilvie." Before the Political Officer had extinguished his lantern, its light had caught Ogilvie's clerical collar. "You make a good parson, at all events in appearance. I wouldn't swear as to the morals!"

"No more would I, Major," Ogilvie answered with meaning.

Blaise-Willoughby seemed to understand. "You refer to your task, I presume?"

"Yes."

"It's a necessary trade." There was a cold wind blowing: Wolseley tucked down into Blaise-Willoughby's neck, staring angrily at the mounted intruder. "Well, we won't waste time on a discussion of ethics. If you'll kindly dismount, I'll take over your horse."

Ogilvie swung himself to the ground. Blaise-Willoughby said, "Follow me," and turned away towards a broken hut where the roof was at least partially intact still. He went inside, hitching Ogilvie's horse to a charred door-post. Ogilvie followed the Political Officer into the gloom of the hut. He heard the scratch as Blaise-Willoughby once again lit the lantern. Yellow light flickered off dirt and decay; clouds of dust rose stiflingly as Ogilvie moved: he gave a sudden sneeze, which made Blaise-Willoughby, whose back had been turned, jump a mile. Wolseley started his angry chatter again, and his master reached up a soothing hand, clicking his tongue at the source of the sneeze. "Careful," he said.

"There's no-one else around, is there?"

"No, but that's not the point, is it?"

"Isn't it? I'd have thought—"

"Oh, don't *argue*, Ogilvie." There was a flash of anger in the Political Officer's eyes as he swung round with his lit lantern, then he seemed to make an effort and shrugged. "I'm a little strung up, don't you know. It's the life I lead—it's not exactly regimental! You'll have to forgive me." He held the lantern up and studied Ogilvie's face. "You can shed that ridiculous moustache now." He reached up and jerked it away with a sudden sharp movement that hurt. "Skin'll have to be darkened—hair's all right. That man of yours did a good job."

"When it starts to grow out—"

"Oh, the job won't take that long—with luck, that is. You'll have to be punctilious about shaving, that's all. Now the skin. You'd better undress, strip right off. You won't need the clerical garb any more, except the boots—hide 'em well clear of Peshawar. I'll take the rest back to Division with your horse." He waved a hand towards a filthy pile of garments in a corner. "Spying order," he said, "to be worn at all times!"

Ogilvie began to undress. "I thought you didn't like the word spy, Major," he said.

"I don't normally, but I suppose you can take a joke. Hurry

21

up now, we haven't got all night—what's left of it." Blaise-Willoughby seemed anxious to be away back to Division, no doubt before dawn came up: he said as much as Ogilvie stepped out of his trousers, adding that he, Ogilvie, was to remain in the village throughout the day, stealing back on his tracks into Peshawar as soon as the next night's dark came down. When Ogilvie was stark naked, the Political Officer produced a bottle of what he said was a vegetable dye. "Quick drying and long lasting, but don't take a bath," he said. "Water won't take it all off, but it'll lighten you. You'll need a dab each day after shaving." With a rag he anointed Ogilvie, who was shivering in the keen night air, cold as the days were hot in these northern hills—not, as the wind blew, so far from the Himalayan and Kashmiri snows capping the high mountains. As it dried out, the dye left him colder than ever: the lantern showed him his darkened skin, a safe disguise for so long as his knowledge of Pushtu and the ways of India held out. Blaise-Willoughby seemed to sense his inner doubts, and uttered words of comfort as he dabbed and smoothed. "You've done it before, and very successfully—"

"As a British arms salesman. Not as a native."

"But it was a deception well maintained. I admit the difference, but remember you're not the first. It's being done all the time."

Ogilvie reflected on the truth of that statement: it was indeed being done all the time in the name of the British Raj, and with a success that was perhaps surprising until one considered the very vastness of the sub-continent, its myriad races and religions and dialects. One was always safe so long as one came from another part of India, barring accidents and the bad luck attendant upon falling in with a genuine native from the district whence you were supposed to have come...one prayed and kept one's powder dry and did one's best and if you were bowled out you accepted your rotten luck, kept your mouth tight shut, and joined the long roll of honour that listed the men, both soldiers and civilians, who had left their life's blood out here on the hills and plains of the Indian Empire to the greater glory of the Queen-Empress and the Raj...

Ogilvie gave a wry grin at his thoughts, his jingoism. The sentiments were those that were customarily expressed in similar phrases by high-ranking officers to the fresh drafts as they arrived on the North-West Frontier from home service: in his own case, they had been uttered by his father, then commanding the First

Division in Nowshera and Peshawar before being appointed to the command of the Northern Army as a whole. They were sentiments passionately held and implicitly believed in by the middling to older soldiers, both officers and other ranks. They were believed in by the younger men also—but those younger men had not, or were beginning not to have as the fresh drafts came out over the years, the same almost religious fervour about them. The funny side of pomposity was beginning to be noted by the irreverent, and, although the loyalest of regimental officers, Ogilvie himself was well aware of his own strong streak of irreverence growing in intensity each time he came into contact with, say, Bloody Francis Fettleworth and the special tone that pugnacious officer used when referring to Her Majesty...

Once again Blaise-Willoughby appeared to be in tune with his thoughts. The Political Officer, as he brought across the filthy native garments from the corner, spoke sombrely. "In the next few days, Ogilvie, you're going to need your patriotism more than when, for instance, you're out on patrol. There'll be no rifles and bayonets, no pipes and drums. I think you understand what I mean, don't you?"

Ogilvie nodded and pulled a stinking robe over his head. "Thoughts of the Raj will keep me going!"

"That's it exactly. That'll be all you'll have—you'll *need* it, as I said. It's something to hold fast to, isn't it? That's one of the reasons why it's all so important, even if Bloody Francis does overdo it on occasions. If you haven't got it, you're no damn use. I'd say—" Very suddenly, Blaise-Willoughby broke off, taking a sharp breath. In a whisper he said, "A sound outside. I'm going for a look-see. Stay where you are."

"I heard nothing, Major—"

"I have acute hearing. It may be just a hopeful vulture." Blaise-Willoughby slid past, stopped just inside the broken, doorless aperture that formed the sole entry to the hut, flattening himself to what was left of the wall. Ogilvie's horse stood patiently, its only sound its breathing. As he waited for what might happen, Ogilvie completed his dressing, inhaling the foul stench from the previous owner of the all-too-authentic garments, a stench of sweat and urine and grease horribly permeated by the heavy and unmistakable odour of bugs. Then, as suddenly as he had broken off in mid-sentence earlier, Blaise-Willoughby came out of cover and crouched in the doorway, his Service revolver in his hand.

There was a slight fall of rubble by the side of a building opposite, then Blaise-Willoughby had fired—once, twice. The explosions echoed off the empty desolation of the standing walls, a shattering sound in the night. The tethered horse jerked its head against the holding rein looped over the post; Blaise-Willoughby went forward at a fast run, his body bent and his gun ready to fire again. Ogilvie came out behind him. With satisfaction a moment later Blaise-Willoughby, upon whose shoulder Wolseley was still miraculously sitting, called, "Got the bugger, thank God! And for my money, he's on his own."

Blaise-Willoughby plunged down into a declivity beside the building. Ogilvie followed: flat on the ground, spread-eagled, was a native form, with lank, oily hair lying across his face and thickly blooded: half the head had been blown away, and brainmatter was oozing. The body was clad in a thick striped garment like a dressing-gown. The British officers looked down sombrely and Blaise-Willoughby said, "Hell and damnation. I'd hoped just to wing him. He'll not talk now, not with his tongue anyway! Or with anything else, since he doesn't look as though he has many possessions."

Blaise-Willoughby knelt by the dead man and riffled through the clothing. Looking up he said dismally, "Not a thing."

"Where was he from, d'you think?"

Blaise-Willoughby stood up, dusting his hands, looking down at the sluggish well of blood. "I don't know, but there's a look of the Tamil, I think—"

"Tamil—from Ceylon?"

Blaise-Willoughby said impatiently, "That's where the Tamils live, yes."

"Ceylon's a long way, Major!"

"A very long way, though not so far from Mysore as it happens."

Ogilvie caught his breath. "Mysore—the Maharajah? Do you suspect a link, then?"

"I've really no idea. I've nothing to go on, have I? But it's interesting, don't you think? Or could be. That is, if I'm right about him being a Tamil."

"Have you any theories?"

"None. It's all too long a shot. All I can say is this: you don't normally find Tamils on the North-West Frontier, and there *could* be a connection with the coming of the Maharajah—and his bloody Dasara!" Blaise-Willoughby's hand strayed up to his

24

shoulder and stroked the patient Wolseley, who uttered a sound of pleasure. "Don't ask me what the connection is, nor why our friend should have been lurking where he was."

"Could he have followed you, Major?"

"What on?" Blaise-Willoughby answered sardonically. "I was mounted, remember!"

"Then it's just chance?"

"Perhaps. And perhaps not. I shall be working on this, Ogilvie. It's just possible there's been a leak, I suppose—that someone knew about our meeting here. I don't like that, I don't like it at all. However, I see little gain for the enemy in the eavesdropping, since the man's dead!"

Ogilvie looked down at the corpse. "Does this mean any change in my orders, Major?"

"No, no change. Except that you should take this as a warning —and keep your eyes and ears even further open than you would have done." Blaise-Willoughby looked up at the sky to the east: dawn was not far off, a faint lightening was noticeable already above the hill-tops. The wind was coming down more keenly than before, but would probably die with the dawning that would bring in another burning day of intense Indian heat. "I've delayed too long already—I'll be off. I'll leave you to bury the dead, Ogilvie!"

"Bury him?"

"You've a long day to pass in his company, and the vultures will be down any minute now. And if there should be any passers by, we don't want him seen." Blaise-Willoughby moved towards his horse, tethered on the far side of the hut they had been using. Ogilvie followed. Blaise-Willoughby said, "Don't dig a grave, just cover him with rubble, that's all." He took the bridle of Ogilvie's horse: he would take the animal to Nowshera on a leading-rein. "Good luck, my dear chap. Do your best. We're in urgent need of information, as you know." He held out a hand, which Ogilvie took. "Three days maximum. Unless you're on to anything by then, it's back into cantonments. You know how to contact me." He turned away and mounted his horse. Moving along the track into Nowshera, he waved a hand; there was a strange air of finality. Wolseley looked back, grimacing, seeming to grin at Ogilvie's loneliness. The hoofbeats faded; horses and rider vanished into the lifting night, heading for the comforts of Division, the luxury of the headquarters mess. Ogilvie looked

25

around at his stark surroundings, the stench of his garments heavy and horrible in his nostrils, the darkening dye seeming to tighten and constrict his skin. As he walked slowly back across the ruination of the central village track towards the dead Tamil, if Tamil he was, he would have given much to hear the distant and approaching sound of the battalion's pipes and drums beating a savage and exultant reminder of Scotland off the frontier hills. Deciding to get the burial over and done with before the full heat of the day struck, he made for the declivity and began knocking the rubble of the tottery hut walls down upon the body. More rubble had to be fetched, and the task took longer than he had thought. Before he had finished the vultures had gathered, their strange telegraph bringing to them the tidings of food. They hovered and swooped and perched precariously on the walls and broken roofs, tilting backward and forward in greedy eagerness, uttering raucous cries, taking not the least notice of the chunks of rubble and stone that Ogilvie flung at them, shouting obscenities as he did so. The vultures he had loathed from his first day in India; so often on active service those birds of prey had formed the only grave, a revolting mobile one, for British soldiers killed along the wicked passes and on the cruel sun-baked hills; at the back of his mind was ever the inescapable knowledge that one day those sharp, blood-stained beaks might tear and rip and tug at his own flesh. Today it was not just the vultures: also before his task was done the ants had emerged—big ones, reddish ones with probosces that dug sharply into flaccid flesh, and ate and carried in never-ending streams.

# 3

A LONELY DAY, passed in the company of vultures and of the dead: making his way across to the declivity to scare away the still-clamorous carrion birds, Ogilvie found that his task of concealment had not been completed as properly as full conscientiousness dictated. From beneath the pile of stones and rubble a hand protruded—or what had been a hand. Now, just the bones were left, starkly cleaned. Ogilvie turned away: death, as such, after his years on the North-West Frontier, no longer sickened him. It was the inevitable marching companion of virtually every extended patrol among the hills of tribal territory, land well watched and jealously guarded by the Pathans, their eyes hawk-like behind the steady jezails, those strange long-barrelled rifles of a former age still in continual use by the men of the warring frontier tribes. Yet even now death was not something with which to pass a day of high sun and heat: as noon passed, the smell was already rising. Ogilvie wished the hours away to sundown; and as soon as the light was at last gone he turned back thankfully upon the track to Peshawar, making his way like a shadow on shod feet across the stones and sun-hard mud: the parsonic boots would be cast and concealed before he reached the outskirts of Peshawar and after that his bare skin would take the brunt. As he plodded on he thought, as for much of the day he had thought, about the dead Tamil: at his first meeting with Major Blaise-Willoughby in Nowshera, it had been agreed that he would act the part of an itinerant trader from the country around Allahabad, a poor victim of banditry who had lost his stock and his mule and was now forced into the indignity of beggardom. The lonely hours had sewn the seeds of a possible

27

change of plan: could he not take over from the dead Tamil, a man from very far away indeed and thus a fairly secure prospect? There was temptation in this, but there were points against: one, though within the terms of reference of the Political Service it was acceptable to alter plans without authority from the high command as circumstances changed, Blaise-Willoughby had made no suggestions as to the Tamil; two, the Tamil could just possibly be known in the district. It would be better, perhaps, to seek to find the dead man's friends or contacts, if he had any in Peshawar, and then try to establish what his presence in the vicinity at this time of important meeting might mean.

*       *       *

It was cold again now: in spite of the exertion of fast movement through the night, in spite of the heavy thickness of the blanket-like garment, Ogilvie shivered as in the silver moonlight he stole back, barefoot now, into the sleazy native city of Peshawar. He shivered from distaste as much as from cold: bare feet were not the best props in any native quarter. He plunged into excrement both animal and human, into dark pools of filth from which the stench rose strong to overlie even that from the garment he wore. He flitted along past close-set dwellings watched now and again by dark faces from the nocturnal doorways. He stepped past sleeping bodies huddled in the shelter of walls, past dead bodies lying beside the foul open drains. He heard the whimperings of children coming from some of the clustered smelly buildings, low laughter coming from others, the laughter of the night-privacy of men and women; from one came a high scream, suddenly cut off into a gurgle of despair and death. Ogilvie moved on, aware of the increased beat of his heart. From a cross-alley ahead of him as he came deeper into the old Pathan city came danger: a large pariah dog, its eyes redly glinting in the moon's light, jaws open and fangs visible, long like knives and probably bearing the germs of rabies.

Ogilvie turned aside and flattened into a doorway: too late. Hackles up, the dog came straight for him, jaws drooling saliva. Gathering up the hem of his heavy robe, he twisted it around a fist which, as the dog sprang, he slammed against the point of the nose. There was a howl, and the animal slunk back, ready to attack again. Ogilvie bent and picked up a large, jagged stone: he hurled it at the dog before the next spring: it caught the forehead, and toppled the brute over. Taking advantage of its dazed condition, Ogilvie ran like the wind. Before he had covered twenty yards the great dog was again after him. As his bare foot stubbed hard against some projection in the rough track between the buildings, he crashed headlong, bruising a shoulder and rolling over to the brink of the drain running sluggish and smelly down the centre of the alley. As he brought himself up just short of the horrible flowing contents he heard an explosion, the single shot of a British Lee-Enfield rifle. There was a howl of pain, followed by another shot: then a military command and the sound of marching feet. An order was given to halt, and Ogilvie looked up from his undignified position to meet the eye of a corporal in command of a town patrol, men wearing the harp and elephant badges of the Connaught Rangers.

"On yer feet, then," the corporal said roughly. "The beast's as dead as a coffin nail. Get up, I said."

"Yes, Sahib." Ogilvie got to his feet. The corporal held finger and thumb against his nose. Ogilvie salaamed. "Thank you, Sahib—"

"You speak English, then?"

"A little, Sahib."

"Where do you live?"

"Sahib, I come from a village to the south of Allahabad. I was attacked, and my mule—"

"All right, all right, I don't want the story of yer bloody life. Hop it—bugger off—pronto. *Jaldi*!" The corporal's revolver was waved in his face.

"Yes, Sahib." Ogilvie salaamed again, then turned away in obedience of orders. The moment his back was to the corporal, an army boot took him hard on his rump, speeding him on his way. He fled, to the sound of ribaldry and laughter, notes of jeering. It was undignified to run from a dog, but it was also prudent when one thought of the germs of madness that could lie in a pariah's saliva... and it was undignified for a Captain of the Queen's Own Royal Strathspeys to be kicked in the behind by a corporal, no matter how illustrious that corporal's regiment! Running, Ogilvie grinned to himself: one day, it would be a tale to tell in the mess after dinner. But for now there were other matters to be considered: ahead of him a man had emerged from one of the sleazy buildings, and stood in his way.

"Stop, friend," this man said in Pushtu.

Ogilvie stopped, eyes narrowed.

"Why do you run so fast? From what, friend?"

"From a mad dog."

"And from the British, I think. I saw."

Ogilvie asked, "You saw the kick from the Corporal Sahib?"

The man spat on the ground, making a sound of anger and detestation. "Sahib is an Indian term of honour, is it not, one that should not be given the infidel." There was scorn in the voice. "Are you a man or a mouse, that you allow yourself to be kicked upon your way, and then run like a jackal?"

"I am but a poor man," Ogilvie said, putting on a whine. "A trader from Allahabad—"

"A long way. Yet you speak Pushtu?"

"It is necessary, since I trade often in these parts. On this occasion I was set upon by bandits. My mule—"

"You have lost everything?"

Ogilvie bowed his head. "I have lost everything."

The man seemed about to turn away, but checked himself. He said, "The British are coming again. Perhaps to deliver more kicks. Perhaps to die."

"Die?"

The man produced a knife from the sleeve of his garment, a long, undulating knife that shone in the moonlight. "I am quicker than they. I shall slit their throats. In the dawn their bodies will be found in the drain, and none shall speak of it afterwards—"

"No." Ogilvie laid a hand on the knife-arm. "You must know the British as I do. Reprisals will come, my friend, and Peshawar will suffer heavily." He paused, deciding to take a risk. "At this time especially, it would be unwise."

The eyes glittered. "At this time?"

Ogilvie said quietly. "The bazaars speak of an important meeting in Peshawar."

"You have heard of this?"

"The very rivers bubble with the news. His Excellency the Viceroy, and two maharajahs."

"Jammu and Kashmir, and Mysore. It is so indeed." The man looked back along the alley as the marching feet of the town patrol crunched closer. "You speak true words, perhaps, my friend. A better time will come, a more productive one. Come, we shall leave the British—for now." Putting a hand on Ogilvie's arm, he drew him a little way ahead and then down into the anonymity of a cross-alley, a narrower way than the main thoroughfare, a place of many doors, of many hovels. Some distance along, the native stopped and looked back: the Connaught Rangers' patrol crossed the end of the alley and disappeared; the footsteps faded. "Come," the man said again.

"Where do you lead me?" Ogilvie asked.

"To food and shelter, such as I am able to offer. It is not much."

"To me it will be all. You are kind, my good friend."

The man looked at Ogilvie's turban, wrapped around the embroidered *kullah.* "You are of the faith—of Islam. Being of the faith, you will know that the Prophet teaches us to respect our neighbours. Is this not written? Do you not expect that I should give help to another of the faith in his distress? Is this not right and proper, with no need to speak, in return, of kindness?"

Ogilvie, as they walked on fast, inclined his head. "It is so."

"Your name, friend?"

"Manzur Zakir Burki."

"*My* name is—Kamruddin Rashti. At least, some call me that." There was a throaty laugh. "You shall call me that, Manzur Zakir Burki, my friend. Have you further questions?"

Ogilvie said, "I have asked none, and shall ask none. What you wish to tell me, that shall you tell me. I am a poor man, a robbed man, and it is not for me to question a benefactor, Kamruddin Rashti."

"It is well." They walked on, slower now, and no more was said until, some while later, Kamruddin Rashti stopped by one of the huts and pushed its door open. Ogilvie followed him into thick darkness, heard him strike a light and saw him put it to the wick of a tallow lamp boat-shaped like an Aladdin's lamp. The flame flickered off bare mud walls, off an equally bare mud floor. In the centre of the room were the remains of a fire, now cold and dead; and in one corner, on a rough bed of rushes, lay a young woman beneath a coarse blanket, a woman now getting to her feet and clutching the blanket tightly to her body and hastily assuming her veil when she saw the stranger.

Kamruddin Rashti told her brusquely to leave them alone: without a word she hastened through another doorway, going as silently as a ghost. The native made no reference to her at all; but clearly she was his wife. Kamruddin Rashti indicated the

31

vacated bed in the corner. "Sleep," he said. "You have come a long way. You are hungry?" he added.

Hunger, in the interest of authenticity, had to be confessed to. Food was brought and forced down: Ogilvie was uncertain of the meal's content. Accompanying the food, which he managed to eat with a hungry air, was water of doubtful quality, but of necessity taken into the stomach. After this Kamruddin Rashti said, "Now sleep, which is as important to a man as food. In the morning, there will be more food. And talk." He made a wide gesture with both arms. "You are my guest, Manzur Zakir Burki."

Taking the tallow lamp with him, he left the room. Ogilvie listened for a moment to his fading footsteps, then groped his way to the rush bed and lay down. Danger, he knew, was all around him: *in the morning, talk.* That could mean many things and too much talk could loosen his disguise and pretence, though he had seemed to convince so far and in fact had a good working knowledge of the district and the city of Allahabad together with an awareness, gained from much study, of the Mohammedan religion and its tenets and practices. To have been seen to be kicked and insulted by the British town patrol had been fortuitous, but its apparent earnest of his status was not to be too far relied upon: Kamruddin Rashti did not look or sound a fool. On the other hand, a lack of suspicion on his part would be far from surprising: the strong undercurrent that was running against the British Raj in the ghettoes and hovels of the poor made it entirely logical for one man in Peshawar to greet another as an enemy of the British. There were the two separate Indias, and Ogilvie was now part of the other one, the one of the starving masses of the sub-continent, the one that was totally distinct from the India of the great princes, the maharajahs knee-deep in treasures of gold and rubies, emeralds and diamonds, the India of Her Majesty the Queen-Empress, of the Viceroy and his court, of Sir Iain Ogilvie and Bloody Francis Fettleworth and their strongly-guarded, luxurious headquarters. Here, though after the dawn he would be able to listen to the distant beat of the drummers and the wailing of pipes and fifes, and the strident bugle-calls over the British cantonments, the edict of the Raj stopped short of holding its sway in the minds of men: in the privacy of their filthy hovels, over the painful rumblings and distensions of their empty stomachs, they could harbour their mutinous thoughts without discovery... Ogilvie checked his ruminations. He was beginning to sound to himself as disaffected as the mutinous native elements themselves and that, for a British officer, would never do. All India did not have empty bellies—yet it did no harm, perhaps, to be aware of those that had! Such indeed was his task, and the more efficiently he became a dutiful intruder among the unfortunates, the more safely Bloody Francis could soak himself in thoughts of glory in an India happy and content to serve Her Majesty in distant Windsor...

After a long time, sleep came.

\*     \*     \*

Like the meal of the night before, breakfast revolted his stomach, but had to be got down: a mess of some kind of maize mixed with berries, after the obedient kneeling before Mahomet in answer to the *muezzin's* dawn call from the high towers of Peshawar. After this, the promised talk. The talk took place in the room alone, no more being seen of the young woman in whose bed Ogilvie had passed the night.

"You spoke, Manzur Zakir Burki, of a meeting of important men. What do you know of this?"

"I told you, Kamruddin Rashti."

"I wish now to be told all. Rumour speaks with many tongues, differently to different people."

Ogilvie shrugged, and did his talking, adding in fact little to what he had said the night before, and, it seemed, adding nothing to Kamruddin Rashti's own store of knowledge. But the native asked a cautious question that aroused Ogilvie's strong interest. Kamruddin asked, as it were casually and carelessly, "In your journey from Allahabad, my friend, did you hear words spoken against this meeting?"

"No, I did not. I fell in with but few men along the way."

"It is a lonely way, not well-trodden," Kamruddin said in apparent agreement and acceptance. "And in Allahabad, and in your own village of—what was the name of your village?"

"The village of Bezar. I heard nothing there, nor in Allahabad." Ogilvie asked his own question, innocently: "*Is* there talk against the meeting, Kamruddin Rashti?"

The man shrugged but gave no answer. He went on, "This side of Nowshera, by way of which city you perhaps came—"

"Yes."

"There is a village named Harazan. Through this you will have passed."

"I do not know."

"A village laid waste by the British." Kamruddin spat thickly into the dead remains of the fire. "Many people were killed, and the village burned. You saw this village?"

"There was one such."

"In this village...was there life?"

"I saw no life, Kamruddin Rashti."

"You are sure of this?"

Ogilvie said, "I am sure. I was struck with its quietness and desolation—if this is the village of which you speak."

Kamruddin Rashti gave a harsh laugh, humourless and grating. "It is the village of which many people speak in Peshawar and Nowshera, not I alone! Also, many people are anxious to know if life was in that village recently. But you cannot help them, Manzur Zakir Burki?"

"I cannot help them."

Kamruddin Rashti brooded, watching Ogilvie from the corner of his eye. "At what time, and on what day—yesterday perhaps—did you pass through Harazan?"

"The village that I think is Harazan...I passed through there yesterday, a little before the sun went down."

Kamruddin made no response to this: he sat on in silence, brooding still, his eyes hooded from Ogilvie. There was a curiously charged feeling in the atmosphere, as though great events waited in the wings. At last Kamruddin spoke again. "Many years have passed since the great mutiny against the British. The Raj is strong, perhaps too strong for its own good, my friend! In their strength, the British grow careless. Many of them give their lives to pleasure. Women, drink, horse racing, pig-sticking, polo." He paused again, then stared directly into Ogilvie's eyes. "What are your feelings for the British Raj, Manzur Zakir Burki?"

Ogilvie shrugged. "I am but a trader, a poor man—"

"Even so, you have opinions."

"Scarcely ones of interest."

"My friend, you belittle yourself." The Pathan leaned forward, frowning. "Each man counts. It is the single ones that make up the whole, and the whole grows and grows until it is vast and cannot be stopped. Myself I am but one of very many in Peshawar. Their voice is not yet heard but their numbers increase

34

so that soon the voice-box shall utter thunder. Too many have been, like you, kicked and defiled by the British soldiers. Even had I not encountered you, you would have fallen among friends had any other man seen you last night. Peshawar is becoming unsafe for the British."

"And will soon erupt?"

"Would you wish an eruption, friend?"

Ogilvie said humbly, "I have no particular love for the British, Kamruddin Rashti, it is true."

"Then lend us your help, that we may be stronger."

"How can I help? I am but a poor trader—"

"So you have said, and said again. A poor trader—from Bezar near Allahabad."

"So?"

Again Kamruddin leaned close to Ogilvie. "Tell me about Allahabad, about the feelings of the people in the city and the surrounding districts, and I shall pass the news to another quarter, Manzur Zakir Burki."

"But how will this help?"

"We must be able to know our strength. Communication between Peshawar and distant places is far from good, as you must know yourself. Occasionally, like you, a man comes, but this is seldom. If the people of Allahabad have feelings similar to ours, my friend, then this will give us extra heart and more power to our sinews thereby... for once the eruption comes, *that* great news will spread fast as it did in the days of the mutiny! Do you not see?"

"Yes, Kamruddin Rashti, I see well."

"Then you will tell me?"

"I have little to tell," Ogilvie answered. "Always it has behoved me to remain on good terms with the Raj and myself I have never uttered against the British. Thus none—or few— have uttered to me." He shrugged. "Naturally there are things that can be sensed by any experienced travelling trader...and I have sensed a certain disquiet, a certain hatred of the lordly ways of the British sahibs, more especially, perhaps, of the mem-sahibs. But that is all. And I must say this: here in Peshawar it still behoves me to remain on good terms with the British sahibs, and therefore I ask you to observe a reticence in speaking of anything I may have said to you, Kamruddin Rashti."

"Such wishes shall be respected."

Ogilvie inclined his head. "If I may be permitted a question…it is this: you spoke of passing my words to a certain quarter. May I know, please, what quarter this is? I have to consider—"

"We all have to consider many things, Manzur Zakir Burki, and one of them is our lives. There must be much discretion, and I cannot reveal anything further. If more is required of you, you will be informed. If a certain person wishes to talk to you, you will be taken to him secretly, but it is unlikely that this will be wanted. Meanwhile you shall regard my home as yours, Manzur Zakir Burki."

\*　　　\*　　　\*

The Pathan left, bound upon some errand the nature of which he forbore to tell Ogilvie. When he had gone Ogilvie found another man sitting in the filth of the alley, blocking the way out. This man said nothing on Ogilvie's approach, but looked upwards grinning: protruding a little way from a fold of his garment the tip of a knife showed briefly, catching the sunlight in a flash of steel. Ogilvie read the message plain: guest was simply a kinder word than prisoner. He went back into the room and sat again on the floor, his back against the wall. The hovel was silent, but outside the day had begun. The alley was thronged with people, men, women and children, the latter yelling at their play and mingling with mangy-looking dogs reminiscent of the brute of last night. Over the medley of sound there came the distant notes of bugles from the cantonments two miles to the west of the teeming native city: out there in peace and serenity the colour-guards of the battalions in their pipe-clayed belts and starched khaki-drill tunics would be presenting arms for the hoisting of the Queen's Colour. Yet from present tokens, mere straws in the wind as they might be, the ever fragile Pax Britannica could soon be shattered into a thousand fragments: if mutiny, jagged, cruel and bloody, was to meet the Viceroy upon his arrival the repercussions would echo around the world and topple governments in Calcutta and Whitehall. *If it happened—and it must not!* Ogilvie, seized with mounting impatience at his own terrible inactivity, understood only too well the implications of his chance meeting with Kamruddin Rashti: that he should so speedily have fallen into contact with potential insurgency, never mind that it was merely the fringe, clearly indicated the extent to which Peshawar had become suborned.

*    *    *

Kamruddin came back when the sun was overhead: the knife-bearer on guard outside was released from duty, and made off down the alley dragging one leg behind him, a withered stick. "You are wanted," the Pathan said to Ogilvie. Something unpleasant had crept into his tone, Ogilvie fancied, some kind of menace. "You are wanted, but not yet."

"When?"

"When the sun has left the sky, that will be the time."

"And for what am I wanted, Kamruddin Rashti?"

"Patience, friend."

The native sat on the floor opposite Ogilvie: he kept a hand inside his clothing, loosely held but, Ogilvie was sure, not far from the handle of a knife. Nothing more was said on either side; after an interval food was brought by Kamruddin's wife, veiled as before, lithe and silent in her movements as she laid down the two bowls and an earthen water-vessel to be shared between the two men. In silence she withdrew; in silence they ate: Ogilvie's nerves were jagged and once again the food caused gastric rebellion held in check with difficulty. After the meal the Pathan went out again and the relief guard returned for another spell of duty that lasted until evening brought some solace from the close heat of the hovel and a lessening of the raucous noises from the alley. Kamruddin returned this time in company: four hard-faced men, as silent as he, all beardless, all with moustaches and turbans and no other clothing save loin-cloths: men with the aspect of *thuggee* about them, as dangerous to the wolf in sheep's clothing as venomous serpents. Forming a watchful semi-circle they sat around the defunct central fire like potential executioners until, when the last of the daylight had faded, Kamruddin Rashti got to his feet and said, "Come, the time is now." He clapped his hands; the young wife came in, bringing a piece of heavy cloth which she placed over Ogilvie's eyes, tying the ends behind his head. He was acutely aware of her body as she performed her task, of the earthy smell of her. Blindfolded he was pushed forward, and stumbled over the fire cinders into the grip of one of the thugs. He felt each arm taken, and as he was pushed on into the alley there was the suggestive prick of a knife in his back. He was led on through the lying filth and variegated smells, unable to tell whether or not the procession was arousing any interest from passers-by; at one moment their progress was halted and he was pulled aside to stumble through a doorway, a rough hand pressed firmly over his mouth: the town patrol, he gathered, had been seen ahead. After this solitary interruption, the way was long and the pace fast. The nocturnal journey ended with Ogilvie being pushed through another doorway, a low one for which he had to bend almost double, and then a progress along what seemed to be a passage of stone or tiles, and a descent of worn stone steps into a cellar. Once down the steps Ogilvie heard muffled music, weird and tinny, Indian wind-instruments, and a monotonous throb of drums. As a door was opened the sound increased: Ogilvie was pushed on into a room heated by a press of bodies and pipes of opium, and aroused emotions. Suddenly the blindfold was snatched away and he saw scenes of orgy: in the dim light of flaring rush torches and a pall of smoke he saw the dancing girls, a dozen of them all stark naked, twisting, flinging up their arms, fondling their breasts, thrusting their pubics forward and wriggling their buttocks in the centre of a horde of entranced Pathans bearing jezails in the crooks of their arms. From the navel of one of the girls a brilliant ruby of immense size blazed red; another had a ring of emeralds fringing her pubic hair and held in place by Ogilvie knew not what agency. The music played, adding to the heady atmosphere of sex: the crowd grew frenzied as Ogilvie watched. Hands reached out to be laid on bare flesh that quickly, mockingly writhed away from the searching hairy fingers. Ogilvie was pushed on through the throng, none of its members paying him or his escort the smallest attention, and led towards a group sitting and watching from a recess at the far side of the cellar.

There were four men in the group: but one stood out.

He wore no turban, he was simply clad in white, a shapeless garment for all the world like a nightshirt but curiously gathered around his knees so that his thin brown legs stuck down like stalks thrust into sandals. The face was the striking force: hairless, as was his head—he was completely bald—it appeared to have an inbuilt shine like polished walnut. A deep scar, long and white, disfigured one side from temple to mouth. The nose was hawkish, the mouth wide, the teeth black and rotten. But the eyes held all the fire of heaven and hell in the boldness of their stare: it was like twin shafts of light, of rays boring into Ogilvie and cutting him through to the quick. A light blue in colour—rare for a Pathan but

38

not unique—the irises were very ice, and were a match for the square firmness of the jawbone.

Ogilvie felt drawn forward by the eyes. He was halted and held in front of the strange figure, suffered a feeling almost of being held in a magnetic field.

"You are Manzur Zakir Burki, from Bezar by Allahabad?"

"That is so."

"And you came yesterday by Harazan."

"That is also so."

"Seeing nothing. Is this also so, Manzur Zakir Burki?"

"It is also so."

The man smiled, a movement of the mouth alone: the eyes remained frozen in their ice. "Then you are a blind man, or one who deals in falsehood—"

"That, I deny."

The strange figure lifted a hand and spoke a few words in a dialect unknown to Ogilvie. At once his three companions got up, bowed, and went away, moving backwards as if withdrawing from the presence of a king or a god. Another gesture and Kamruddin and the four escorting thugs also withdrew. The man said, "Now we are alone. If you have anything to say, say it, and without falsehood, for I shall recognise falsehood for what it is."

Ogilvie met the magnetic eyes. "I have nothing to say beyond what I have said already to Kamruddin Rashti."

"Then I shall myself speak. But first, this." The man reached into a fold of his clothing and brought out his hand balled into a fist. Lifting the hand, he opened the fingers: something dropped to the cellar floor, and rolled. "Pick them up," the native ordered.

Ogilvie obeyed: kneeling, he scrabbled around. After a short search he found the dropped objects, and stood up with them in his hand: two bullets...two bullets from a cartridge of a pattern fired by a British service revolver.

"Removed from the body of a Tamil from Ceylon," the white-clad man said ominously. "A Tamil found dead in the stricken village of Harazan. Perhaps you can explain?"

Ogilvie licked his lips. "Master, I do not understand. How did these bullets reach Peshawar?"

"A watcher, a man concealed behind the crags upon the heights. A man friendly towards us and our ideals. This man espied a native emerging from a broken hut at daybreak yesterday, and casting stones to form a burial cairn upon a body. After dark,

39

when this native had left along the track into Peshawar on foot, the watcher descended from the heights and examined the body, and found what you now hold in your hand, Manzur Zakir Burki. Today he reached Peshawar." The eyes grew even colder. "Why have you told falsehoods, if you are a poor trader from Bezar with no apparent purpose in uttering lies about Harazan?"

Ogilvie lifted his hands in a gesture of despair and apology. "I was afraid, Master. Much afraid that I would be blamed for the death of the Tamil."

"You—to possess a revolver of the British Army? And why should you suspect that the death of a Tamil from Ceylon should cause us to blame anybody?"

"Because Kamruddin Rashti had spoken in particular of an anxiety to know if there had been life in Harazan...and thus I judged that the Tamil, whose body I confess I had indeed seen and given decent protection in death, was a part of your plan against the British."

"And this you swear?"

"This I swear, by the Prophet and upon the Koran."

There was a pause: behind Ogilvie the music continued, the dancing girls performed, the aroused Pathans murmured hoarsely in their pent-up passions that mounted now to a sound of climax. The weirdly god-like man said, "So be it. We shall see. We shall put you to the test, Manzur Zakir Burki." He gave a loud hand-clap: Kamruddin Rashti and the men of *thuggee* came back to the recess, swift, silent and utterly threatening. Once more Ogilvie was seized and hustled away, out through a door opening off the recess into another passage. This time there was no blindfold: when Ogilvie was thrust into a damp-smelling, vaulted chamber with walls of solid stone, he saw with a terrible clarity. In the centre of the room was a table, and behind it a chair. In the chair sat what appeared to be a major of the Bombay Light Infantry in full-dress uniform with epaulettes and gilded sword-belt, the white facings of the tunic dark with blood. Propped by some invisible means one arm, the hand that of a white man, rested on the table; the other, the right arm, was fixed rigid at the salute. But the saluting hand backed against no forehead, for the major had no head. The neck stood raw, cleanly cut, blood still welling, and the various tubes running from the torso to neck gaping white and flaccid.

# 4

SHAKEN TO THE core, Ogilvie stared at the terrible thing seated at the table: with a supreme effort he had held back on his first natural impulse, which had been to utter words of shock—in English. But his face, his eyes, were the give-away. Kamruddin Rashti and the man in white had come round from behind and looked.

"You are horrified, Manzur Zakir Burki from Bezar."

He answered in Pushtu: "It was a surprise. A headless man is not a usual sight."

"You are horrified because he is a British officer."

"No. Because I am a man of peace."

There was a laugh. "This you must prove. Are you not curious as to how the major came to lose his head?"

"If you tell me, I shall listen."

"Very well. It is a symbol. This major was easily taken, whilst riding with a mem-sahib and a guarding trooper outside the cantonments last night. The mem-sahib and the trooper were killed on the spot, and their bodies disposed of. The major was brought to this place, and beheaded this evening—"

"Do you not fear reprisals, a tooth-combing of all Peshawar?"

"We expect this in due course, but we do not fear it. This place is secure, and so far the search has not begun. I assure you, it will not immediately do so—"

"Why not, Master?"

The man in white smiled his cold and humourless grimace, giving a cryptic answer that puzzled Ogilvie: "Because the British are very respectable people, that is why!"

Clearly the man had no intention of elaborating. Ogilvie,

ashen-faced beneath the brown vegetable dye, said, "Master, you spoke of a symbol, but I fail to understand your meaning."

"The headless Raj," the man in white said softly, his eyes shining in the light from the torches held by the thugs. This time Ogilvie could not fail to take the point: within days now His Excellency the Viceroy of India would arrive in state, accompanied by all the panoply of imperial power, represented by the full-dress uniform upon the dead body in the chair. Major that body might in fact have been, or might not; in any case he would not have been out riding in that uniform. The man in white would no doubt have plenty of ways of obtaining British uniforms, even of having them made to his order by native regimental tailors—and the uniform would have been placed upon the major after capture to complete the symbolism of the headless Raj, and the fulfilment of the symbolism was to lie in the murder of the Viceroy.

*　　　*　　　*

Earlier, the man in white had spoken of Ogilvie being put to the test: and Ogilvie felt that they were still unsure about him. He had not given himself away entirely: though they might not see him as a recruit, he believed they had as yet not the smallest suspicion that he was a British officer—rather, they believed he could be on the British side, a loyal native supporter of the Raj; in which case, of course, they might still come to the correct conclusion that he was a spy for the British. In the meantime, though he remained closely guarded by the four thugs and kept in the presence of the headless body, there seemed to be no haste. Kamruddin Rashti and the man in white went back to the main cellar, presumably to continue their enjoyment of the dancing girls. As time went by Ogilvie began to shiver: here in this part of the cellar, and this he had noted on first entry, the air was cool. No doubt they were well below the level of the ground; the heat in the main cellar would have been due to the close-packed bodies and the aroused emotions. Watched by the four guards, whose knives were ready drawn, Ogilvie maintained a calm face but inwardly pondered with a degree of hopelessness on what form the 'test' might take: there were varying degrees of torture in the Indian armoury of horror. He had heard of many, had seen the results of some: wax tapers thrust beneath the finger-nails and lit to burn to their ends; the ripping off of the toe and finger-nails intact; the crushing of ankles by means of iron clamps; the crushing of other parts of the body, the testicles being one; in the case of women, other and perhaps more terrible atrocities. This was no more than a selection: the Indian mind was inventive and knew no bounds to cruelty and pain. For the sake of his sanity Ogilvie forced his thoughts away from horror and tried to concentrate on his mission for Major Blaise-Willoughby. It could now be considered certain that the splendid meeting between the Viceroy and one or both of the two maharajahs was to be the rallying-point for some powerful strike of war against the Raj, also that His Excellency was to be the prime target for the rebels. The time, the place and the man ... though far from certainty as to time and place. The revolt, the mutiny, might start at any time after the Viceroy's arrival in Peshawar or could be delayed until after he had left for Kashmir, even until his arrival in Srinagar. There was much yet to be learned, but unless he could get away the knowledge would never reach Division. Things had gone very badly wrong ... Ogilvie pulled himself up on that negative thought as well: things had not gone wrong yet; what had happened—the headless body apart—was only what was to be expected. Spies had to establish themselves. That had yet to be done. In the meantime he could only pray to his own God to intercede with the Prophet on his behalf. Thoughtfully he fingered his upper lip where once his moustache had been, felt the sprouting stubble, and lowered his eyelids against the stares of the thugs squatting on their haunches before him: the Prophet might not take kindly to God's pleas. It was still up to mortals, and something might yet be done to circumvent the test: Ogilvie was no hanger-back in battle, but knew his limitations. Every man under torture had his breaking-point: it was largely a matter of luck if death came before disclosure. And he knew it was vital to the defenders of the Raj that they should not be known even remotely to suspect any evil intentions against the Viceroy such as would lead them to send in a spy. It was of course true that every native bazaar in all India was from time to time the hunting-ground of the British Political Service and its agents; but of all times this was the one for the Service not to lift its head ...

Ogilvie opened his eyes and spoke to one of the thugs. "I have words for Kamruddin Rashti," he said. "If he will consent to come, I shall speak of matters of importance to him."

\*          \*          \*

The Pathan came, and stood looking down at Ogilvie, a wary gleam in his eye. "You wish to speak," he said in Pushtu. "Then speak, Manzur Zakir Burki."

Ogilvie inclined his head and moistened his lips. "I wish to speak more about the burned village of Harazan."

Kamruddin's eyes narrowed. "Speak, and quickly."

"It was not only the Tamil that I found. Upon reaching Harazan, great hunger overcame me, and I searched for scraps of food, anything that might have been left."

"This is natural. Yes?"

"In my search, I came upon what I did not expect to find. I found a sheet of paper, a letter. I have insufficient English to know the import...but the letter was from the great British General, Ogilvie Sahib, in Murree."

"And addressed to whom?"

"To another general in Nowshera, Fettleworth Sahib."

Kamruddin's eyes were hard. "Why did you not speak of this before?"

"I have said, I do not meddle in great affairs. I had no wish to be found in possession of such a paper, therefore I left it where it was. As to telling of it, it did not seem important that I should—"

"Then why speak now?"

"Because it is now clear that there is to be a blow struck against the Raj. If that is the case, I wish to help our people rather than the British. The paper came back into my mind. What does one general write about to another general, Kamruddin Rashti, but of military matters? Is it not possible that movement of British soldiers is mentioned on this piece of paper? And if His Excellency the Viceroy is coming to Peshawar—"

"Yes!" There was a savage note in the Pathan's voice now, and he paced the cellar, back and forth past the grisly thing at the table. "You shall tell me where this paper is, Manzur—"

"The village is derelict, all broken into rubbish as you know. To tell you will not be easy, and much time—"

"Then you shall come with us and show us. I shall speak now to the Mullah, who will be angry that you have wasted time." Kamruddin Rashti strode from the cellar, leaving Ogilvie to ponder on new information: the man in white was a Mullah! Mullahs, self-appointed though they were, did not grow upon

44

every bush. At momentous periods of eastern history, they manifested themselves as leaders of great causes either religious or secular. When discontent threw up a Mullah, it was time indeed for the British in India to watch closely to their defences and their armouries: this was something that would cause much alarm at Division. Mullahs, who seemed perennially to be ignited by a burning flame from within and to have immense sway over the minds of natives, rousing them by impassioned oratory to extreme violence, had not so far, to Ogilvie's knowledge, disturbed the serenity of Bloody Francis's high command; now he was going to burst a blood vessel.

\* \* \*

Blindfolded once again, and now with his hands tied behind his back, Ogilvie was brought up to ground level on the Mullah's order and lifted into a mule. A man rode on either side of him, steadying his body and keeping the mule on its course out of Peshawar for Harazan. The blindfold was removed when they came to the outskirts. They left the city unmolested, this time seeing not even the soldiers of the patrol. It seemed the Mullah had been right: there appeared to be no search parties out looking for the dead major. They made fair speed into Harazan, lying bright beneath the moon. Ogilvie was assisted down from the mule and his hands were untied. "Where is the paper?" Kamruddin Rashti asked.

Ogilvie pointed down the rubble-strewn track. "That way, Kamruddin Rashti. The third hut—at the back of it. Or perhaps the fourth."

"You shall make the search," the Pathan said. "Have a care for speed." He paused, looking closely at Ogilvie, and then asked, "During your search for food, you found nothing else in Harazan?"

"Nothing else. The letter only."

Kamruddin nodded, grunted, seeming satisfied. "Very well, Manzur Zakir Burki—the letter!"

Ogilvie turned away with the thugs and Kamruddin following close behind. He made for the third hut's ruins, going round to the back and pushing stones aside, ostensibly looking with care and concentration. He took his time; Kamruddin grew impatient, urging him on with sharp words. The moon was bright, showing every detail clear and starkly outlined but leaving deep shadow

45

behind such walls as still stood. Exhausting the possibilities of the third hut, Ogilvie moved on to the fourth and started again, patiently shifting the stones and rubble, sifting through the deep piles of dust drifted like sand up against the walls by the wind out of Himalaya. He was waiting for his chance and it seemed to come when the four thugs were momentarily out of contact around the eastern edge of the back wall.

"I believe I have found it," Ogilvie exclaimed.

"Where?"

"There." He pointed. "Do you see, Kamruddin Rashti? In a crevice of the wall, blown perhaps by the wind."

"I see nothing." Angrily, impatiently, the Pathan moved ahead of Ogilvie, bending for a better look. Already Ogilvie had a heavy chunk of rock in his hand. Striking hard for the head, he heard the crunch of bone as the skull stove in like an egg. As the body fell forward, he rolled it over quickly and grabbed for the knife, then called to the guards.

"Kamruddin has fallen and hurt himself!"

Heads appeared round the wall. One man came forward followed by another. The first man bent over the Pathan's body, fell slack as Ogilvie thrust the knife with full force into his stomach. The second man, coming on at the rush, met death the same way; then the remaining two had closed in, their knives gleaming in the moonlight. Ogilvie seized the knife-arm of one of the men and held it high in the air away from his body while the thug writhed and kicked. Before he had got a grip on the other man's arm, a knife had slashed down Ogilvie's right side, parting the skin beneath the thick garment. He felt the run of blood and a blinding pain, then he had his grip. Steadying himself against the double writhing, he lifted a knee and drove it with all his strength into the groin of one of the attackers. The man dropped screaming. Ogilvie bent to seize the knife, then started whirling the last of the thugs round and round, using the arm as a pivot. The full momentum gained, and using a final burst of effort, he let go and the thug crashed heavily and head first into the wall behind. The snap of the neck was loud enough to be heard. Panting with his exertions Ogilvie saw, just in time, the man whose groin he had kicked coming for him. He turned, holding the knife-blade steady: the thug ran full tilt onto it, though the final jerking thrust was Ogilvie's. With blood gushing from his neck, the man went down flat. Breathing hard, Ogilvie mopped at his sweat-streaked face with the sleeve of his garment. It had been a bloody night and God alone knew what next day would hold. But work he knew there would be: the Pathan's tone when he had asked him if he had found anything else in Harazan had intrigued him. A full-scale search might yield interesting results.

*     *     *

Patient, plodding work did yield those interesting results: by a little before noon next day, Ogilvie had found something totally unexpected yet something that slotted into place neatly enough. Buried beneath the ruination of one of the hovels he came upon a canister with British Army markings, a canister of TNT. Then another...and another, and another. More and more and more were laid bare as the sun crossed the sky. Not TNT alone: there was dynamite, gelignite and simple gunpowder, plus the more volatile fulminate of mercury to act as a detonator. Ogilvie did some fast thinking: he could perhaps make Nowshera before the Mullah sent out a search party to find his missing prisoner and escort, and there might be time for a detachment of sappers to come out and re-possess the pilfered British stores. On the other hand, there were four bodies...and it would be better from Blaise-Willoughby's point of view, no doubt, if the Mullah could be left in some doubt as to what had happened to them. Given something upon which to go, the Mullah might well be left to make an intelligent if wrong guess that would leave the British clear of any thought on his part that they had had access to his secrets. Ogilvie looked around, assessing the lie of the land and the possible cover. That cover was minimal but it was worth a risk: he could run fast. Quickly he broke open four canisters of gunpowder, leaving a pile of freed powder in the centre of the explosives, and ran a rough fuse-trail of powder from there to a point some thirty yards clear. This done, he manhandled the bodies of Kamruddin Rashti and the thugs, already half consumed by the eager vultures, from behind the wall and dumped them on top of the explosives, pursued the while by the slashing beaks of the infuriated birds: by the time he had finished he was covered with his own blood. Finally, using the bush lore learned along the frontier he made fire with dried sticks and the sun's heat, just enough to ignite a gathered bunch of withered grass. This he touched to the end of his fuse-trail and made sure the trail was running.

Then he too ran. He was still running when the dump went up. He was blown flat, for a brief moment concussed. When he lifted his head the air above the dump was heavy with a pall of smoke and the descending pieces of fragmented vultures. The bang had been stupendous, enough to be heard in Nowshera, and the bodies would be as fragmented as the vultures. Ogilvie started along the track towards Nowshera. He had covered little more than a mile when he saw the dust-cloud ahead, then heard the pounding of hoof-beats. Soon he recognised the uniforms of Indian cavalry, the Bengal Lancers galloping at full stretch. Seeing the tattered native, the squadron commander lifted his hand to bring the riders to a halt. Ogilvie was held at lance-point as a *duffardar* rode up to him and speaking in Pushtu asked him who he was and what had taken place along the track.

To the astonishment of all, the tattered native disregarded the *duffardar* and smartly saluted the squadron commander.

"I'd like to be taken at once to Division, Major," he said. "And in the meantime, I'm afraid, no explanation—but very still tongues on the part of all your men."

# 5

"THERE'S ONE THING," Blaise-Willoughby said, sitting back in a comfortable chair in his office at Division and flipping his cigar-end towards a heavy brass ashtray. "There'll have been enough mess made for the Mullah to suppose your body's been fragmented with the rest. That's quite a point, apart from your description of the Mullah himself." The Political Officer had pounced on that description: the Mullah, it seemed, had raised his head before, though only fractionally. Virtually all that was known of him was that he was a Kashmiri, which in the present circumstances could be considered relevant in itself. Blaise-Willoughby went on, a note of disparagement entering his voice now, "Yes, your report's pleasing so far as it goes, but it doesn't go far enough really, does it? You should have stayed longer, you know."

"In Harazan? If I had—"

"No, *no*, Ogilvie, in Peshawar. The Mullah—he's the boy! He might have confided in you."

Sarcastically Ogilvie asked, "Can you think of any reason why he should, Major? He was half-way to being sure I was up to no good anyway. Besides, there's another point: I didn't want to risk being made to talk."

Blaise-Willoughby looked impatient. "The best way not to talk is—not to talk, Ogilvie."

"Thanks! Have you ever been on the receiving end?"

"No, but I'd grit my teeth—"

"If you had a head to grit them in. That dead man—"

"Yes. You've no ideas as to his identity?"

"None. There was the uniform, of course—assuming he really

was a major, that could be a pointer, but an unreliable one, to his regiment. Any full-dress uniform would have suited the Mullah, I imagine. Haven't *you* any ideas, anyone reported missing?"

"Yes," Blaise-Willoughby said after a moment. "I fancy your body was a genuine major all right, a genuine British major—and indeed it looks possible another mystery's solved itself now. I have word from Peshawar of a major in a line regiment being reported missing—and not on his own either!"

"With his wife?"

"A charitable way of putting it, Ogilvie. No—with his mistress! At any rate, with the wife of a captain of sappers, along with the infantry major's corporal of bearers—no doubt a discreet servant and sworn to secrecy. And that, I think, checks with what the Mullah told you." Blaise-Willoughby gave a leer, which Ogilvie found unpleasant in the circumstances. "One wife and one husband are going to have a shock they didn't expect when the news is out, eh?"

"It seems so. In the meantime, something else is explained: why my Mullah was so sure there wouldn't be a search!" Ogilvie's tone was scornful. "God, we do protect our lilywhite reputations, don't we?"

"Yes indeed, and rightly. We don't want a public scandal," Blaise-Willoughby said, looking virtuous. "Of course, now that we *know* ... but if we hadn't, well, it would have been glossed over for as long as possible and no hornets' nests poked. But Harazan, Ogilvie—the hidden explosives. Any theories?"

Ogilvie nodded. "Yes. One in particular. Harazan's not far from the railway line from Simla, and His Excellency's arriving by train."

"A blow-up on the track?"

"Not the track precisely. The bridges. The Indus, the Sohan, the Jhelum bridges."

"Well, it'll not happen now—you did well there, Ogilvie."

"That may not be the only explosives dump, Major. But it's no more than theory, of course. I wouldn't necessarily place too many eggs in that basket."

"Why not?"

"I can't really say. It's just a feeling." Ogilvie got up, walked over to the window and looked out towards the Divisional standard flying from the flagpole. "I may be entirely wrong, of course, but I think the Mullah's after something more spectacular—"

"By God, Ogilvie, His Excellency being blown up to heaven on a railway bridge would be spectacular enough for anyone, Mullah or not, surely?"

"I don't know. But I wouldn't concentrate too much on the railway bridges. There are other areas of danger, you know."

"Yes, indeed." Absently Blaise-Willoughby ruffled Wolseley's fur: the monkey began scratching, an action that dislodged its master's hand. Blaise-Willoughby was about to speak when a knock came at the door and a corporal of the headquarters staff entered.

"Sir—"

"Yes?"

"The General's compliments, sir. He'll see you and Captain Ogilvie now, sir."

The Political Officer waved a hand and the corporal turned smartly about and went off. The two officers made their way along an impressive corridor, red-carpeted, its walls hung with prints of old Indian life largely from the days of the East India Company's rule and thus pre-mutiny. Looking at them as he had on past occasions looked but with different eyes, Ogilvie thought of the horrors of mutiny, a very much more terrible affair than mere civil riot confined mostly to one town. Mutiny presupposed a continent-wide rising, a vast and bloody total upsurge against the very root and branch of British power both military and civil. With so many women and children in the Indian garrisons, the prospect was appalling. He and the Political Officer advanced into a square hall, carpeted like the corridor, with busts of former Divisional Commanders staring from their stone pillars along the walls and a massive portrait in oils of Her Majesty Queen Victoria seated regally upon her throne immediately over the portals of Lieutenant-General Francis Fettleworth's room.

A sentry came to attention and presented arms while a subaltern who had been waiting turned and opened the doors wide.

"Major Blaise-Willoughby and Captain Ogilvie, sir."

The two officers went forward, passing the subaltern, and stood to attention facing Bloody Francis, who was seated behind an immense and important-looking desk with the stomach of his scarlet tunic overflowing its top.

51

"Well, come in, come in—" General Fettleworth broke off and his sky-blue eyes bulged in their sockets. "God, not that bloody monkey! Get him out!"

"Sir, I—"

"Shut up, Blaise-Willoughby, and get him *out*! Get him out this instant, I say!" Bloody Francis fairly yelled the next word: "Popham!"

The subaltern came back. "Sir?"

"That damn monkey, Popham. Take him!"

"Sir!" Deftly Popham took Wolseley, allowing the animal to scamper up his arm to his shoulder, where he sat looking sadly with immense eyes at Blaise-Willoughby. Fettleworth appeared to be on the verge of a stroke: Ogilvie made the correct assumption that this was not the first time Wolseley had been brought into the presence.

"Now!" the Divisional Commander snapped. "Sit down, both of you. Over there." He pointed at a row of gilded straight-backed chairs to the left of his desk. When the two officers were seated, Fettleworth said, "Now, Ogilvie. What have you found out? Hey?"

Ogilvie reported the facts: Bloody Francis was shaken by his description of the headless major, seemed even more shaken by Blaise-Willoughby's interpolated identification. "Harris of the what-is-it...poor feller, poor feller! What a tragedy. And Bellamy's wife...damn fine-looking woman, don't blame Harris in the least—but how terrible. Just an assignation, and then for that to happen! They'll be damn well revenged, of course, I'll see to that personally. Well, go on, Ogilvie."

Ogilvie elaborated, making reference to the possibility that the railway bridges might be under threat but repeating what he had said to the Political Officer about other areas of danger.

"Be precise, Ogilvie, be precise."

"I believe the Maharajah of Mysore may be in danger, sir, as well as His Excellency—"

"A joint assasination—but why?"

"Because it would have a greater impact, sir, and also because there may be an involvement of religion, Muslim against Hindu."

"But surely that would scarcely be the way to unite the Indians behind a rebellion, Ogilvie?"

"There has never been unity between Muslim and Hindu, sir."

"But to succeed, a revolt *needs* unity."

52

Ogilvie said, "With respect, sir, I disagree. You speak of unity. This Mullah would never, in any case, get the support of the Hindus for a Muslim plot. He *has* to act without Hindu support. Suppose he were to see some advantage in, as it were, capitalising on his limitations?"

"I don't follow," Fettleworth said pettishly, and turned to the Political Officer. "Do you, Blaise-Willoughby?"

"I fancy so, sir. If a prominent Hindu were to be assassinated whilst in the presence of His Excellency, whilst under British protection, it's not unlikely that some of the opprobrium would rub off upon us. More than that—I suggest we might be accused of complicity—"

"Complicity!" Fettleworth gaped. "Stuff-and-nonsense, my dear fellow! Would we kill His Excellency—I ask you!"

He appeared to have scored a point: Blaise-Willoughby flushed and looked put out, and murmured something about no specific threat having been made in words against the Viceroy: it had been merely Ogilvie's assessment.

"Pah!" Fettleworth snapped. "Ogilvie spoke of that poor fellow —the threat of a 'headless Raj' was what he said! That's good enough for me."

"Yet, sir, a headless Raj could still be the *result* of any attack upon the Maharajah—"

"You suggest the Hindus being turned into cats'-paws for the Muslims, is that it, Blaise-Willoughby?"

"It's possible, sir. And we mustn't forget the Maharajah of Kashmir—true, his people are Muslim, but himself he's—"

"Another bloody Hindu," Fettleworth said witheringly, and put his head in his hands. Looking up again he said, "Well, if you *are* right, then there will be no showing of hands on the part of the rebels whilst His Excellency's en route from Simla—they'll wait till Lord Elgin and Mysore meet in Peshawar. From that time on...Good God, it doesn't bear thinking about! All the bloody way to Srinagar!" He stared vacantly, his protuberant blue eyes full of horror, twin mirrors for inner reflections upon total disgrace. In the British Army failure was the cardinal and unforgivable sin, and the higher the rank the more the ignomy. He, Lieutenant-General Francis Fettleworth, Commander of Her Majesty's First Division in Nowshera and Peshawar, would go down in history books for schoolchildren to read about as the officer who had permitted a Maharajah and a Viceroy to be

53

slaughtered by a bunch of dirty loin-clothed natives in the very heart of a British garrison! Worse: he would be written down with contumely as the man who had lost the Indian Empire, wrested from the imperial crown of Britain in fire and blood and wholesale slaughter of soldiers' families. Bloody Francis Fettleworth, ever since the first day of his arrival in the sub-continent, had been haunted by the fear that one day the terrible scenes of the mutiny would be repeated.

\* \* \*

Next morning, with James Ogilvie back one again in cantonments, the Divisional Commander's anxieties had, after due consultation with his Chief of Staff and with Sir Iain Ogilvie in Murree, been transmitted into orders for the garrison, brought to Peshawar by a mounted runner from Division. When these orders reached him via Brigade, Lord Dornoch at once departed to attend a briefing by the Brigadier-General; and on his return after luncheon summoned his officers for a conference.

"I'll put it in a nutshell, gentlemen," he said, his voice sombre. "His Excellency's due to arrive by train, as we all know, at 9 a.m. the day after tomorrow. He's to spend the morning on an inspection of the cantonments, and luncheon will be followed by the review, which takes place for the Maharajah's arrival at 3 p.m. Currently, the Maharajah's a little more than half-way from Rawalpindi." Dornoch paused. "The General's view is that nothing will happen before the meeting, and may well not happen until His Excellency and His Highness are started upon their journey north into Kashmir. That, however, is not to say he's complacent—far from it. Full precautions and heavy security have been ordered. Captain Black?"

"Colonel?" Black stood up smartly.

"Our own brigade is under orders to provide a part of the security. Two companies of ours, two of the Connaught Rangers, and two of the Border Regiment will be taken out of the line for the review. They'll be used to strengthen the barrack guard and to provide a perimeter guard for the whole cantonment area. You'll see to our share in that, Captain Black, if you please."

"Very good, Colonel. And the city?"

"Battalions from the other brigades will provide companies to reinforce the town patrol and ensure that the entire city is given coverage from midnight tomorrow until after His Excellency and His Highness with their retinue and escort have left for Kashmir. We ourselves are to provide a half-company under Captain Ogilvie to join the town companies but to remain in the guard-room in the city, for identification and questioning by Captain Ogilvie of any men, any natives, apprehended by the patrols."

"Is rioting expected before His Excellency's arrival, then, Colonel?"

Dornoch shrugged. "We don't know. We're working on theories so far, Captain Black. In any case, since there may be hotheads who'll show their hands as the time approaches, the General intends to leave nothing to chance. The town companies will be under strict orders to provoke nothing, but to be on instant alert for trouble. If trouble comes, it's to be put down firmly, and if necessary the whole garrison will be turned out. But the feeling at Division and Brigade is that all will be quiet until the important persons reach Peshawar. That's all for now, gentlemen. Except that you're all to observe the fullest secrecy. Nothing is to leak out that we suspect trouble beyond the ordinary. Captain Ogilvie, a word in your ear. And you also, Captain Black."

The two officers remained whilst the others left. Dornoch moved over to the window and stood for a moment looking out across the parade-ground towards the immaculate sentry on the main gate, marching his post with his rifle at the slope, turning smartly about at the end of his beat and marching back again. In that sentry, in the Colonel's view, there was personified and given flesh the whole spirit of the British Raj: the alert watchful-ness, the smartness and precision, the visible accoutrements of the Queen's service, the military strength and the correctness of attitude.

Glancing at Black and Ogilvie, Dornoch said with a faint smile, "A symbol, gentlemen—the sentry. One to set against that dread-ful headless body, James!"

"Colonel?"

Dornoch smiled again: a wry smile. "We must keep the *good* in mind. We must never adopt the standards of the enemy—to do that is all too easy once civil trouble starts. It's a very different thing from frontier activity against the tribes, as you'll discover."

"Yes, Colonel."

"There's always a temptation to play a dirty game. We must remember our honour as a regiment—and remember, too, that the support for the British is in fact vast. We must not lose goodwill. But enough of that!" Lord Dornoch turned from the window. "What I wanted to say to you, James, was this: thanks to your prompt obliteration of those thugs in Harazan, General Fettleworth believes this Mullah of yours won't necessarily expect anything to have been leaked. It's Division's hope that he'll put it down to an accidental explosion. The General expects this advantage not to be thrown away. Therefore you'll act with the utmost restraint and circumspection when on duty at the city guardroom, you understand?"

"Yes, Colonel."

Dornoch nodded. "Right! Any questions?"

"Only about the railway bridges, Colonel. They *could* be threatened, no matter what I—"

"Agreed. The General's taken note. The Lincolnshires and the Sherwood Foresters have been ordered out to the bridges from Rawalpindi. The garrison here is somewhat badly stretched, but we shall cope." Dornoch turned to the Adjutant. "Andrew, I want all men to remain in cantonments until further orders, and that includes the officers. I want the guard on the married quarters reinforced and the restriction on movement to apply to the women and children as well."

"Very good, Colonel. Will this not alert the natives, that we—"

"A risk I must take, and never mind Division. Far worse would result from any molesting of women in the city, and frankly I don't believe it'll cause comment. It'll not be the first time movement has been restricted to cantonments, and it'll be put down simply to routine security requirements for His Excellency's visit, as indeed will the strengthening of the town patrol." Dornoch pulled out his watch. "That's all, Andrew, for now. We'll have further orders shortly regarding the onward escort, which is now clearly going to be heavily strengthened."

*       *       *

That evening a subtle difference was noticeable in the atmosphere. Following upon the Colonel's order, the barrackrooms and married quarters were more than usually full. There were no riding parties out, no gay bachelor roisterings into Peshawar city for an evening of wine, women and song in the safer parts: the wise men avoided the other areas at the best of times, since danger lurked in every doorway, in every dark alley, the danger of injury or death from *thuggee* or other elements of banditry. Ogilvie, sitting in a basket-work chair on the verandah outside his room, looked across towards the married quarters of the Other Ranks, the clean but comparatively primitive living-places for the wives and women and children; the officers' ladies lived in the luxurious, well-spaced cantonment bungalows with gardens and stables and many, many servants. But Other Ranks, although in India waited upon by native bearers, did not have ladies; NCOs had wives, the men had women as stated in Queen's Regulations for the Army. Monarch of all in those married quarters was the Regimental Sergeant-Major, and Mrs Regimental Sergeant-Major Cunningham was queen. Unlike the rest, the Cunninghams had their own bungalow, one virtually indistinguishable from those of the commissioned officers and with as much garden and as many bearers...As Ogilvie watched idly, he saw the RSM marching across from his quarters towards the Seargents' Mess, back straight, glengarry precisely angled, kilt swinging rhythmically, pace-stick beneath his arm, Sam Browne belt stretched tight across the broadly-set shoulder-blades. Getting to his feet, Ogilvie called across the parade:

"Mr Cunningham!"

The Regimental Sergeant-Major halted with a crash of boot-leather and swung his right arm in salute. "Sir!"

"One moment, if you please, Sar'nt Major."

Cunningham altered course for the verandah: Ogilvie went out to meet him. "I'll not detain you, Sar'nt-Major—"

"That's all right, Captain Ogilvie, sir, that's quite all right."

"I wanted a word about the married quarters' security."

"All in hand, sir. I've done the rounds myself."

"Good. How are the families taking it, Sar'nt-Major?"

"Variably, sir. Some are philosophical."

"And the others?"

The RSM met his eye. "Scared, sir. *Shit* scared, if I may use the phrase. They've read too much about the mutiny, sir. You'll know the stories, sir: the spitting of babies on the bayonets at Kabul, sir. They're a shower of bastards, sir, the natives are." His eye, unusually angry and emotional in the presence of an officer, dared that officer to contradict.

Ogilvie refrained from contradiction: it would have been pointless in any case. He said, "Calm their fears, Mr Cunningham,

57

rather than make them worse. Stories of the past, exaggerated over the years, don't help now."

"The spitting of babies was the truth, Captain Ogilvie."

"I know. But some of the stories are not true. We're in for a difficult time, Sar'nt-Major. Let's concentrate on keeping the women and children safe."

Cunningham glared frostily, then smiled. "Aye, sir. I've no doubt you're right really. They'll be well guarded."

"I'm sure of it. How's your good lady taking it?"

"Like a Cunningham, sir, like any sergeant-major's wife. But just the same, she's not happy, sir. She loves Scotland, and she sees it coming close. If you take my meaning, sir."

Ogilvie nodded in understanding: Cunningham was not so far off being a time-expired man, due within the next year for Bombay, the *Malabar* and the voyage home to Portsmouth Hard and then his last farewell as a serving Warrant Officer of the regimental depot at Invermore on Speyside. It would be a sad day for both Cunningham and the regiment, but the Scots wife he had married twenty years ago when he was a corporal and entitled by his age to marry 'on the strength' would be glad of it. Cunningham underlined the fact: "It's her hope and mine, sir, that she'll be seeing Scotland again."

"Mine too." Ogilvie reached out and clapped Cunningham on the shoulder. "Off you go, Bosom. I'm sorry to have kept you from your whisky!"

"Sir!" Cunningham saluted and turned about. He strode away, right arm swinging from the shoulder, boots hitting the ground precisely at the correct infantry pace. He marched straight into the sunset, the blood-red orb sinking above the roof of the Sergeants' Mess, down into the Afghan hills. As he went, the peace of the parade-ground was shattered very suddenly: from the direction of the married quarters a scream ripped out into the still air. Running towards the source, Ogilvie glanced across at Cunningham. The RSM had swung round, his mouth was open, his arms crooked and fists bunched, the whole man seeming enveloped by the red rays of the sunset. Momentarily as still as a statue, he got on the move a second later, a bulky man running at full speed, and as he did so the cantonment came alive with men.

# 6

FIRST ON THE scene apart from the immediate neighbours, Ogilvie looked down upon the dead: a young woman whom he had known as pretty and vivacious—one Mary Abbott, a corporal's wife, now cold and still with a short-handled knife sticking out from her chest, her dress blood-soaked. Her children, a small boy and a smaller girl, were crying in the arms of one of the sergeant's wives, a woman staring at the body as though she couldn't look away.

"The children!" Ogilvie said. "Take them away at once—indoors, sharp!" He looked round. "Where's Corporal Abbott?"

"On guard duty, sir, with the town patrol."

"Who did this?"

"He did, sir." The speaker, a sergeant, pointed with a jerk of a thumb at a body half visible inside a door. "He's dead, Captain Ogilvie, sir. His neck's broken."

"Who killed him, Sergeant?"

The sergeant said simply, "I did, sir."

"You may have to answer for it, Sergeant Thomas."

"*Answer* for it, did you say? Man, the bastard murdered Abbot's wife... what else would you have me do?" Thomas's voice rose. "Officer or no, I'll bloody—"

"All right, all right!" Ogilvie snapped. From the corner of his eye he saw the RSM coming up, and Black overtaking. "You have witnesses... witnesses to say you acted to try to save Mrs Abbott?"

"The two bairns, sir, and Corporal Morrison's wife."

Ogilvie nodded: such witness was fortunate. Life was held cheaply enough in India, but even murderers could not be murdered without witnesses to say it had not been an act of simple revenge. Black came up officiously. "What's happened, Captain Ogilvie?"

"Look for yourself," Ogilvie said. He took a deep breath. "This is the start. We're all in for trouble now."

Black nodded dourly. "Statements," he said. "That's the first thing. Captain Ogilvie, then to the Colonel." The RSM, panting heavily, halted beside the two officers, stared down at the pathetic body on the sandy ground. No salute: none expected in the circumstances, but all the same a curious omission for Cunningham. Ogilvie glanced at his face: it was white beneath the tan and in the eyes there was the sparkle of tears. In all his years with the regiment, Ogilvie had never seen such reaction from the RSM. The face was savage; when trouble in the wider sense came, the rebels would get no mercy from Cunningham.

*       *       *

The Colonel's formal enquiry, held next morning after the preliminary investigation by the Adjutant and Corporal Abbot's company commander, elicited the simple facts: Mary Abbot had given her bearer an order accompanied by a reprimand, an order to see more thoroughly to the cleaning of the kitchen. At once the bearer had attacked in the presence of both children and the wife of Corporal Morrison. Sergeant Thomas, happening to pass, heard the screams and rushed in to find the bearer at Mary Abbot's throat. Too late to save her, he had hurled himself on the native and in the course of the struggle had broken the man's neck.

"I consider you acted properly," Lord Dornoch said. "This must go to Brigade and then Division, but my report will reflect my views. In the meantime," he added, turning to the Adjutant, "Sar'nt Thomas will carry out full duties."

"Very good, Colonel."

Dornoch nodded. "All right, Sar'nt Thomas, that's all."

"Thank you, sir. Thank you indeed. That bugger—"

"That'll *do*," the Regimental Sergeant-Major roared. "Salute, about *turn*, quick *march*, left-right-left..." Outside his voice dwindled and broke off. Dornoch turned to Andrew Black.

"Justice having been done," he said wryly, "we must hope we're not accused in the streets of Peshawar of white-washing our own men. Not that it *wasn't* justice..."

"I agree, Colonel."

"Well, now there's another matter to consider afresh, and that's the safety of His Excellency. This business is going to exacerbate feelings on both sides of the fence, undoubtedly. There'll be trigger-happy fingers in the city and along the processional routes...I'd be happier if His Excellency decided to cancel, frankly."

"So would we all," Black said gloomily, "and especially, I have no doubt, General Fettleworth." He shrugged. "It'll be up to him to recommend it, Colonel, in the light of your report this morning. It's out of our hands."

*       *       *

Fettleworth was indeed glad to seize the chance. Sending for his Chief of Staff, Brigadier-General Lakenham, he thrust across the despatch from Brigade brought in to him by his ADC.

"Well, Lakenham?"

"Well, what, sir?"

"The Viceroy, dammit! We've represented the potential danger to Simla and been disregarded. But this is different, don't you think?"

"Possibly, sir, but I doubt if His Excellency will see it as such."

"Why not?"

"Lord Elgin is not a man to scare easily, sir, and he is a stickler for keeping his word. In the meantime, His Highness the Maharajah is virtually upon our doorstep—and it's a long journey from Mysore!"

"Oh, damn His Highness!" Bloody Francis drummed worried fingers on his blotter. "Surely to God the safety of the Viceroy is more important to the Raj than letting a damn maharajah's journey not be wasted?"

Lakenham stifled a sigh. "Perhaps to God, sir. Not, I think, to Brahma or His Excellency—"

"Well, that's your opinion. It's not mine! There's no time now to refer this to Murree and wait upon Sir Iain Ogilvie, so I'll act on my own, damn it—"

"How, sir?"

"Why, by informing His Excellency, of course! Draft a despatch, Lakenham, a warning despatch about that murderous native. It shall go immediately to Simla, by telegraph and in code." Fettleworth opened a drawer and brought out a sheaf of papers. "In case His Excellency should decide to continue notwithstanding, you should send despatches to Peshawar now, indicating the details of the onward route orders into Kashmir, and the extra escort that'll be required. Then there's the elephants." Even viceregal elephants could not be put in quantity aboard the train, and Division had been ordered to supply this requirement from stock. "Hey?"

"That's been dealt with, sir. A full muster of elephants with howdahs and mahouts will be at the railway station at Peshawar by 8.30 a.m. tomorrow."

\*     \*     \*

During the afternoon the funeral of Mary Abbott threw a blight over the Royal Strathspeys' cantonment: all officers and NCOs who could be spared from duty attended, walking behind the crepe-muffled drums and the pipes playing 'Lochaber No More' and the firing-party with their rifles reversed. At the graveside in the military cemetery the coffin was lowered to the sound of the rifles and the bugle strains of Last Post and handfuls of Indian sandy soil cast down by the Chaplain. As the funeral party moved away, back to cantonments, the pipes and drums played lighter tunes and Ogilvie caught the eye of Corporal Abbott. The man's face was stiff and white and he seemed scarcely aware of his surroundings. He would do no more duty that day and Ogilvie's guess was that he would drink himself into a state of temporary forgetfulness in the canteen: no officer or NCO would notice the result, and Cunningham, that experienced amalgam of mentor, driver, nursemaid and father-figure would see to it that Abbott's friends and a junior NCO would in any case keep him well on the safe side of trouble. The army was mostly a machine, hard and soulless when it had to be; but it also had compassion and understanding. Lord Dornoch had felt the tragedy deeply: the 114th Highlanders came from a sparsely-populated if geographical wide recruiting area, and few of the officers and men in the regiment were total strangers one to another at home in Scotland. That night, when under Ogilvie and Colour-Sergeant MacTrease, the half-company as detailed marched out of cantonments for the city guardroom, the soldiers' faces showed a grim resolve that the natives would get away with no more killing: as had been forecast earlier by the Colonel, fingers were going to be ever a-squeeze against the triggers of the rifles notwithstanding firm orders given personally by Black. Ogilvie, understanding as he was of the reasons, felt a strong sense of unease as the half-company reached the end of the two-mile march from canton-ments and came into the city's outskirts. Perhaps word had spread along the strange wires of the bush-telegraph, word that the Scots soldiers in particular were in fighting, hostile mood: at all events, the native population was not too much in evidence and the tramp of feet inside the network of alleys and hovels was mostly that of the battalions ordered to back up the town patrol. Outside the guardroom MacTrease halted his half-company and turned them into line to face the whitewashed steps as the Officer of the Guard, a captain of the Middlesex Regiment, came down to greet Ogilvie.

"Any reports of trouble?" Ogilvie asked, climbing the steps with the Englishman.

"No, all quiet."

"Too quiet, d'you suppose?"

"I don't know. I'm thanking God that it is, frankly!"

Ogilvie said, "On the frontier, it's usually not a good sign." He paused. "D'you mind if I offer a word of advice? It's your show, not mine, but my battalion's seen a good deal of service up here, and—"

"Go ahead," the Middlesex captain said.

"Then I'd suggest you specifically warn your patrols to watch their backs. An instinct for self-preservation may well have told them that already, of course, but if it hasn't, you may get casualty reports sooner than you think." Ogilvie grinned. "Hope you don't mind?"

"Any advice gratefully received! This is all rather a change from Colchester, you know." They reached the small room reserved for the Officer of the Guard: the captain, who had introduced him-self as Williamson, gestured to a chair. Ogilvie sat, taking off his revolver-holster. Williamson said, "Now you're here, I wonder if you'd mind taking over for a while?"

"From you?"

"Yes. I'd like to make contact with my patrols."

"If I were you, I'd detail a sergeant."

"I'd rather go myself."

Ogilvie shrugged. "It's your decision. Take an escort, though."

"You really think I should, Ogilvie?"

"I'm certain of it. Any officer in uniform walking the alleys alone tonight is asking for it. As you said yourself—this isn't Colchester!"

Williamson nodded and handed over the guard duty, promising to make a speedy reconnaissance through the city and come straight back. For a while Ogilvie sat in the officers' room: a corporal came in with a mug of tea, his bayonet-scabbard hanging below the brown leather pouches and shoulder-belts of his Slade-Wallace equipment.

"Thank you, Corporal," Ogilvie said. "What's it like out there?"

"Quiet, sir. Nothing seems to be moving, sir."

"Watch like a hawk, Corporal. I'll be out directly."

"Yessir."

The corporal saluted and withdrew. Ogilvie drank the tea, hot, sweet and strong. On a wall a clock ticked loudly, a cheap clock; the only sound in the night's curious stillness apart from the foot-falls of the sentry marching his post at the bottom of the steps. The tea drunk, Ogilvie took up his glengarry, strapped on his holster, and went out to the verandah above the steps. The moon was high and bright: Peshawar was bathed in silver, its buildings starkly outlined, its squalor lost in the contrast of light and deep shadow...shadow that, all over the city, could hide the men with the knives until the very moment of attack. Despite the sentry below, despite the men in the guardroom ready to turn out at a moment's notice, Ogilvie was struck by a feeling of intense loneliness; pacing the verandah he felt like the Officer of the Watch aboard a ship at sea, pacing a lonely navigating bridge with no company but a quartermaster in the wheelhouse below, communicating by means of a metal tube, a waste of seas around and a star-filled sky overhead. The sky over Peshawar was in fact full of stars, a pattern of intense, almost luminous brightness, God's lanterns hanging so low that in fancy a man could reach up and grasp them. Such a sky was seldom seen in Britain, land of cloud and mist...Ogilvie paced on, listening, watching, thinking about the Mullah and the man Kamruddin Rashti, and the headless body in the chair in the cellar. Where were those men tonight, his captors? He would give much to know, much to find that cellar again, but recognised the wisdom of high command that had decided against a search—an almost certainly useless search and one that would immediately have alerted the rebel leadership. Meanshile the unreal air of quietness persisted: the only movement was the falling-in of reliefs for the various patrols, and the return of those whose spell of duty was done.

All the reports were negative: Peshawar was sleeping and brooding, its teeming ant-like native population withdrawn to the ant-hill. There were no arrests for Ogilvie's interrogation. After an absence of two hours, Williamson marched back with his escort of a corporal and four privates, and his report added nothing to the scanty sum of knowledge.

"Quiet as the grave, Ogilvie." There was an odd tension in his voice. "Damn it, it gives a man the creeps!"

Ogilvie smiled. "It's a feeling you'll get used to in the next few years! Not often in the cities, but when you're away on extended patrols its the norm. Only the sounds of nature disturb it—night animals, birds. When you hear the Pathan, it's usually too late."

"But in a city—"

"I know. It's unnatural. It's not all that late."

There was a pause, then Williamson said, "I have a flask of whisky, Ogilvie. Care for a drop?"

Ogilvie nodded. "Thanks, I would." They went inside. After the nightcap, Ogilvie shook down for a few hours, ready to be called should he be required to take his half-company of Scots to any scene of action or difficulty. He remained unwoken right through the night: when he was called it was 7 a.m. The day was bright and Peshawar was alive again, its alleys and market-places thronged. Yawning, Ogilvie got up and had his half-company fallen-in before the guardroom and then marched back to cantonments to the beat of the drum. In a sense it had been a wasted night; yet it had sent its message and the message had been received and understood: Peshawar was on the brink of explosion.

\*      \*      \*

"Word from Brigade, Andrew. It's as expected, but it's still unwelcome!"

"Colonel?"

"His Excellency will not change his plans—I didn't think he would at this stage, of course." Lord Dornoch waved a sheaf of documents at the Adjutant. "I have the route orders for the Kashmir escort now, in some detail. The whole brigade's ordered

65

out, not just us. We shall have cavalry and artillery—two mountain batteries, two field batteries, with a support column. The cavalry and guns join us at Rawalpindi—we entrain as far as there, and our brigade acts as sole escort meanwhile. Also at Rawalpindi, Sir Iain Ogilvie will join His Excellency's entourage —travelling as a passenger, taking a back seat for once! From Rawalpindi we march direct for Srinagar, being met a few miles outside the city by a native escort provided by Pertab Singh in honour of His Excellency and the Maharajah of Mysore."

"Back across the bridges to Rawalpindi, Colonel." Black shook his head mournfully. "I don't like it, I don't like it at all."

"No more do I—nor does Fettleworth, I gather—but there it is." The Colonel shrugged; he looked anxious. "The three bridges will continue to be guarded by a brigade from Rawalpindi, which leaves Peshawar itself in the hands of Harrison's and Dermot's brigades. The General is not depleting Nowshera, it appears, but the routine drafts and reliefs from home, now on their way from Bombay, have been allocated to reinforce Peshawar. I can only hope they'll be enough."

"They'll be grass green, Colonel."

"It can't be helped. They'll know how to fire a rifle at all events!"

"Indeed I hope so. I have the families in mind."

"So have I." Dornoch's tone was brisk but his heart was heavy; it would be hard to leave women and children behind to face the potentially enormous threat, and the knowledge that they were doing so would tend to weaken morale on the march into the Kashmiri hills. "I know General Fettleworth is not unmindful."

"Are further troops coming in from Murree, Colonel?"

"Not immediately. They'll be available if and when required, but of course we must remember Murree has its own requirements and commitments—which also include women and children."

"Ootacamund?"

Dornoch shook his head. "Ootacamund may well be faced with similar problems if trouble starts here. In India events spread fast. The GOC Southern Army is stretched and can offer no assistance outside his command—and in any case, Andrew, it's a devil of a long train journey up to Peshawar or Murree! No, we have to cope with what we have. It's a tall order, but—"

"Cannot His Excellency be yet prevailed upon to—"

"To back down, for that is what a change of plan would be seen as, Andrew? He's adamant, apparently, and I understand why." Dornoch blew down his pipe-stem: fragments of burnt tobacco flew. "Think, Andrew: all India will be watching. If the Raj should be seen to bow to threats which in point of fact have not yet materialised...what happens then? We deliver ourselves, our whole power to decide, into the hands of the dissidents, do we not?"

Black nodded. "I suppose so, Colonel. So we entrain and march—along with Dasara!"

"Along with Dasara indeed," the Colonel said, grim-faced. Dasara, for His Highness the Maharajah of Mysore and his retinue, would begin, so said the orders from Division, at a time to be decided after leaving the train at Rawalpindi and would culminate beyond the Kashmiri border inside the territory of His Highness's brother Hindu: and the panoply of religious observances, in British eyes disorderly ones, were certain not to prove the most propitious background against which to preserve the peace and the lives of important men against attack.

# 7

HIS EXCELLENCY THE Earl of Elgin, Viceroy of India, stepped from the train followed by the Vicereine and the Commander-in-Chief, Sir George White, the latter resplendent in scarlet tunic with orders and decorations, and with white ostrich feathers pluming his cocked hat. Salutes were exchanged with Lieutenant-General Francis Fettleworth and his staff, the National Anthem was played, and then His Excellency proceeded in state towards the elephants, who were kneeling obediently to bring their howdahs closer to ground level, the mahouts executing their balancing tricks behind the immense flaps of the animals' ears. It was a brilliant day of sun with a welcome light wind from out of the Himalayan foothills as the procession made its way to the British military cantonments, accompanied by a Captain's Escort of Skinner's Horse with a battalion of infantry marching in front with drums and fifes, and more infantry lining the whole route, standing rigidly at attention as the Viceroy passed by. Upon arrival at cantonments. Their Excellencies were lowered to the ground by reverse action of the elephants, and General Fettleworth accompanied the Viceroy and the Commander-in-Chief and their combined staffs upon their inspection of the military station: an exhausting business, involving the introduction of many colonels and adjutants and a lengthy walk of barrack-rooms and parade-grounds in the mounting heat of the sun. As that sun reached its zenith Bloody Francis began to pant; an hour later he was in urgent need of the *chota peg* which, in His Excellency's presence, he took in the anteroom of the Royal Strathspeys who, as a Scottish regiment, had been accorded the honour of providing luncheon for the Viceroyalty the current holder of which high office was himself a Scot. Sweat poured into the collar of General Fettleworth's tunic, a sticky stream of discomfort; luncheon worsened his condition, but he bore it all stoically, looking forward to the delights of the afternoon and the splendour of the great review stage-managed by himself and his Chief of Staff: Bloody Francis, as ever, was confident as to the effects that would be produced by that review upon the mind of the native and of the potential rebel in particular. A show of strength was his panacea: and the afternoon would bring such a show of strength as had not for a long time been seen upon the parade-grounds of Peshawar.

\*     \*     \*

If the state arrival of Their Excellencies and the Commander-in-Chief had been a thing of splendour, the entry of His Highness the Maharajah of Mysore was a riot of dusty pomp, something from out of the Middle Ages, a story-book coming of power and riches, riches and goings-on that Her Majesty Queen Victoria had never dreamed of: Buckingham Palace, Windsor Castle, Balmoral...none of these were for poor men; but none of their rooms and cellars was stacked from wall to wall and ceiling to ceiling with precious stones and metals; nor did the good Queen maintain the male counterparts of the many wives and concubines awaiting, as soon as he should become old enough, the desires of His Highness of Mysore. A little late, the long procession, behind a guard and band found by a native infantry regiment of the Indian Army, straggled onto the parade-ground like a colourful circus: the way had been immensely long and though hurry had not been part of it and the interludes of rest had been many, the colourful uniforms of His Highness's private army were thick with dust and damp with sweat; high caste men and women nodded with sleep in the elephant-borne howdahs; the tinny music of flutes and native pipes, the clash of cymbals, the beat of the drums, seemed muted by a natural tiredness. The horses and mules, the elephants themselves, plodded doggedly rather than stepped with pride; and at the distant rear of the procession the commissariat personnel with His Highness's kitchen utensils, his cooking-stoves and his food moved along in the carts without a care in the world for the British brass that stood waiting on the dais by the ceremonial red carpet: they slept, they lolled, they grinned and grimaced and they kept themselves comfortable. As the procession turned in order that its head might lead past the dais for the disembarkation of the youthful Maharajah, the tail end rode into full view across the parade-ground and General Fettleworth found his gaze riveted. He clutched at the arm of his Chief of Staff, and rudely pointed.

"Lakenham, that cart. That man! What the devil is he doing?"

"Making water, sir."

"That's what I thought! Can't somebody stop him?"

"He's an Untouchable, sir, a sweeper."

"Yes, but that damn well doesn't mean—" Fettleworth broke off: urination was not strictly his responsibility, however unpleasant it might be in full view of the assembled ladies, wives and women of the garrison: and His Highness had now drawn level with the dais, the procession coming to an imprecise halt behind the guard and band. The scene immediately in front of Fettleworth more than compensated for the rest of the long and variegated column: the Maharajah and his personal retinue were breath-taking: rubies and emeralds sparkled in the afternoon sun; sky-blue turbans, white turbans, peacock's feathers, jewelled jackets, brilliant saris—it was a never-to-be-forgotten scene as His Excellency the Viceroy, equally colourful, stepped forward and, as once again the National Anthems crashed out from the combined brass bands, saluted a subject-prince of the Indian Empire. His Highness, slight, slim, a child in the guise of a potentate, returned the salutations, standing at the salute himself as The Queen was played, remaining motionless in the shafts of sunlight as next the bands played the General Salute, a few bars of Garb of Old Gaul.

Then, with a deep bow and heels together, he greeted Her Majesty's representatives, was led to the dais, the assembled officers and their ladies were introduced and, as the native procession moved away, the ceremonies of review began with a nod from Bloody Francis to Brigadier-General Lakenham. It was an emotional scene, very highly-charged as a result of the deep fears of the British officers as to what was threatened: never mind that the whole district was under close surveillance or that much military might was close at hand. From now on every moment was potentially the one that could bring the danger. Fettleworth, as the march past began, felt as though he were sitting on a pile of dynamite with persons unknown hastening towards him with

70

matches: his was the responsibility until the Viceroy was outside the limits of his command, and it was an awesome responsibility. But he would bear it, supported and steadied by thoughts of Her Majesty the Queen. There was a deep rumble and a cloud of dust as the guns moved past the Viceroy, now standing at the salute: field guns, siege guns, mountain batteries went past with a clatter of equipment and a creak of shining harness-leather, great tubes of war pointing astern behind the brightly-polished limbers and the riders in their full-dress uniforms. After them the representative cavalry of the Indian Army, two squadrons each of The Guides and the Bengal Lancers, splendid men in turbans and highly-polished knee-length boots set off by the colourful shabraques, with the guidons fluttering from the lances and the mounted band ahead of them playing the cavalry canter, Bonnie Dundee, as they increased their pace spectacularly to wheel away across the parade and let the infantry come up in their place. There was a mist in front of Bloody Francis's eyes as the foot soldiers marched past to the music of the fifes and drums: Fettleworth was scornful of the guns, useful as they might be at certain times and in certain places; he tended to regard them as a physician might regard the butchery of the surgeons: mechanics to be called in grudgingly as a last resort, stealers of the glory of those who had done the ground-work. The cavalry he mistrusted: they were at times too dashing and vainglorious, mere limelight seekers. But the infantry...ah, the infantry was the queen of battles, soldiers marching doggedly upon their own economical feet, their commissariat requirement taking up less room upon the march than the mountains of feedstuff needed by the cavalry and artillery animals; solid and dependable men for whom Fettleworth, who had himself been an infantryman in his regimental days, had the highest regard. His chest swelled with pride behind the scarlet and the gold and the many-coloured medal ribbons as the English county regiments marched past with heads high beneath the helmets, scarlet and blue and white and gold upon their bodies, each regimental colour held proudly by the colour-guard and displaying the battle honours which of themselves formed a whole volume of British history and glory, and of valour in the name of Empire and the Monarch. As the sun began its journey down the sky, sinking over the cantonment buildings towards Afghanistan, the atmosphere was vibrant with sound yet curiously muted as though all the noises of military splendour were confined, cocooned in this the farthest-flung outpost of the Empire set right upon the very edge of civilisation. It was an odd moment: the sandy parade-ground with its backdrop of the trees' dusty green and the distant shadow of Himalaya, gleamed red, a moving red of uniforms, like blood slowly running out towards the sunset...but it was not sunset yet in either sense of the word, and Fettleworth gave himself a vigorous shake and firmly set his jaw: there would be no sunset while he was there to prevent it!

*      *      *

"Captain Ogilvie!"

Ogilvie, crossing the parade-ground, halted and turned: Black was hurrying towards him, kilt swinging. "Captain Ogilvie, a word if you please."

"Yes?"

"A full attention to detail, nothing left to chance. Whilst on the march, you are to see to it that your colour-sergeant has a close eye upon the men throughout. Also that there is no mixing between the men and the natives of the Maharajah's retinue."

"Why so?"

"I would have thought the reason obvious enough. We wish no excacerbations of religious feelings upon the march, and no altercations. Besides, it is the natives from whom the threat comes, and we can trust none of them—"

"Oh, come!" Ogilvie broke in impatiently. "They're all Hindus —they're not going to take that sort of risk for a Muslim mullah, even if they subsequently join his mutiny—"

"There can be such a thing as infiltration, can there not?"

"I doubt it—on this occasion! A Muslim would stand out like a sore thumb until we get to Srinagar."

"Nevertheless," Black said frigidly, "you have your orders. The natives will be held in isolation so far as that is possible, Captain Ogilvie. I shall be informing all company commanders to this effect."

"Very good." Ogilvie saluted the Adjutant, and turned away, going on towards his company's lines, frowning. Black was, as usual, fussing, though there was sense in trying to avoid mutual exacerbations. It was Black's tone as much as anything that irritated: the man was petulant and could never leave the men, or the officers either, alone to carry out their tasks. He was always there to chivvy, frequently interfering in the proper authority of company commanders and getting in the way even of the Regimental Sergeant-Major ... Ogilvie shrugged and dismissed Black from his mind: the Adjutant was the Adjutant and had to be suffered and that was that. Moving on, Ogilvie watched the preparations for the forthcoming march, starting at dawn next day with the entrainment at the railway station. Now there was a difference in the air from the ceremonial of the afternoon: there was workaday movement of men in shirt-sleeves, sweating men supervising the loading of the ammunition and commissariat carts by the regimental camp-followers and bearers; the organising by the sergeant cook of the field kitchens; much work upon the horses and mules by the teams under the farrier-sergeant. Surgeon-Major Corton and his medical orderlies made ready for any sickness or action on the march, though the battalion would be joined by a reinforcing medical column provided by Division. Colour-Sergeant MacTrease and his NCOs inspected rifles and kit and tents, a last-minute check to ensure that every detail was correct. There was scarcely any grumbling, even from the married men: Ogilvie noted an acute awareness of crisis. His tour of inspection completed, Ogilvie left his colour-sergeant to carry on and went back towards the Officers' Mess. Taking off his Sam Browne belt he entered the anteroom for a *chota peg* before changing for dinner; but before he could order one he was again approached by Andrew Black, in the Mess less formal than on the parade-ground.

"Ah, James. All company commanders to the Colonel, at once."

Ogilvie lifted an eyebrow. "What now?"

"The Colonel has just returned from Brigade, where he had words with His Excellency." Black said no more, but left the anteroom hurriedly. Ogilvie made his way to the Colonel in the battalion office, last of the company commanders to report. Dornoch nodded briefly at him, then got to his feet behind the desk.

"I'll not keep you long, gentlemen. I am ordered to tell you of the particular reason for His Excellency's visit and for his meeting with the Maharajahs." The Colonel paused: the lamplight, reflecting in yellow brilliance from the crowns and stars on the shoulders of his mess dress, also showed strain and anxiety in his face. "This is to be no mere state visit but the occasion of a vital

73

conference in Srinagar. There are pressures from Russia—you may say there is nothing new in that, but this time there is a difference. Reports reaching Calcutta and Simla over the last few weeks have indicated that Czar Nicholas is building up armies inside Afghanistan. Units have crossed the frontier from Turkestan, through the Safed Koh—small units but many of them, that appear to be coming together in the plains about Kandahar."

"Is their composition known, Colonel?" Ogilvie asked.

"From the reports, which tend towards a certain vagueness and a possible duplication—several divisions of cavalry with infantry and artillery support and a considerable supply train. And that's not all: another army is reported massing in the north—in the mountains of the Hindu Kush between the Khatinza and the Agram passes above Chitral, and is positioned to march down upon Ghilgit. If they do mean harm, then it's only too likely they'll have the support of the Afghan hordes—and you all know what that means, gentlemen."

There was a buzz of talk, shushed at by Black. Lord Dornoch went on, "Neither the British Army nor the Indian Army has the current numerical strength...extra drafts have been asked for from home, but the voyage to Bombay takes time. Thus His Excellency hopes to persuade more support from the native armies of Kashmir, and a northward movement of those of Mysore, to give us an availability of strong reserves in this area. Either that, or a promise from Mysore that he'll relieve our own troops in garrison in the Ootacamund command." Dornoch pulled out his watch and glanced at it. "Questions, gentlemen?"

The one question came from the second-in-command, Major Hay: "Is a connection seen between the Czar's movements and the threat from this Mullah, Colonel?"

"At present, John, the official answer's no. That's not to say a link will not emerge. It's a coincidence, and I distrust coincidences. We must be vigilant upon the march. That is all, gentlemen, except that I would like to see all officers clear of the Mess by ten p.m., and gone to their beds."

*     *     *

The imponderables were many: but it took little imagination to foresee the certain result, at this time, of a large-scale mutiny along the North-West Frontier. Such would bring in the Russian divisions as though drawn by a magnet. There was indeed a strong chance that the end would come for the Raj: and, whatever the Colonel had said—and in fact he had seemed to hint at a personal disbelief of the official view to date—it was very highly unlikely that the thin, blue-eyed man in that Peshawar cellar, the Mullah whom Blaise-Willoughby had said was a Kashmiri, could be unaware of the stir of events over the border inside Afghanistan. The next morning early, Ogilvie met B Company, paraded for his inspection before the regimental column moved out to entrain, with a heavy heart. Slowly he walked down the ranks, checking equipment and ammunition and here and there a rifle. He had a special word with the men married 'on the strength', a word of encouragement and hope: but read in the eyes the gnawing anxiety for wives and children that would go with them all the way into Kashmir...

Outside the vacated Officers' Mess, Lord Dornoch sat his horse, with Captain Black a few paces in front. Faces looked from stores and barrack-rooms: those who were being left behind as the skeleton of a holding company, the non-combatants, the sweepers, loyal Indians but not required on the march into active service; and from the married quarters the women and children, a tight little group trying to look cheerful for their men's sake but clearly afraid. Mrs Cunningham was there, as ramrod-like as her husband, talking to Lady Dornoch. One by one the companies of the battalion were reported ready to the Adjutant: when all the reports were in, Black turned his horse and rode the short distance to the Colonel.

He saluted. "Battalion ready to move out and entrain, Colonel."

"Thank you, Captain Black. Move out, if you please."

Another salute, and the Adjutant rode away towards the waiting line, caught the eye of the Regimental Sergeant-Major and of Pipe-Major Ross. Ross gave a barely perceptible nod; the pipers lifted their instruments, the drummers poised their sticks. In a loud voice Black gave the orders: "Battalion will advance in column of route. Into column, right... *turn!*"

As the whole battalion came round as one, Lord Dornoch rode his horse forward to take his place at the head of the column behind the pipes and drums, with the Queen's and Regimental Colours and the colour guard behind him. Officially the colours had not been taken into active service since those of the Northamptonshire Regiment, 48th and 58th of the British line, had been carried into action at Laing's Nek in the Drakensberg in 1881; but because of Sir Iain Ogilvie's personal wishes in the matter, they were still carried by the Royal Strathspey and to date officialdom had turned a blind eye. Lord Dornoch gave the order: "Bugler, sound the advance." As the strident notes streamed across the cantonments, the bugles of the brigade battalions also sounded out into the still air of the morning. The last marching order was given; the pipers stepped out briskly, puffing air into the bags beneath their left arms. The ranks moved away in column past the women, their rifles at the slope and the pipes sadly yet hopefully playing.

> "We're no' awa' tae bide awa',
> We're no' awa' tae leave ye ...
> We're no' awa' tae bide awa',
> We'll aye come back and see ye ..."

Dust curled up around the marching feet, dimming the shine of the boots. The wail of the pipes and the drumbeats echoed off the cantonment buildings, and across the parade as the highlanders marched away a child started crying. At the same moment a young woman, white-faced and hysterical, rushed across the parade-ground, her arms wide, and one of the privates fell out, going to meet her with his rifle at the trail. At once Black rode down the column, his face stiff, shouting.

"Fall in, that man! You there, woman, get away back to your quarter this instant!" The young woman stopped, tearful, irresolute in the face of military anger. The private, her husband, called out to her, "Go back, Jeannie, go on back and dinna fret. Awa' wi' ye, lass!"

She stayed where she was, face now hidden in her hands. Black stood in his stirrups. "Sar'nt-Major, that man's name. He's to go on report, d'you hear, Mr Cunningham?"

"Aye, sir, I hear." Cunningham's voice was sharp with disapproval, but dutifully he hazed the man back into the ranks. The pipes and drums continued playing; the men kept their eyes front, compassionately not noticing the distress, and the column marched through the cantonment gates and away.

# 8

THERE WERE THREE trains to take the entourages and the escorting brigade, one ahead and one in the rear of that carrying the Viceroy and the Maharajah. The trains were overcrowded, stuffy, uncomfortable for the rank and file. Soon it would grow unbearably hot: as the engines chuffed away from the railway station at two-minute intervals all the windows were down, with the Scots leaning out from the centre train to catch what air they could. Now there was laughter and cheering: the single men at all events were happy; and since they were vastly in the majority the departure was a stirring one. The entrained pipes and drums were of necessity silent, but there was vociferous singing of 'Soldiers of the Queen' after the brass band on the platform had played them out to the melanchony strains of 'Auld Lang Syne'.

Once they were away, with the Maharajah and the Viceroy and the more important personages of their retinues sitting luxuriously in drawing-room coaches reminiscent of those used by Her Majesty for visiting Balmoral, the sergeants and corporals moved along the train, shouting at the men from the windows.

"Come along there, move away—get sat down those that can. We'll not want to block the fresh air for the others—"

"Or the bloody dust!" A raw-boned Jock turned from his window. "God, the dust!"

"You've been long enough in India—"

"To swallow dust and like it—I know, Sergeant." The Scot swatted at flies: they all swatted at flies, right along the train's length. Crawling, tickling, irritating, inflaming tempers even before the real close heat bit into the packed troop train's sweating occupants. None was immune: in his carriage Lord

Dornoch swatted with his officers: only the Indians of the Maharajah's entourage bore the flies' attentions passively, though the Maharajah himself sat beneath the busy fans of two young eunuchs whose charge was to keep His Highness free of the unworthy insects' investigating probosces and hurrying legs. At the rear of the long, slow-moving train the flies had their field-day: there in open trucks travelled the commissariat, both British and native, watched and attended by low-caste Indians. Behind them again came the horses, eight to a truck. Behind again, in the guard's van, a section of the Royal Strathspeys, under a subaltern and a sergeant, bore with fortitude the smells that wafted back upon them as the train ground slowly along: even with two engines in front to haul and one more behind to push, progress was diabolical. Slow enough indeed for the Adjutant occasionally to get down to the track-side and walk along by the open trucks to communicate with the rearguard section and with the section that, with its rifles and fixed bayonets, guarded the front engines and tenders. There was much vigilance in the air as the troop train pulled into open countryside, and a good deal of tension as it began the approach later to the first of the river bridges, the one spanning the Indus. Some two hundred yards short of the bridge, the trains were halted and contact was made with an officer from the Rawalpindi brigade acting as guard upon all the bridges. This officer, a major, reported to Lord Dornoch, who had got down upon the track.

"All safe, sir."

"No tribes around?"

"None, sir. We've scouts out over a very wide area, and they've all reported peace and quiet, not a sight of the Pathan anywhere."

"What d'you make of it, Major?"

"That's hard to say." The Major pulled at his moustache. "It could mean...almost anything. A genuine intent to leave His Excellency alone—or the other thing, of course!"

"Luring us on to more favourable pastures—for them?"

"Exactly, sir."

"And your Brigadier-General?"

"Feels it's safe enough to cross the Indus at all events. We're in full control here!"

"No explosives found?"

"No, nothing at all."

Dornoch nodded. "I'll report along those lines to my Brigade

Commander, then, and you can assume we shall proceed. Thank you, Major."

The Major saluted and turned his horse; as he rode off to his own brigade HQ, Dornoch climbed back aboard the train and made his way to his Brigadier-General, who was travelling with the Viceroy. He made his report; the Brigadier-General passed the order to carry on. Leaving the royal coach, Dornoch found Black waiting for orders.

"We move, Andrew, dead slow. Pass the word to the trains ahead and in rear, if you please."

Black saluted. "Very good, Colonel." He went off towards the lead locomotive, had words with the driver: a moment later the steam-whistle shrilled out a signal of two long blasts and the Adjutant walked back to his carriage. As he swung himself aboard, the train jerked and moved on slowly for the bridge. As they inched out across the Indus River there was a feeling that every man was holding his breath. No matter what the security, here, surely, was the ideal chance for mutinous natives to act. Yet Ogilvie for one felt it would not come now: there was still the Maharajah of Jammu and Kashmir to join the party. He stared down at strong military detachments armed with rifles and Maxims, some on the nearer bank, some on floating pontoons around the piles that carried the railway track across the river. Mud swirled, a brown flood running to the distant mouths of the delta below Karachi, bearing dead branches of trees and animal carcases moving sluggishly down-stream. In the event the trains crossed in safety, coming within the protection of more soldiers on the farther bank. Once across, speed was increased. At intervals along the track, dispersed troop formations of section strength presented arms as the viceregal and princely coaches rolled past them. A little before luncheon a message came to Lord Dornoch and his officers, requesting the pleasure of their company for a glass of sherry in the Maharajah's coach. Led by the Colonel and Major Hay, the officers attended in a body. The scene was within its physical limits a splendid one: two thrones, even, had been fitted into the coach, side by side facing the engine, the Viceroy's slightly larger and more splendid than the Maharajah's and bearing on its back the Royal Arms of Great Britain. Such of the 114th's officers as had not already been presented in Peshawar were presented now. Ogilvie felt the keen interest of the Viceroy, was aware of Lord Elgin's shrewd and appraising look, a look that swept him from head to toe as he bowed formally and then shook hands with the seated personages.

"Sir Iain's son, of course," Elgin remarked.

"Yes, Your Excellency."

Lord Elgin smiled. "I trust one day you'll serve some future Viceroy in the same capacity and as faithfully as your father serves me."

"Thank you, sir. If I command the battalion I'll be pleased enough!"

"Yes, yes, indeed. A family tradition, and one I'd like to talk about, Captain Ogilvie. When I can manage a few minutes, I'll send an ADC to you."

"Thank you, sir." Ogilvie gave another formal bow and turned about, yielding place to another of the company commanders waiting to be presented. It was all something of a mêlée, the coach was too crowded, and it was hard to keep one's feet against the swaying motion: the springing was perhaps too good, the track undoubtedly had too many bends in it for comfort. Ogilvie, handed a glass of dry sherry by a bearded servant carrying a tray of solid gold, had difficulty in finding the elbow room in which to raise it to his lips: and when he had done so the effort seemed scarcely worth while. The sherry was execrable, so dry as to be both tasteless and colourless, and of poor quality. His Highness of Mysore, currently rising from his throne to drink a fruit juice, would be no connoisseur of wines. Presumably no Hindu would be; but in his place Ogilvie would have beheaded his wine-chooser! Reflecting upon Lord Elgin's words, he steadied himself against the back of an armchair, one of several set upon swivels and with fine views from the wide windows of the swaying, rattling coach. The Viceroy, he believed, had been seeking an excuse: his interest lay not in the military traditions of the Ogilvies but in the brief undercover activities of their most junior member... Ogilvie's attention wandered to His Highness as the youthful Maharajah spoke to the Colonel and the Brigadier-General. In the West, one was not accustomed to child rulers, still less to feudal monarchs who ruled in the direct and positive sense that the Maharajahs of India ruled their subject peoples. This child's advisers carried a high responsibility, one that they might or might not be discharging to the good of their dependent people: here in India there was much opportunity for nest-feathering. It was not the duty of a captain of infantry to speculate on such matters, but

Ogilvie could not help but reflect upon the apparent fact that the threat to British India directly involved a native prince. The would-be mutineers, the followers of the Mullah from Kashmir, had no more love for the native princes than they had for the British, and the courts of the maharajahs would become blood-baths along with the cantonments and residencies and the outly-ing forts and the hill stations. The disparities of wealth were too great, the contrasts of splendour and misery too apparent; yet innocence should not be made to suffer death, and at the age of eleven His Highness of Mysore could scarcely be held in guilt. Talking to a staff major now, Ogilvie found his eyes wandering again towards the Maharajah and the boy's remarkable self-possession, far beyond that of any British boy of similar age. To all appearances he was holding his own in conversation with the senior officers, and Ogilvie's guess was that that conversation would not be of school, and cricket, and rugger as would have been the case with a British prep school boy. But British prep school boys did not rule great tracts of country and millions of men and women: they were still learning to rule an Empire, and boyish things came first... Ogilvie was watching the Maharajah when there was a sudden violent jerk: the train's brakes had been slammed on, hard. All the occupants of the drawing-room coach went flat, the Maharajah himself vanishing in the chaos of jumbled bodies. Overall there was a hiss of escaping steam, and the shouts of men, and then a crackle of rifle fire from ahead, joined by the stutter of a Maxim. Ogilvie scrambled to his feet, his right shoulder sore and aching from hard collision with the floor of the coach. With the rest of the Scots officers he jumped down to the track, his revolver in his hand, and ran ahead towards the sound of the rifles. The train had been passing through a rift in the hills, and the sides were steep: looking up as he raced on, Ogilvie saw no signs of life, no watching Pathans with jezails to fire down upon the train. It seemed unlikely they had been ambushed, and surely any frontal attack upon the locomotives would have been supported from the flanks, especially in such a place between the hills? Ahead of him Ogilvie caught sight of Robin Stuart, E Company Commander, and called out:

"What's happened up there?"

Stuart turned, shouted briefly, "Body on the track. We've got one of the buggers who put it there—the rest got clean away." He turned back to face front, running out of sight ahead of the

81

leading train. Ogilvie went on through the clouds of steam and smoke, past the craning necks at the windows, overtaking men crouched along the track behind their ready rifles. Coming round the locomotive he was brought up short by a sight of the cause of the trouble: the body lying across the track, the scarlet tunic, the gaping empty neck-band, the headless major, now very decomposed.

*　　*　　.　*

The man shot by the locomotive guard was dead, with a bullet in his throat. Of the others there was no sign: Stuart said there had been three more, wild-looking Pathans who had rolled the dreadful corpse down the hillside to the railway line. Search parties, sent out on both flanks and ahead, reported nothing, and the Brigadier-General, after consultation with Lord Elgin, gave the order for the trains to move out: there was no point in delay, but there was possible danger in remaining below the hills. Shortly afterwards Ogilvie, sooner than he had expected, had his private talk with the Viceroy in the latter's bedroom carriage.

"The same body, Captain Ogilvie?"

"So far as I can say, Your Excellency. The regimentals were the same, certainly."

The Viceroy nodded: headless bodies were hard to identify. "You referred to a symbol. I'd like you to expand a little on your earlier report, which of course I've seen."

Ogilvie said, "Frankly, sir, there's little to add. The headless body, the headless Raj." He hesitated. "A threat to yourself, sir, very directly, in my view."

"No doubt. Yet on this occasion there was no attack, either upon me or anyone else."

"No, sir."

"Why?"

"That's hard to answer, sir."

"Make an attempt, Ogilvie. You've had contact with these elements—even with this Mullah. I haven't—yet! I'm interested in your personal appraisal."

"I've little to offer, sir." Ogilvie hesitated, feeling awkward under the Viceroy's close and expectant scrutiny. "On the surface, what's just happened seems pointless. Yet the Mullah would have seen some point, I'm sure."

"Well?"

"Sir, the Mullah is a man of symbols, as I put in my report. This could have been another—a scaring tactic, to impress our troops and also the local natives, and our own camp followers and bearers. It's possible the Mullah may believe something's leaked— if he doesn't in fact accept that my body was amongst those blown up in Harazan, he'll know for certain there's been a leak. He may see a need to impress the men—a kind of earnest, sir, a sample of what he can and will do."

The Viceroy laughed. "Then he must think again, Ogilvie! He'll not weaken our resolve in such a way—what does he imagine the Raj is made of?"

The question required no answer. Ogilvie waited, reflecting on the inadequacy of his own response to His Excellency. It was possible, he fancied, that the Mullah's curious gambit may even have had the opposite intent: the *hardening* of the British resolve, of the Viceroy's own resolve, to continue to Srinagar—rather than be seen to fear headless, decomposing bodies! The Viceroy got to his feet and looked out of the window as the train pulled on for Rawalpindi. He remained by the window until they came clear of the hills, their sides shallowing and falling away to reveal a broad stretch of sun-dried plain and a metallic blue sky that hurt the eyes. The heat was intense: Ogilvie spared a thought for the rearguard down-wind of one of the horse trucks: into an open truck in a crate emptied of foodstuffs had gone the body of the headless major, packed tight in ice provided from the viceregal commissariat's ice-boxes. The corpse would last as far as Rawalpindi, where it would be placed in the cool of the garrison mortuary pending further orders. An officer of the Army Medical Staff would no doubt be required to issue a post-mortem report, an unpleasant task. Lord Elgin swung round from the window and faced Ogilvie once again. "This Mullah," he observed coolly, "must be taught a lesson. I am not impressed by him. We continue from Rawalpindi into Kashmir, and I have no doubt we shall arrive and return intact."

\*     \*     \*

The remaining river crossings were made without incident and under strong bridge-guards as before. The viceregal train pulled slowly and ponderously with much creaking of woodwork into the railway station at Rawalpindi, the leading train being signalled into a siding until Their Excellencies and His Highness had disembarked with the Royal Strathspeys. As at Peshawar, the station, cleared long since of unauthorised natives, was resplendent: Lieutenant-General Sir Iain Ogilvie, Northern Army Commander, meticulously uniformed and booted for the ride with the column even though he was to be merely an onlooker, was there to greet the important personages, and a battalion of infantry had been paraded on the platform. Outside the station waited a Captain's Escort of The Guides. A military band played, bugles sounded the General Salute. It was late afternoon now, but there was to be no delay overnight: the procession was to move out for the Kashmiri border within the hour, making camp at sundown and continuing with the first light of dawn, at which time the ceremonies of Dasara were to begin. As speedily as possible the stores of food and ammunition, the horses and the mules, were detrained: the fresh elephants were brought up, as were wagons for the commissariat. The rank and file sweated in the last of the day's full heat, lashed by the shouts of the NCOs and the commands of the various adjutants and quartermasters as they worked at the loading of the wagons and the assembling of the long column of march. The guns and the cavalry now joined, with more regiments of the line to reinforce the vital escort into the Kashmiri hills. Cunningham worked like ten men, overseeing the 114th's share in the march and getting the Scots fallen in by companies in the lead to act as vanguard and to provide the advanced scouting parties and the pickets in the hills, the eyes of the column who would be its first protection from attack. When all was ready the many reports were made: coloursergeants to company commanders, company commanders to adjutants, adjutants to colonels, colonels to brigadier-generals, and finally brigadier-generals to the Major-General appointed to the command of the special force, one Major-General Sir Thomas Lee, late the 10th Hussars. Sir Thomas gave the order to move out, and the column got under way to the skirl of the pipes and the beat of the drums. In the lead the face of Pipe-Major Ross was a study in sheer disbelief as the stirring tune of 'The Campbells Are Coming' was, despite the Indians' love of Scots pipe music, overlaid in a most disorderly fashion by a cacophony of flutes and bells and tinny-sounding apologies for drums coming from the colourful hordes of the native retinue.

*      *      *

"Captain Ogilvie!"

Ogilvie turned: Andrew Black was riding down upon him, silhouetted against the last of the daylight and the stark backdrop of the northern hills through which they would pass on the morrow. Camp had been made half an hour previously, and the regimental lines were taking shape, an orderly scene of row upon row of white canvas with the Maharajah's entourage safely positioned between the two escorting infantry brigades with the attached cavalry and artillery on the flanks. Two of the tents stood out beneath the standards of their exalted occupants—the Maharajah's and the Viceroy's, each with a strong personal guard mounted upon them.

No doubt because of the presence of the exalted persons, Black was on edge.

"Your company is to provide the night perimeter guard for the van, Captain Ogilvie. Kindly make your dispositions, and see your men fully alert."

"Very good. Who's the stand-by company?"

"E Company will provide the stand-by, Captain Ogilvie, and will turn out at a moment's notice." Black stood in his stirrups, and looked all around the camp's perimeter. The Major-General had chosen his site well: they were in open country, nicely clear of the hills, and the moonlight should see to it that no-one approached unnoticed. There was no cover anywhere beyond the little provided by scrubby bushes and a few trees. After tonight, it would be different, and Black's long look towards the northern hills was an anxious one. With less formality than he had used so far, he expressed his anxiety.

"I do not like it, James. That body with no head...a terrible thing. There is a bad wind blowing for the Raj!"

"We shall weather it."

Black's teeth gleamed in the fading light, a stretch of lips into a nervy grin. "I hope so, I hope so indeed."

"Surely you haven't any real doubts, Andrew?"

"I have never had doubts until now," Black said in a low voice, "but when all's said and done, we British in India are very, very few against so many hundreds of millions of the natives." He gave a sudden shiver. "Despite all assurances, Canute failed, did he not, to turn the tide?"

85

Ogilvie stared: Abruptly, the Adjutant pulled his horse round and rode away towards the Colonel's tent. It was Ogilvie's moment now for worry: Andrew Black was a cold man and a moody one, given to bolstering his courage with the whisky-bottle and not over-keen to expose his body to action—but not precisely a coward, for he valued his reputation beyond his skin when it came to the point. And he had never spoken in such terms before. To Andrew Black, as to every man in the regiment, to every ordinary soldier throughout India, the Raj had been impregnable; the high command, with its wider knowledge of the world balance of power and of the aspirations of such men as the Czar of All The Russias as well as of the insidious effects of native dissidents, may have had their doubts—but not the officers or men of the combatant units. Black's reaction was an alarming one, and if he could have it, so might others. Riding towards his company lines, Ogilvie thrust Andrew Black from his mind. Seeking out Colour-Sergeant MacTrease he passed the orders for the perimeter guard.

"Sir! I'll draw up the roster immediately, sir. What strength is the guard to be?"

"Twenty men, two NCOs, one officer. Two-hour watches. I shall be taking the first and last two hours myself, and Mr Baird and Mr MacIver the middle spells."

"Aye, sir. Are there any special orders, sir?"

Ogilvie shook his head. "No, Colour-Sar'nt. Just a full alertness, that's all. But we'll do well to remember the large number of natives in out midst, which is something beyond the normal in our experience."

"You mean, sir—"

"I mean this," Ogilvie said crisply. "They could panic if the alarm's given, or they just *could* contain subversive elements, Colour MacTrease, according to the Adjutant. Either way, they'll need to be watched as carefully as any Pathan in the passes!"

*     *     *

A solitary piper of the 114th Highlanders, after Last Post, played Lights Out over an already darkened encampment, its tents shining white and stark beneath the climbing moon. Tradition was being kept up: every night since the regiment had been formed in the Monadliath Mountains of Speyside, a piper of the Royal Strathspey, like a kilted ghost in the shadows, had held men's attention with the sad, thin notes of 'The Flowers of the Forest'. Every night from the battlements of the depot in Invermore, and from wherever the battalions had been serving: over Stirling Castle, over Edinburgh Castle and the winding, narrow streets of the Old Town lying steeply below the age-old walls ... over the great bastions of the Rock of Gibraltar standing gaunt beneath the low-slung stars; over the grim brown-ness of Aden; over the long-ago battlefields of the Peninsular War, the Crimea, the Mutiny itself; in Africa, Hong Kong and Singapore, and along the North-West Frontier. No exception was made to-night: the camp was in any case open and visible. Ogilvie, moving restlessly along the perimeter upon his watch, was moved as ever by the piper's inherent poignancy. The tune symbolised the regiment and the many dead over the years of war and the turbulent years of keeping the Pax Britannica, which, for those who had died on Indian service was, in truth, very war ... The tune ending, the piper stood for a moment like a statue, outlined against the hills, then put his pipes beneath his arm and marched away. Ogilvie listened to boots striking against the hard ground, a fading sound in the night, precise and disciplined. A small thing but heartening: throughout the army in India, the discipline would hold, that was certain. Whatever was to come would be met with courage and steadfastness and with faith in the fighting qualities of the British line.

# 9

"A NICE PEACEFUL night it was, sir." Cunningham rubbed at
weary eyes: he had had little sleep himself, lying wakeful in his
tent with his revolver handy, getting up at intervals to make his
own survey of the camp's perimeter, the act of a man whose one
fault lay in the direction of over-conscientiousness. "But I'd not
be too sure about today—and I don't mean the Pathan, Captain
Ogilvie, sir!"

"Then what, Mr Cunningham?"

"The priests, sir. Dasara! Already you can't hear yourself think!
Or *I* can't, and that's the truth."

Ogilvie laughed. Cunningham was exaggerating; the sounds of
the various native musical instruments were irritating but were
largely absorbed by the sheer space round them or overlaid by the
sounds of the troops as they prepared to march out. There was a
ragged line of men at their ablutions in a running, clear stream,
others were shaving, their mirrors propped before them in cleft
sticks. A clatter of pots and pans and kettles came from the
field kitchens, and appetising smells were wafted on a slight breeze
out of Himalaya, cold and freshening. Orders were being shouted
as various details fell in under the sergeants and corporals, and
the tents were struck and packed away. Thus was Dasara muted,
but the Regimental Sergeant-Major was still disapproving.

Ogilvie remarked, "Live and let live, Sar'nt-Major!"

"That's all very well, sir. God's God, Mahomet's Mahomet—"

"Wrong religion, Sar'nt-Major."

"With respect, sir, I was going on to say, their gods are their
gods—once you can sort them out, which is not easy." Cunningham rose and fell on the balls of his feet, chest out,

stomach in as far as he could manage, a hand teasing the waxed ends of his moustache. "They're perfectly free to worship them at the proper time, but I think they should not hold religious festivals upon the march, sir. I think the Commander-in-Chief should have issued orders stopping it, sir—"

"It's their religion, and their country, you know."

"I do know, sir, and I do not deny it. But they're going to be a perishing *nuisance*, sir!"

"The cross we must bear into Kashmir, Sar'nt-Major. Ours not to reason why...and all that!"

"Sir!" Cunningham, looking huffy at platitudes and clichés, swung a vast hand to the brim of his Wolseley helmet in a salute that vibrated before a red, simmering face and glaring eyes; then turned about with a crash of boot-leather and marched away, left-right-left, to begin shouting for the colour-sergeants. Ogilvie sighed, then smiled to himself. Like the Black Watch, like the Argyll and Sutherland, the Royal Strathspey had in the possession of its Sergeant's Mess a much honoured and long embalmed ram's head with silver-tipped horns, a strong face and glazed eyes. On guest nights this defunct animal was by custom placed upon the table before the Regimental Sergeant-Major: and there were occasions, this early morning being one, when there was a most remarkable resemblance between RSM and ram, and about as much sense to be got from the obstinacy of the one as from the embalmed state of the other. In the meantime it seemed that Dasara was on other minds as well as Cunningham's: Ogilvie was making his way towards the trestle table set up for the officers' breakfasts when he was approached by the Colonel's runner.

"Captain Ogilvie, sir. The Colonel's compliments, and he'd like you to attend his tent, sir."

"Very well, thank you." Ogilvie returned the man's salute and headed for the Colonel. The other company commanders were already present, together with Major Hay and Black.

Lord Dornoch, seated on a collapsible camp-stool, nodded an acknowledgment of Ogilvie's salute. "I'll summarise, James. Brigade's had representations from His Highness's major-domo or whatever he's called. Assistance is wanted."

"With what, Colonel?"

"Dasara, I'm afraid. This is not to be taken lightly, I might add. The assistance as requested is of a somewhat negative nature—

which is why I stress it must not be allowed to become a matter for laughter." The Colonel paused. "You know, of course, that as from dawn the Maharajah has gone into what I might call retreat."

"Confinement to his tent and howdah, Colonel?"

"Yes. Normally he'd be in his room, but being now mobile...if he's seen by the human eye at the wrong times, Dasara's wrecked. Well, we don't want to be accused of wrecking Dasara, gentlemen, and Brigade tells me that British eyes are a damn sight more wrecking than native ones. To cut this short, the men are not to look towards His Highness's tent or howdah. If they must be in the vicinity of either, they are to avert their eyes, if necessary making their approach backwards as they come up, and then turning front once they're past." Lord Dornoch's face was as straight as a die. "You are to inform your colour-sergeants that they are to interpret the order with the utmost strictness and be vigilant that it is obeyed at all relevant times, which to be on the safe side they are to interpret as *all* times. Furthermore, there is to be no unnecessary shouting of orders...I gather there was a direct reference here to our RSM. Well? Are there any questions?"

There was a silence, a rather stony one. Ogilvie broke it. "One only, Colonel. Who is to tell Mr Cunningham?"

Dornoch's face twitched. "I think we can leave that duty to the Adjutant, James."

\*     \*     \*

"...and there is another thing, Captain Ogilvie, sir, in fact two things, the orders for which have just reached me."

"Well, Sar'nt-Major?" Ogilvie's face was as straight as the Colonel's had been, but with an immense effort: Cunningham was seething. "What are these other things?"

"A shroud of heavy canvas, sir, and a thunderbox."

"*Shroud?*"

"For invisible transportation, sir, of His Highness from tent to howdah at dawn and conversely, sir, from howdah to tent at nightfall. His Highness will enshroud before transferring, then deshroud in privacy. Sir!"

"And the thunderbox?"

"His Highness has observed the officers' thunderboxes, sir, and wishes one of his own, but more elaborate. A thunderbox with a surround, sir, a wooden screen."

"Which he'll enter and leave in his shroud?"

"That is correct, sir."

"But surely he's made arrangements for such things, Sar'nt-Major?"

"I gather there was a gold po, sir."

"Well, then!"

Cunningham shook his head. "No, sir. That was for use en route from Mysore to Peshawar, at which point, sir, Dasara had not begun. I don't know the ins and outs, Captain Ogilvie, but it's my opinion there's been poor staff work, one of his retinue slipped up. And now he's relying upon us, sir. God Almighty! The things the British Army is called upon to do! Sir!"

Saluting, the Regimental Sergeant-Major turned away and marched off to organise shrouds and thunderboxes. Orders came down from Sir Thomas Lee that the march was not to be delayed by construction work; and the Maharajah was handed, through his tent flap, a large sheet of canvas in which for now he could enfold himself for lifting into the curtained howdah. The long column formed up by battalions in route order, with men under the Farrier-Sergeant of the 114th working on the encased thunderbox in the back of a rumbling, lurching commissariat wagon. When, as they moved towards the pass into the hills, singing started in the ranks, a hasty conference was called around the Major-General's horse; within minutes the various adjutants were riding down the column with orders for the company commanders: no singing upon the march. This was Dasara, and the voice of the heathen was unwelcome.

\*     \*     \*

From the Major-General, in the lead ahead of the pipes and drums of the Royal Strathspey, now as silent as the men's voices, the scouts were seen, a file of two doubling back with a corporal and an apparent prisoner. Sir Thomas Lee put up his field-glasses, as did Lord Dornoch.

"Well, Dornoch? What d'you make of that?"

"I think we'll have to wait and see, Sir Thomas."

There was a grunt. "I suppose you're right. In the meantime we'll not alarm His Highness, or His Excellency either."

"No stand-to?"

91

"It's not necessary. We'd have had word on the heliograph of an ambush." They rode on in silence, were rejoined by the Brigadier-General of the 114th's brigade who had ridden down the column for a word of cheer to his battalions. The Major-General waved a hand towards the approaching scouts, but said nothing. He continued riding ahead as the corporal saluted and made his report.

"What looked like a native, sir, apprehended as he descended the hillside from the west, sir, into the pass—"

"*Looked* like a native, Corporal?"

"He says he's a Political Officer, sir, from Murree, sir."

"He does, does he?" Sir Thomas looked down searchingly at the ragged figure still held by the privates of the escort. "Speak up for yourself, man. Who are you, and what are you doing?"

"Major Butler, sir, attached Northern Army Command...now *de*tached as you can see."

"I suppose you carry no identification?"

"Hardly, sir. But I can stand up under questioning."

"I trust so." The Major-General looked keenly at the speaker. "You're finding standing up difficult at the moment, I fancy!"

"I've walked a long way, sir, and without food."

"Quite so, quite so. The name of your senior officer at Murree?"

"Colonel Fitzjames."

"H'm. Know his wife—do you?"

There was a sardonic smile. "Colonel Fitzjames is single, sir."

"Indeed he is. Your regiment before you were seconded?"

"First Punjabis, sir, Colonel Henderson commanding." The man staggered a little as he walked along, was held straight by his escort. "Sir, there is a matter of urgency—"

"Yes, yes. Well, sir, you sound English enough to me, to be sure." Sir Thomas signed to the escort; they fell out, but stood by to assist the Political Officer should he be in need. "Make your report, if you please, Major Butler."

"Sir, I found movement in the hills, well ahead of your line of march and a little to the west. A body of native horsemen, Pathans, well armed and riding purposefully—"

"Purposefully?"

"I know the Pathan, Sir Thomas. I know when he has a purpose, and when he is merely roving with an eye to the main chance."

"And their purpose? Were you able to assess that?"

Butler, leaning now on the arm of the corporal as he moved

along beside the General's horse, said, "I know who they were at all events: the man known as the Mullah, sir, and his personal guard."

"The Mullah!" Sir Thomas Lee reined in his horse and called to his bugler. "Sound the Halt!" As the notes of the bugle sounded loudly on the still air, the long column came to rest behind the General, bunching a little towards the rear. In the centre the Maharajah's entourage and commissariat bulged out sideways: orders from the Brigade Commanders sent company officers riding up and down the column on both sides in an effort to contain the natives on the track. The Major-General dismounted and called to his Chief of Staff to send for a doctor and orderlies and to prepare a casualty wagon for Major Butler. "Now, Major," he said. "How sure are you that it was the Mullah you saw?"

"Very sure, Sir Thomas. A full description was passed to me some days ago, by the telegraph to Srinagar and a runner sent out—"

"Captain Ogilvie's description?"

Butler nodded. "It was a good one. In any case, I've met the Mullah before, a little more than a year ago. In those days, he was not especially eminent ... but it seems that times have brought him more renown!"

"Did he see you?"

"No, Sir Thomas. I'd seen the riders coming, and I was in good cover when they passed by—"

"Heading where, d'you suppose?"

"Srinagar—that's a guess, but I fancy it's a good one. They'll have confederates there, and the Mullah is at home with his Muslims in Srinagar. It's his old stamping-ground."

"Major, this threat of attack—of mutiny. Have you any information for me or His Excellency?"

"That depends how much you know already, sir, but at the moment we have little to go upon but rumour and the bush telegraph." Butler rubbed at weary eyes. "If, as I've suggested, the Mullah's making for Srinagar, then it seems likely enough Srinagar's where the trouble will come."

"In Srinagar, rather than upon the march?"

Butler shrugged. "I'd not rule out some kind of attack en route by over-enthusiastic tribesmen!"

"I see. Well, there will be a conference of my staff officers

93

directly you've eaten. After that I shall draft a despatch for the field telegraph to Rawalpindi."

As the Chief of Staff rode up with a medical officer and a small cart, Lee passed the order for the column to fall out for a rest period: the men sat down for a smoke and to take welcome water from the bottles of the regimental *bhistis*. Within half an hour Sir Thomas Lee had held his conference and drafted his informatory despatch: and within ten more minutes was approached by his Signal Officer with a report that the lines of the field telegraph, laid on the march by the sappers, had been cut.

"Cut, by God! Are you sure?"

"Quite sure, sir. There's no communication at all. We can send men back—"

"No, no, I can't accept such a delay—the cut could have been made many miles back and the line can be cut again." There was always the likelihood that the field telegraph would be cut on any march, and the facts had to be reckoned with; nevertheless there was a naked feel about being thus out of communication and the Major-General's face was anxious enough as he summoned all brigade and battalion commanders to attend upon him. They were given word that the Mullah was ahead of them and that their reception in Srinagar could be a hot one.

"This confounded madman," Lee said, "will without doubt seek our total destruction. If he does..." He had no need to put it into words: the column was a massive one and had seriously depleted the reserves at Murree and the other garrisons. If they should be defeated, it would be hard to put another army into the field until it was too late for the Raj. Lee's face was grim and anxious as he rode down the column to make his report to Lord Elgin and to receive any further orders from that high source. He was quickly back: there was, he said, no change. The march continued: it was too late to draw back, and the dangers were in any case well enough known. There was one fresh order: Major Butler was to accompany a cavalry probe ahead to catch up with and identify the Mullah's party, who were to be engaged and the Mullah taken alive. Lee had represented to His Excellency that the Political Officer was in no fit state to ride immediately and would require rest. The matter being in the Viceroy's view most urgent, Captain Ogilvie was to ride in place of Major Butler.

*　　*　　*

As the column marched out encumbered by the native horde, James Ogilvie rode ahead with a squadron of The Guides and a mule-borne battery of mountain guns. Butler had given him his direction: straight along the pass into Kashmir. Butler was certain the Mullah's party had been heading for Srinagar and that when sighted they had in fact been making for the main track.

"They have a good start on you, Ogilvie," he had said, then turned to the Captain commanding the mounted squadron. "You'll have no time for rests."

"We'll ride till we catch them," the cavalry officer said, meeting Ogilvie's eye: Ogilvie, returning the look, had found more than a trace of superciliousness. He was being stared up and down, and had found himself reacting against it. However, this was no time to indulge in umbrage. Riding now along the track northwards, Ogilvie learned that Captain Simon Quentin had little more than a year's Indian service, having transferred from the Blues, the Royal Horse Guards.

Ogilvie made conversation: "You find things rather different out here, no doubt."

"Indeed I do, Ogilvie, indeed I do. A different kind of officer, don't you know, no real connections—I refer to the Indian Army, of course, not the British regiments, though I'm bound to say the Household Cavalry..."

"Yes?"

"Oh, never mind," Quentin answered in a lofty tone. "As I was saying, the Indian Army...its British officers mostly came out for the extra pay, which really doesn't make for a good spirit—"

"And you?"

Quentin shrugged. "Not the pay, my dear chap! There seemed to be more scope, that's really why. A wider life. Things can get... *narrow*, in London society. One's a little too close to the Court at times." He said no more after that, seemed to feel he had already been too forthcoming to someone he had not met before. Ogilvie smiled inwardly: he suspected an involvement with a woman, probably a woman who would have proved unacceptable to Her Majesty's Household Cavalry—very likely an actress. If an officer of the household troops should wish to marry an actress, he was expected to send in his papers; an open indiscretion short of marriage even, at any rate if it should happen to reach the ears of the old Queen, could result in a transfer to the limits of Empire. And somehow Captain Simon Quentin had not the look of a man who would be at home on the North-West Frontier but rather the look of one who missed the London drawing-rooms and the debutantes and the stage doors. Yet he seemed competent enough and seemed also to have the respect of his squadron *duffardar*-major, a ferocious-looking man with a thick black beard whose superb horsemanship made him appear one with his horse. They rode on as fast as the terrain would allow, drawing well ahead of the van and scouts of the column winding its tedious way across the Kashmiri border. Soon the pass deepened between the great rock sides, cutting off the sun's rays, bringing virtual twilight to the track itself. The mounted men, and the gunners tending the mules that carried the stripped-down mountain battery, moved in a kind of vacuum, a vacuum in which their own sounds were the only ones to disturb a brooding atmosphere of hidden menace. Quentin gave an uneasy laugh. "A fine place for an ambush, Ogilvie," he said. "We wouldn't have a hope, against a strong attack."

"It won't be us they'll attack. They'll keep that for the main column—if at all. There'll still be no certainty in their minds that we know about the Mullah and his threat, and in the meantime they'll not be putting any straws into a wind that would blow them into our faces!"

"So you're still putting your money on Srinagar?"

Ogilvie nodded. "Yes, that's so."

"And the headless major, Ogilvie?" Quentin gave a hard laugh. "Was that not one of your straws?"

Ogilvie shrugged: in giving his unconvincing answer to a similar question from His Excellency, he had suggested that the Mullah might in fact have suspected that his plans were partially known to the British, but this was still supposition. They had so few straws, and nothing positive. Ogilvie was about to respond to the cavalry officer's question when there was a shout from behind.

"*Sahib . . . Captain Sahib, the peaks to the west!*"

Ogilvie and Quentin looked up: along the crests above the narrow, rock-strewn pass four great boulders were teetering back and forth. Quentin gave a gasp: already smaller stones were flying, bouncing off the rock sides, coming down in a shower.

Quentin stood in his stirrups. "Ride!" he shouted. "Fast as you can!" With Ogilvie and his subaltern he went ahead at a gallop, spurring his horse with desperate rakes of his rowels. There was a noise like thunder above the small force as the boulders got on the move, spinning and bouncing in a death-dance down into the floor of the pass.

# 10

IT WAS COLD between the hillsides, but the men and horses were in a lather of sweat. It seemed a miracle that they got through: all, in fact, did not. Two gunners and two mules at the rear of the force went straight into the fall of one of the spinning boulders, and were crushed to red pulp. A *sowar* of The Guides had broken his neck when thrown from his stumbling horse, three more had been badly injured in similar falls. The rest, once they were past, were ordered to dismount and take cover and to fire independently at anything that showed itself on the crests above. Nothing did: there was a curious silence and an utter lack of movement. Even the horses stood motionless, even the mules for a space.

"Now what?" Quentin asked, staring up at the deserted crests. "Do we continue, or ride back and warn the column?"

"We stay here," Ogilvie said, "and act as an advanced guard—to ensure they don't try the same sort of thing when the column comes up." He stared back along the pass. "A word of warning might be appreciated. I suggest you detach two of your *sowars*, Quentin, with a message for the General."

"Or as targets for."

"We'll cover them. This is vital."

Quentin glowered, but consented. He called to his *duffardar*-major and two *sowars* were detailed to ride back and report. With no time lost they galloped towards the south. As they went firing started from the crests and puffs of smoke showed. The bullets struck off rock, harmlessly: the men of The Guides took aim towards the smoke-puffs. When a head showed briefly, half-a-dozen rifles fired at it. There was a cry, and a man fell spread-eagled, a wild-looking Pathan whose body bounced like the boulders earlier, to a messy death on the jagged rocks of the pass. With the riders quickly out of range and safe, the fire from the crests was turned upon the cavalry and the guns. The men, horses and mules were settled down into all the cover that could be found: for the time being, protection was better than wasting ammunition upon an invisible enemy. At last the movement of the advancing column was heard: the escorting brigades were marching now to the pipes and drums of the Royal Strathspey, the music coming to the waiting men ahead even of the forward scouts.

"I thought," Quentin remarked to Ogilvie, "the General was respecting Dasara?"

Ogilvie grinned. "I expect my Colonel had something to do with the disrespect. When action's in sight, we Scots have a high regard for the pipes, and there's no military point in silence now."

"Well, I hope they get through bloody fast, that's all!" Quentin was studying the hill crests through his field-glasses. The column was a long one and would pass but slowly in fact; the lumbering elephants, slow and ponderous beasts except when stampeding in panic, would see to that with their nodding howdahs, as would the heavily laden commissariat carts and wagons. Quentin cursed under his breath: the time of danger would be long. Meanwhile his squadron had the crests nicely covered: but they would need sharp eyes and quick reactions. The Pathans would show themselves, if they showed themselves at all, only very briefly. The column came on; already now the scouts had made contact with the advanced force, breaking off to join the latter in their cover positions. At this stage there were no pickets out; the hillsides were too steep for climbing and for the construction of the temporary sangars that would normally have been roughed-out from the stones and broken rock on the slopes. The van came into Ogilvie's view, the pipes and drums sounding loud, beating off the close-set walls of what was almost a canyon. There was a slight climb towards the concealed cavalry position, and Ogilvie was able to look down upon the column. It was a splendid sight, a microcosm of Empire. Behind the colours and the proudly swirling kilts of the Royal Strathspey were the turbans and guidons of the Bengal Lancers with the gilded shabraques on the flanks of the horses; there was the native splendour of

Mysore with the richly caparisoned elephants and jewelled turbans and peacocks' feathers in the lurching howdahs behind the mahouts; and there were the dark shapes of the guns behind the polish and sparkle of the limbers. Above all was His Excellency the Viceroy of India and his train, like Queen Victoria's court trundling through the frontier hills. It was an extraordinary sight and an impressive one: Ogilvie was well aware that he was looking down on history in the making and that if the Mullah from Kashmir had his way then before many more days had passed a new page, and not a pretty one, might be written into the continuing story of the Empire, and that this wondrous caravan could prove the last chapter of the old.

*　　*　　*

"Not a damn thing," Sir Thomas Lee said, and said it again: "Not a damn thing—they must have allowed their courage to fail them, and simply made off!" He twisted in his saddle. "Where's Captain Ogilvie?"

"Sir!" Ogilvie rode up alongside the General, saluting.

"What d'you make of it, Ogilvie?"

"I doubt if their courage failed them, sir."

"So do I, frankly! But why not attack?" The General swung an arm above his head, towards the boulders on the crests. "There's plenty more ammunition, isn't there, all nicely poised!"

"Yes, sir. In my submission, sir, they simply didn't want to attack His Excellency here in the pass. I believe theirs was no more than a holding task—to stop The Guides overtaking the Mullah."

"Very possibly, very possibly." Sir Thomas gave a vigorous nod. "Coincidence, or foreknowledge, d'you suppose?"

"I don't know, sir. Perhaps simply an intelligent guess, when they saw cavalry moving ahead of the column, and moving fast. Faster than they'd normally move over such ground." Ogilvie paused expectantly. "May I ask what the orders will be now, sir?"

"The same, Ogilvie. Kindly rejoin Captain Quentin's squadron, and do your best to make up the time lost."

Ogilvie saluted smartly and turned away, making towards the waiting cavalry. As he went his ponderings were slightly rueful: there had been no rebuke from Sir Thomas either in word or tone, but the phrase 'make up the time lost' had stuck in Ogilvie's mind. The chase of the Mullah had been delayed, as it had turned out, unnecessarily ... Ogilvie rode on, rejoining the cavalry squadron and repeating the General's order to Quentin. The trumpeter sounded the Advance, and once again The Guides moved out along the pass. Behind them, the column's advance continued. Soon, with no further attack from the surrounding peaks, Ogilvie moved out into a wider section where the hillsides fell away to less steep inclines and above the riders the sky opened out, a shimmering steel-blue around the blazing sun.

*       *       *

In his Divisional Headquarters in Nowshera, Lieutenant-General Fettleworth read a despatch from Calcutta in growing alarm. His protuberant blue eyes switched their gaze from the sheet of paper to his Chief of Staff standing beside his desk.

"Those damn Russians!" he said. "Who does the Czar think he is, I'd like to know! Linked by marriage to Her Majesty—it's damn disgraceful!"

"But nothing new, sir."

Fettleworth's stare was vacant. "What?"

"We've faced threats from Russia before now. Marriage alliances seldom reduce national ambitions—"

"Then they damn well should!" Fettleworth interrupted energetically, swinging his stomach round towards the Chief of Staff. "If any son or daughter of mine contracted a marriage and then—and then—"

"Shall we stick to the point, sir?"

Fettleworth gaped. "What d'you mean, Lakenham?"

"You are not the Monarch, sir."

"Don't be impertinent, sir!" Fettleworth's face deepened in colour and his eyes bulged dangerously, sky-blue sapphires in royal purple. A fist thumped the rich leather top of the desk. "I will not be spoken to—"

"I apologise, sir," Brigadier-General Lakenham said frostily. He indicated the despatch. "There are decisions to be made at once, and Calcutta to be answered."

"Damn Civilians. God, how I detest the Civilians!" Fettleworth picked up the despatch, held it at arm's length and read it through again. The implications of its contents were frightening:

further intelligence had reached the Secretariat through extended Political Officers and other functionaries, among them the British Agent in Kandahar and the Resident in Kunarja. The infiltrating Russian forces were coming together between Kabul and the western mouth of the Khyber Pass more massively than had been feared and all the indications were that a vast expedition was in course of formation; also that the army waiting in the mountains of the Hindu Kush between the Khatinza and the Agram Passes had been greatly strengthened and was starting to move towards Chitral. It could not escape the attention of the Commander of Her Majesty's First Division that these armies were nicely poised to strike not only at the Peshawar and Nowshera garrisons, currently much depleted, but also down from the north via Chitral and Ghilgit to Srinagar, where shortly the Viceroy was due to make his entry. Calcutta, as ever, was being devious: the bloody Civilians, Fettleworth thought vengefully, always avoided decisions when they could, so that they could the better blame the military when things went wrong. Currently, the despatch was for advice only, a merely informatory document; but woe betide the General Officer who failed to act upon the words hidden between the lines! And with the Northern Army Commander en route for Srinagar in the Viceroy's company, the responsible officer was Lieutenant-General Fettleworth...

"What the bloody hell," Fettleworth enquired, "do they expect me to *do*?"

"One thing only at this stage, sir," Lakenham answered.

"What?"

"Inform Sir Iain Ogilvie by the field telegraph, I would suggest—"

"But he's not actually commanding the column, Lakenham."

"I see no difference, sir, since he still commands the Northern Army, but if you wish, then inform Sir Thomas Lee, who will undoubtedly refer the matter to Sir Iain, who will—"

"Yes, yes, yes! What's the Commander-in-Chief doing, I'd like to know! Hiding behind the damn Civilians in Calcutta?" Fettleworth fumed: he sensed a degree of unfairness in the breeze from the capital, and was not mollified by his Chief of Staff's suggestion that Sir George White had always been a man to leave what in effect were as yet local decisions in the hands of his local commanders. A time might come, but had not yet done so, when the overall Commander-in-Chief would take personal direction: and the inference of the phrase 'had not yet done so' was also obvious, and Fettleworth put it into words: "It's the bloody Civilians again, Lakenham! If the Commander-in-Chief becomes involved, then so do they—so they've tied his hands. Great God, what a place India is!"

"Yes, sir. May I suggest, sir, a despatch be drafted for the field telegraph, informing—"

"Yes, of course, I've already decided upon that, have I not? See to it at once, if you please. Then we must think about reinforcements—a matter of extreme urgency now. You shall draft another despatch, this time to Ootacamund for action with a copy to Murree for information: to hell with Southern Command's commitments—*this* is the area under immediate threat! I am in urgent need of strengthening by no less than four infantry brigades and ancillary support—and cavalry..."

\* \* \*

The despatches were drafted, approved, encoded for transmission by cable to Ootacamund and Murree and to the Major-General commanding the column on the march: the signallers at Division tapped out a call along the lines of the field telegraph trailed behind by sappers of the Royal Engineers accompanying the Viceregal procession. They received no response and finally Brigadier-General Lakenham reported to the Divisional Commander.

"The field telegraph appears to have been cut, sir. We're out of contact with His Excellency."

"Good God Almighty!" Fettleworth put his head in his hands. "Out of contact... *we can't be*! How the hell can that have happened?"

"Very simply, sir. A pair of wire-cutters—"

"Oh, shut up, Lakenham! The Raj stands in its greatest peril and you offer nothing but impertinences!" Fettleworth got to his feet and prowled about the room savagely. "A party must be sent at once—from Rawalpindi, that's nearer—sappers, to locate the break, with infantry support—a company, I think. And two men to ride to overtake His Excellency with my despatch." He lifted his arms in the air, and shook desperate fists. "If only I'd had the men...I'd have had the line guarded throughout its length, damned if I wouldn't—"

103

"Thus, sir, negativing the purpose of the field telegraph."

"What?"

"They could have *shouted* to each other, sir."

Fettleworth gaped, his mouth hanging slack, "Messages by word of mouth, d'you mean?"

"Yes, sir." Lakenham kept his face straight. "Send three-and-fourpence, we're going to a dance."

"What?"

"The unreliability of the human factor. That's what happens when you pass a message saying send reinforcements, we're going to advance. I think the field telegraph is a better thing after all, so long as it remains unbroken."

"You—you—"

With asperity the Chief of Staff said, "No army in the world has the men to spare for uninterrupted surveillance of a field telegraph line, sir, and we must accept the fact. In the meantime I suggest we make our dispositions against attack through the Khyber. I think Peshawar must be told to put all available men into the field to contain any advancing army beyond Fort Jamrud, with the assistance of the Khyber Rifles in the peaks. The women and children should be brought together in one cantonment with as strong a barrack guard as can be spared from the field."

\* \* \*

Rest periods were time lost and Ogilvie intended to ride through the night: nevertheless, and despite the urgency of the Mullah's arrest that might well lead to the collapse of the threatened mutiny before it had begun, it was of necessity that the horses were rested. Ogilvie, himself no cavalryman and anxious to press on, recognised that sheer necessity. The men and horses were rested for an hour during the intense heat of the afternoon, and water and rations were issued frugally. Shortly after dark another halt was called, and weary men flung themselves on the ground, too tired to notice the hardness, glad only to be out of the saddle for however short a time. Ogilvie fell into a sleep of exhaustion; Quentin remained on guard with his *duffardar*-major. The watch was wakeful and alert, but when trouble came, it surprised the guard: Ogilvie came out of his sleep with a jerk. There was a loud neighing from one of the horses, a sound of terror ending in a cry cut very short, and then the soft pad of bare feet on rock close at hand.

# 11

THE ALARM WAS up: Ogilvie found the *duffardar*-major at his side, the Royal Arms on his tunic-sleeve darkened by a spreading well of blood. The shadows behind the rocks were lit by spurts of flame as the rifles went into action; in the open the moon's light showed confused fighting, with oiled bodies darting like flies among the slower-moving *sowars* of the cavalry. Not far off, a horse screamed—another horse, with its throat slit by a knife. The scream ended in a gurgle and a sound of choking as the blood entered the gaping windpipe. Ogilvie brought up his revolver and fired straight into the face of a near naked, straggle-haired man who was coming for him with a captured cavalry sabre: the face burst into a mess of blood but the body hurtled on. Ogilvie side-stepped and the corpse crashed into a rock behind. There was no sign of Quentin. Bodies seemed to be everywhere, the wounded, the dying and the dead. The attackers, men who knew blindfold every inch of their terrain, had come out of the night, in silence, materialising as it seemed from nowhere. Ogilvie, fighting off another attack on his person, found a moment to look down the pass towards the guns of the mountain battery, two of which had been assembled to cover the resting men when the order to fall out had been passed: they had been given no chance to go into action and were now standing, clear beneath the moon, without their crews as the fighting surged and swayed around them. As the *duffardar*-major beside him went down bloodily from a knife-thrust, Ogilvie used his last revolver bullet in the gut of the NCO's killer and grabbed for the heavy sabre, coming upright again just in time to parry another knife: using the sabre like a butcher's cleaver, he took off the knife-arm below the shoulder in one savage stroke that went on to mangle the native's flank and cut down into the hip-bone. Then, as the fighting moved away from his vicinity, he looked again towards the silent guns and began running towards them, keeping so far as possible in the shadows thrown by the moonlight. If he could reach the guns...it would not be possible at the moment to open fire without slaughtering as many of The Guides as of the enemy, but a time might come, and better that the guns were in any case denied the attacking tribesmen. Ogilvie moved fast, keeping an eye open for Quentin: still there was no sign of the cavalry captain. There was no further personal attack: the cavalrymen had rallied a little now, and the Pathans were fully occupied. Ogilvie bore down upon the guns, saw a man lying across the barrel of one of them, his head pouring blood from a wound in the neck. He was not quite dead; gently Ogilvie lifted him to the ground and laid him flat, and then, once again, he was back in the thick of the fighting. A tall, bearded man was coming for him full tilt behind a snaky bayonet on the muzzle of a jezail. Once again Ogilvie dodged aside and the man ran on under his own impetus, the bayonet striking sparks from the breech of the gun. The Pathan went head-over-heels across the barrel, recovered, stood up, and lost his head to Ogilvie's swinging sabre. Even in the heat of the fight it was a sickening sight: the body stood, the severed head fell to the gun-barrel, dropped to the hard ground of the pass, and rolled. Then the body went down, crumbling at the lifeless knees. Ogilvie crouched behind the ready-loaded gun, swung it round to point into the heart of the mêlée and tried to find a target on any groups of the Pathans separated from the fighting. It was not possible. As he watched, he saw Quentin coming towards him at a staggering run, fall over a rock, and collapse.

Leaving the gun, Ogilvie ran forward.

Bending, kneeling, he saw the face, white and blood-streaked and with blood-matted hair falling over the forehead. The breathing was laboured, a curious sighing sound accompanying each exhalation. Quickly, as gently as possible, Ogilvie felt inside the tunic: he found a weak heartbeat, a mere flutter. Hearing the distant but closing sound of horses' hooves, he got to his feet: riders were coming along the pass from the north, more tribesmen, moving fast, a horde of men. The fighting mass parted, scattering to left and right. Ogilvie lifted the dying cavalry officer and laid him down behind a rock nearby where he would be safe from the flying hooves, and then dashed back towards the gun still aimed along the pass. He fired point-blank into the thundering ranks of horsemen and the shell took the leaders and ploughed on to explode in a shattering roar in their centre, sending up earth and fragmented rock and pieces of flesh that had a moment before been men and horses. When the smoke and débris cleared, the moon showed the complete rout of the mounted attack. There was a sudden trumpet call and The Guides began to rally as the notes sounded out along the pass; but before they could achieve anything another wave of horsemen was heard coming in, and Ogilvie, desperately searching around the guns, was unable to find more ammunition. Scattering the Indian soldiers of the Raj like ninepins, the fresh riders swept along the pass, loosing off to the front and to the flanks with their jezails or cleaving the air with their sabres. They rode down on Ogilvie, still standing by the useless gun. As they parted ranks to surround him, he saw the closely-guarded man in the centre: a man in a shapeless white garment, a hairless man, scarred, with a hawk's nose and a wide mouth and extraordinary eyes that seemed to reflect cold silver from the moon, the Mullah from Kashmir.

As Ogilvie was herded by the horses and the blades of the sabres, the Mullah smiled. "The end of the day, I think, Captain Sahib, and victory for me!"

"But not for long."

There was another smile, though the eyes had narrowed. "I think for very long, Captain Sahib. I think this is the beginning of the end for the British Raj—"

"The slaughter of a squadron of The Guides and a mountain battery? Is *that* the Raj, in your view?" Ogilvie gave a hard laugh. "They died like men, and there are many men to take their places, and—"

"Of course! And those, too, shall die." There was a curious look in the Mullah's face, a reflection of wonder and of a rising urge to sadism: the eyes shone more than ever, burning into Ogilvie. "Have you more to say, Captain Sahib?"

"For now, no."

"For now, no!" the Mullah repeated softly. "But for soon, plenty." He gestured to his horsemen, who moved in closer, the animals' nostrils almost touching Ogilvie's body. "You have said

enough for now, Captain Sahib, and not for your own good!
The uniform, the colour of your skin—these were unfamiliar.
But..." He laughed suddenly, a harsh and humourless sound in
the night.

"But what?"

"But I never forget a voice," the Mullah said.

*       *       *

They rode through the night, with the barefoot Pathans on
the pillions and Ogilvie led along roped to his horse, his hands
tied. There was no talking; almost all questions had remained
unanswered. There was grim purpose in the air, in the intent
and alert bearing of the riders, hard-faced men visible as the
dawn came up. A turn to the west off the main pass had been
made some four miles beyond the point of the night attack. The
dead had been left behind and the guns blown up, the breeches
shattered. The wounded had been despatched by the sabres to
join the feast for the circling vultures. When the Viceroy's column
marching behind came up and found the evidence, it would be
too late for any withdrawal through the passes, any fallback
on Rawalpindi. If they should decide upon retreat, they would
need to fight their way through. The one piece of information
volunteered by the Mullah had been the word that a large
force had already cut the main route inside the Kashmiri border.

"Many thousands of tribesmen and guns, Captain Sahib," he
had said. "Very strategically placed along the crests, and in good
cover on the hillsides. It would be a holocaust."

It could have been bluff, but Ogilvie fancied it was not: it
was a logical and understandable part of the master plan, whatever that might be. It was possible the Mullah would not wish
to be forced into destroying the Viceroy in the mountains, before
the meeting with the Maharajah of Jammu and Kashmir that
would put Srinagar in the dead centre of the world stage—but
he would be ready to do so rather than risk an anticlimax.
Ogilvie rode stiffly, awkwardly on behind a leading-rein, trying
to think things out, to plan what should be done if ever he
got the chance. He had made no confession to the Mullah that
he and the itinerant trader from Bezar were one and the same:
he had scoffed at the suggestion, but knew that he was not
believed. Though he had contrived so far to brazen it out, the

Mullah had appeared certain of his facts. Close questioning was obviously to come, and Ogilvie recalled his conversation with Blaise-Willoughby: how far could he go before they broke him down?

Above them now the sides of the pass began to close in; here the growing dawn scarcely seemed to penetrate. The pace of the horses was slowed as they picked their careful way between the rocks, riding through a valley that was virtually a chasm. They emerged later into the heat of a high sun, coming out of the valley onto a track that wound its way around the side of a mountain, climbing now with a sheer drop to one side above the dark green tops of trees and the savage points of rock lying like avenging teeth where the trees were thin. On their other side the mountain rose sheer and vast to the shimmer of the sky. The horses, crowded together on the narrow track with its sliding surface of loose stones and rubble, made but a slow speed still. They had progressed some two miles from the valley up the mountain-side when the Mullah halted his party and pointed down into the far distance to the east.

"The Raj, Captain Sahib," he said. "The Raj, moving to its destruction. You see it?"

There was a splash of colour, presumably from the Mysore section, and metallic reflections of the sun like winking heliographs as, briefly, the column showed itself in a gap of the hills.

"Soon now they will find your dead, Captain Sahib, but they will not find us."

"You're very sure of that, aren't you?"

The Mullah smiled. "As you say—very sure!" He sat his horse in silence, looking down on the actuality and the vision of passing British power, keeping his band as still as himself in case movement, despite the great distance, should attract the attention of field-glasses. Ogilvie looked down in bitter frustration as the column went by, so unsuspectingly. A diversion—his heels hard into his horse's side, and a mêlée on the high track that just might be seen? Probably useless enough, but perhaps worth a chance: he was about to act when the Mullah gave the order to move on again, and Ogilvie saw that the tail of the column had passed and the gap stood empty of life and movement, and the chance had gone. They rode on for several more miles, twisting up the mountain and then down the far side into another valley with sides as high as the earlier one but set farther apart and with a climbable gradient. Another couple of miles into the valley, and the Mullah gave an order in Pushtu.

The armed tribesmen turned aside, riding the horses up the slope to the north, following one arm of a watercourse that trickled down the rock fissures to a stream below, clear and fresh, cold with the flow from the snow-line where it had its origins. Some three hundred feet above the floor of the pass they turned right, heading in between two great pillars of natural rock. Again the sun's light vanished; the party advanced in single file along a narrowing cleft that led into a pool of total darkness, total blankness. The horses were walked in very slowly, their hoofbeats echoing off distant rock. When the first half-dozen men were inside, matches were struck and torches flared. In the increasing light, Ogilvie looked around and gasped in surprise and alarm: they were in a great cavern, high and long, and its sides were stacked deep with arms, ammunition and explosives. Piles of rifles, thousands of them, some of British origin, some of Russian; Maxims, small pieces of artillery, many of them old but apparently well cared for and something that would have to be reckoned with when the time came for the Mullah to bring them out into the light of day: this, clearly, was the armoury, or one of the armouries and dumps for the attack on the Raj.

From the shadow flickering around the torches Ogilvie heard the Mullah's voice: "You are surprised, Captain Sahib?"

"Not surprised. There are avenues of supply, and you would naturally prepare—"

"For what, Captain Sahib?"

"To carry out your plan...whatever that may be."

"I think you know it well, in aim at least."

Ogilvie shrugged. "There have been rumours—"

"It is not rumour on which you base your knowledge— Manzur Zakir Burki from Bezar!" The Mullah, who had been behind Ogilvie until now, rode his horse around to the front: the eyes, caught in the flaring torchlight, looked colder and more penetrating than before, shining with that almost insane glare of dedication and sadism. "Soon you shall talk. In the meantime, while my men and I find rest and food, you shall reflect upon your future and that of the British Raj. In each case, Captain Sahib, the future is but short. Look around you. You see enough explosive to blow up all Peshawar and Rawalpindi, Nowshera and Murree. You see arms enough, backed by what I have in

111

other places, to equip all the men of all the tribes along the frontier. Already there are armies in the field, and behind us, Captain Sahib, as perhaps you know, there is the powerful Russian bear, poised with tooth and claw ready to rend the Raj asunder!"

Ogilvie looked coldly at the native. "You have a short memory," he said. "Was not the great Sepoy Mutiny of 1857 met and contained, and finally beaten? And has not the grip of the Raj tightened considerably, as a direct result? Is it your wish to bring down upon your peoples an even further tightening?"

"It will not happen, for we shall succeed."

"Do you not forget our strong armies here in the north, and our reserves in Ootacamund and in other places—and at home?"

"They will not be found enough. Here in India we have many millions more than the Raj can bring together in a thousand years, and we shall be fighting in and for our own land. The Raj is doomed, Captain Sahib." The Mullah gave a laugh, quiet and confident. "Nevertheless, you shall assist its speedier doom—"

"I'm afraid you'll ask that in vain."

The native shook his head. "Not so. You will see! I spoke of reflection—you will do well to heed what I say. It will help me if I know the exact disposition of your armies, and also what the intentions are of the leaders of the column bringing the Viceroy and the Maharajah of Mysore to Srinagar. And I think, when you have reflected, and used your imagination, you will tell me."

"Never!"

There was another smile. The Mullah backed his horse away a little, and called to one of his Pathans. The rope binding Ogilvie to his horse was cut, though his wrists remained tied. Once again the hard-eyed Mullah rode forward: this time, coming up close, he struck out at Ogilvie with the back of his hand, a hard and sudden blow that took the British officer off his guard. He lurched sideways, but kept his seat in the saddle. The moment he was upright again, a Pathan struck from the other side. Ogilvie lost his knee grip on the horse and fell to the ground, helpless with his wrists tied fast by the rope. The Mullah stared down at him, face gaunt in the yellow flares. "Another symbol— the fallen Raj! There you shall stay, under guard. Do not move, especially your head, Captain Sahib." He spoke to his horse,

112

quietly, using some native word that Ogilvie failed to recognise. The animal moved forward a pace and then, halting, lifted a front hoof and held it crooked, poised no more than an inch above Ogilvie's head. Ogilvie felt the sweat pour, though the cavern was cool, almost cold. There was a dead silence: the horse stood immobile. Time seemed endless. Then the white-clad leader spoke again, as quietly as before, and the pastern-joint un-crooked, the hoof touching the rock floor of the cavern several inches from Ogilvie's head. For the moment, the danger was past. With another word of warning that he was to remain where he had fallen, the Mullah rode away towards the entrance, the hoofbeats fading. Two Pathans remained behind, armed to the teeth with jezails, bayonets, knives in their belts, and cavalry sabres loosely held to the same belts by leather loops around the guards. They sat, with a torch thrust into a rock crevice, staring balefully at Ogilvie, their eyes seeming in his imagination to hold all the pent-up hatred of the Raj of which the wild men of the North-West Frontier were capable. It was an almost physical violence, and he knew without being told that the moment he made any movement actual physical attack would result. His tied wrists denying access to his watch, Ogilvie had no real idea of the time; but the two sentinels were relieved at one stage, replaced by others, and the vigil went on. It was perhaps three hours after their arrival that the Mullah rode back into the cavern and told Ogilvie to get to his feet.

Stiffly, he stood up. His uniform was rumpled and dirty, the khaki-drill tunic harsh with sweat that had dried grittily, the starched linen collar of his shirt still clammy beneath the tunic's neck-band. His head ached and he felt sick from an empty stomach, dry in mouth and throat from lack of water.

"You have reflected, Captain Sahib?"

He said, "I didn't need to. I've told you already, I've nothing to say about British troop movements."

The Mullah shrugged. "This, I believe, will change, and soon. You are utterly within my power, Captain Sahib. Do you under-stand?"

"Yes, I understand. Your people have a reputation for bar-barism."

"You are not afraid?"

"All men suffer fear," Ogilvie answered indifferently, "but all do not succumb. I'm not telling you anything, and if you kill

113

me, at least I'll know you won't live long yourself to boast about it."

The Mullah smiled. "Fine words, and brave ones. But we shall see. You have a saying: the proof of the pudding is in the eating thereof. Soon the eating shall begin, and it will begin with a demonstration." He turned aside, nodding to Ogilvie's guards. As the Mullah rode his horse out into the afternoon's brilliance, Ogilvie was seized by the Pathans and hustled after him on foot. Beyond the rock-sheltered entrance to the cavern, the Mullah had turned up the hillside and as, behind him, Ogilvie came over the crest to a biggish expanse of flat land, a plateau bare and open to the sun, he saw the rest of the Mullah's band of brigands, sitting their horses in hollow square around a native pegged stark naked to the ground. This man writhed and twisted against his binding ropes, but comparatively silently, for he was gagged: a high moaning came from his lips and that was all. This apart, the only sound was the hoofbeat from the Mullah's horse. There was a total silence as the Mullah halted by the pathetic figure stretched out in the sun. Then the Mullah spoke, addressing Ogilvie.

"Captain Sahib, this man is to die. He is a man of little faith, who attempted to leave me and join the British force that brings your Viceroy and the Maharajah to Srinagar. He is to be made an example to my followers—and to you. You shall watch his death, and in it see your own."

He backed his horse off a few paces, then gave a single hand-clap. From the ranks of the horsemen four men dismounted and went towards the tethered figure, cut the ropes securing him to the pegs, and lifted him to his feet, holding him fast. When the gagging cloth was removed from his mouth, a babble of sound came out, high, hysterical, incoherent. The staring eyes pleaded; but the Mullah's face was expressionless, unheeding: there was to be no mercy shown. At another signal there came the beat of a single native drum, a sound like a knell that echoed in weird solemnity off the farther crests. At the first beat a man rode forward, approaching the doomed Pathan slowly with a long, thin-bladed knife in his right hand. As he reached down from his horse, two of the native's guards took the head in their hands, holding it firm and square. The knife was pointed towards the face. The man screamed, a terrible sound that ripped across the mountains.

114

Sweat poured down Ogilvie's face.

\* \* \*

India was a cruel land: cruelty lay deep in its very nature even to its man-eating tigers, its trampling wild elephants, its silently winding snakes with their bags of deadly poison; even to its treacherous mountain crags and its deep ravines, its crop-destroying floods and tempests and droughts; but man had added the dimension of deliberate, calculated sadism. Afterwards, when the spectators had withdrawn back to the cavern, the scene was vivid still in Ogilvie's mind. First the wretched victim's eyes had been shelled out with the knife, then his roped limbs had been torn from the trunk by horsemen and the remains left in the sun. Ogilvie glanced at the faces of the Pathans: they were unreadable, but Ogilvie guessed the Mullah's object-lesson had sunk home well enough and that these men would keep their faith with him, had almost certainly not been disposed to break it in any case. Once again in the light of flares, the Mullah spoke to Ogilvie, held still by his guards in front of the leader.

"Now is the time for speaking, Captain Sahib."

"I shall not speak."

"No? Then I shall say this to you: it has come to me that there are more useful things than speaking to me, Captain Sahib, of matters of military movement!"

"What do you mean by that?"

"Listen and you shall learn." The Mullah, dismounted now, paced the rocky floor for a few moments, then swung round again on Ogilvie. "Before your capture, some of the *sowars* of The Guides were questioned. It was told to me that the British infantry officer in the many-coloured trousers was a young man of high connections...that he was the son of the Lieutenant-General Sahib, commanding the army in Murree. Do you deny this?"

Ogilvie shook his head. "I don't deny it. But that won't help you. My father's not the man to be impressed by hostages and threats."

"Perhaps not. This, I understand. I do not seek to use you as a hostage."

"Then what are you asking?"

115

"I *ask* nothing. I instruct—instruct under threat, Captain Ogilvie Sahib! There is a mission for you, and failure in this mission, or any revelation to your father the Lieutenant-General Sahib, will mean deaths for persons important to you, deaths similar in all respects to that you have seen today."

"Whose deaths?"

The Mullah smiled, his face devilish in the glow of the flares. "I shall send messages across the hills to Peshawar, which is presently but poorly garrisoned. I am told that your regiment is from Scotland, the Royal Strathspey. My people will attack the women's quarters, and take a number of the women and children, and bring them here to me as fast as possible through the mountain passes. The message will go with the speed of a forest fire, by smoke signals from crest to crest, and the women and children will be upon their journey here whilst you are traversing the passes to rejoin your column."

# 12

THE THREAT WAS no idle one and it would not be difficult in the execution: a strong night infiltration by dedicated Pathans moving silently in the shadows, a swift thrust towards the married quarters after despatching the quarter-guard by the exercise of *thuggee*, and then away into the hills with their victims across the saddles of horses that could be held in readiness outside the cantonment area—it stood every chance of success against the heavily depleted Peshawar garrison. The Mullah, looking down at Ogilvie in the torchlight, smiled as he saw in his face the realisation of the facts.

"You're asking me to make contact," Ogilvie said, "with the column in the pass. If I refuse—"

"Then your women and children will still be brought here—and then, I think, you will quickly change your mind."

"But if I were to go...how would you know I rode for the column, and not for Peshawar? Or if I rode for the column, how would you know I had not reported your whereabouts?"

"As to the first question," the Mullah answered, "I have many men in the hills, watchful men. From the moment of your leaving, you will be under observation. As to the second question, whether or not you tell your father of this place will become known to me by the action that follows, for the column will be watched as it has been watched all the way through the passes. Already the field telegraph line has been cut, and any rider with despatches, or any force that may be detached, will be hacked to pieces within an hour of leaving." The Mullah's steady stare seemed to burn into Ogilvie. "Captain Sahib, you must know that the hills are always alive with men, with my Pathans, seldom though they show themselves to the marching soldiers of your Raj. You know this to be the truth."

"Yes, this I know. What do you want of me?" Ogilvie met the Mullah's stare boldly. "Why do you wish me to make contact with the column?"

"Ogilvie Sahib, fresh news has reached me, news sent down from the north by horsemen." The Mullah paused. "What this news is, I shall not tell you, except to say this: it is not happy news for the British Raj. However, it is necessary to make a small delay in our plans. I wish you to delay the Viceroy's column, and to urge the Lieutenant-General Sahib to make camp where the hills give way to the valley of the Jhelum, twenty-five miles west of Srinagar."

"To be a sitting target for attack?"

The Mullah shrugged. "A risk that must be taken! I urge you to think about the women and children of your regiment, Captain Sahib."

Ogilvie stared back in silence, thinking fast. On the face of it he had no alternative but to agree: the women and children would be taken anyway, but their survival, as it seemed, was in his hands alone. And he could achieve nothing by remaining in captivity, that was certain. He asked, "What do you propose, then, that I should report to my father?"

"In the first place, you remain silent as to this cavern, and about myself. Of this there will be no report, Captain Sahib. Instead you will say that your force of cavalry was attacked and overcome by independent bandits, that you alone escaped, but that whilst in the hands of these bandits, you learned that they held another British officer captive. His name and regiment you do not know, but you know this: he was riding to overtake the column with word that a reinforcing army is marching north from Lahore upon the express orders of Sir George White Sahib. The column is to await the arrival of this army and until it makes contact is not to continue the march to Srinagar."

"And if I report the truth? Do you really expect that I shall not?"

The Mullah smiled, his eyes blazing in the flares' light. "What passes privily between you, Captain Sahib, and the leaders of your column, I cannot in truth control. But I can control the results." He shrugged. "It will be your choice, and yours alone. I have

118

given you an excuse for halting the column in camp. If you choose otherwise, you kill the hostages, for they die at the first approach of any British force. I say again, the choice will be yours alone."

*      *      *

His alone! Ogilvie rode out within the next half-hour, reflecting upon that choice and its consequences whichever way he should decide. The women and children were part of the regiment, and the regiment was his life, and Lord Dornoch's, and his father's. Riding along the pass, Ogilvie kept a watch for the hidden observers of his progress, the men who would hand him on, as it were, from one to the other and immediately send back the word to the cave-bound Mullah if the British officer should deviate from his proper path. Ogilvie saw nothing but knew they were there behind the crags with their jezails and snaky bayonets. Soon after he had set out, the day began to fade. In the increasing darkness Ogilvie followed the Mullah's route orders: some four miles ahead along the track he would come upon a pass leading east; this pass would bring him out ahead of the column marching north along the route from Rawalpindi. He could not, the Mullah had said, lose his way, for the pass was the only one that carried the track to the east, and indeed he found it without difficulty, its high peaks and crags reaching to the star-hung heavens, lonely, threatening and silent. There was much to bring Scotland to Ogilvie's mind. This desolate Kashmiri landscape was not unlike a progress through the lonely Pass of Glencoe from Kingshouse on Rannoch Moor to Ballachulish on Loch Leven, and he could almost imagine himself there, among the ghosts of dead MacDonalds slaughtered two centuries ago on King William's order. He shivered: ghosts abounded! His thoughts moved to the Monadliath Mountains, home of the regiment's depot at Invermore. It was largely from the Monadliath Mountains that the Royal Strathspey was recruited—from the crofts, from the larger farms, from the great houses and castles. They were close-knit, their homes and families well known to one another and in many cases joined by marriage. The women and children, the innocents, could not be allowed to suffer. There would be no welcome and no peace of mind on Speyside for whoever caused them harm, when one day the regiment entrained for the troopship at Bombay and the return to Invermore.

*     *     *

Ogilvie made his contact two hours after the next morning's dawn, emerging from the easterly track into the main pass to hear the skirl of the pipes away to the south. Soon a small party came into view, with a single piper and drummer, the advanced scouts whose music might be considered sufficiently far ahead of the Maharajah of Mysore as not to interfere with the cere-monies of Dasara. A subaltern of the 114th, Lieutenant Coutts, was in command, supported by a sergeant.

Ogilvie waved down the track: in the strong sunlight, his uniform could be clearly identified. Coutts waved back and the scouting party advanced towards him.

"James! Well, I'll be damned! What happened to you?"

"It's a long story, and one for the Major-General. How far ahead of the van are you?"

"Four miles, just about." Coutts stared at him. "We found the remains of battle, back there." He waved a hand along the pass to the south. "What a shambles!"

"You may well call it that, David! What action did Sir Thomas take?"

"Probes into the hills—we found nothing. A force was sent along a side pass after we moved out, but again nothing, so we came on. Do I take it you're alone now?"

Ogilvie nodded. "Quite alone. I'll ride on and join the column. Keep alert, David—just in case!" He turned away, aware of the curious stares from the Scots. The time for decision was close now, and still he was far from certain in his mind as to what he should do. Duty demanded that he make a full and truthful report—this he did not doubt. Humanity, he felt, demanded otherwise, and so to some extent did sheer expediency: once the report was made, the word could spread, and they might even have a different kind of mutiny on their hands, a mutiny of Scots soldiers who would storm off on a foray to cut out their women and children, and thus cause their deaths. There was the rub! With the head of the column now in view, Ogilvie eased his horse's pace, instinctively putting off the moment of decision.

120

As he approached, he saw signs of wonderment in the van and as he saluted the Major-General the latter stared in considerable surprise.

"Captain Ogilvie, by God! Where the devil have you been, young man?"

"Sir, there was an attack—"

"I know that. I saw with my own eyes, damn it all! Terrible— terrible! What have *you* to report?"

"Sir, if I may...I request a word in private."

"In private, Captain Ogilvie? I'll be damned! What's all this about?"

"A matter of extreme importance, sir. I must insist, sir, that it be stated in private."

"You insist, do you? Damned impertinence!" Sir Thomas's face reddened dangerously. "You'll make your report here and now, and in front of my Chief of Staff."

"No, sir." Ogilvie stood his ground, his face and mouth hard. "For reasons that you'll appreciate when I've made my report, I refuse to make it except to you alone."

The Major-General's mouth opened and shut again, and he stared, frowning blackly, into Ogilvie's face. Then he said abruptly, "Very well, but woe betide you, young man, if—" He broke off and turned to his Chief of Staff. "Halt the column, if you please, Brigadier-General. I shall ride ahead with Ogilvie. Come!" His face rock hard, he put spurs to his horse and rode northward. Ogilvie followed as the bugles rang out over the long column, echoing from the hillsides. A hundred yards clear of the van, Sir Thomas Lee reined in his horse. "Well, Captain Ogilvie?"

"First my apologies, sir—"

"Oh, never mind that! Get on with it."

"Yes, sir. I've come from the Mullah—"

"*The Mullah!*" Lee was clearly shaken. "The bloody man himself, and you—"

"Sir, with respect, discretion's called for. I—"

"By God, Captain Ogilvie—"

"Sir, please hear me out." Ogilvie sweated, felt his fingers shake as he gripped the reins of his horse. "By now the Mullah will be holding hostages—women and children from my regiment in Peshawar—"

"What?"

"I think it better if the facts are not known to my regiment, sir."

"I begin to follow," Lee said in a quieter tone. "Let's have it all, Ogilvie, as fast as you can."

"Very good, sir." Briefly, concisely, Ogilvie reported the facts of the murderous attack, of the dismembering of the native and of his own subsequent conversation with the Mullah. "If I may suggest it, sir, I think the truth should be known to you alone as military commander of the column, and perhaps, at your discretion, to His Excellency."

"And Sir Iain?"

"I think not, sir. My father does not command the column as such, he is virtually a passenger—"

"He commands at Murree, damn it! He's my superior officer."

"But can be disregarded for the purposes of your own command, sir—"

"But why? I fail to see the point!"

"My father's a Royal Strathspey, sir—"

"I'm aware of that!"

"And has the regiment very much at heart, sir. If he knows, I fear the consequences."

"Kindly be more precise."

"I believe he'd take over the command, sir. And then I believe he'd lead an attack on the Mullah's stronghold. As a result—"

"Slaughter of the non-combatants! Yes, I take your point, Ogilvie. Damn it, you did right to speak in private." Lee rasped at his moustache. "All the same, I think you underestimate your father. He'll know the dangers well enough and is experienced enough to act accordingly."

"I think not, sir. This would become a personal matter. I may be wrong...but I believe the risk is too great."

Ponderously, Lee nodded. "You're suggesting I appear to accept the story put to you by the Mullah, are you? You're landing *me* with the nasty decision?"

Ogilvie coloured slightly. "I'm sorry, sir—"

"Oh, don't worry! I'm the officer commanding and decisions are up to me—I've no complaint! On the other hand, you've presented me with a bloody nasty dilemma, Ogilvie, and I'll not deny it. But on the other hand, the answer's plain enough and unavoidable: we must on no account halt the column at the Jhelum valley."

"But the hostages, sir—"

"I'm sorry, Ogilvie, truly sorry, but that's my decision. Think, man, think! Did not this Mullah tell you he had had fresh news of something he would not mention further?"

"Yes, sir."

"Well," Sir Thomas Lee said harshly, "I'm making a guess and acting upon it. My guess is that the Mullah's not ready yet. From that, in my view, it follows that the Czar isn't ready to move his army down from the north-eastern spur of Afghanistan—or alternatively that that army is taking longer upon the march south than was expected."

"It was thought they would only march upon Ghilgit, sir, according to Division's assessment up to the time we left—"

"Division can be wrong and time brings changes," Lee said. He swung his horse round. "*My* assessment is that they intend to follow on south and drop upon us like a nutcracker, and that the Mullah's intention is to delay us until they get there, which we shall not do. We march on for Srinagar as planned. I shall not risk His Excellency in the open field." He reached out and put a hand on Ogilvie's shoulder, and his face was solemn as he said, "I'm very sorry. The whole Raj is in danger, its security in the balance, and if it falls, then millions will die. Think about it and you'll understand—and not a word to anyone else as to the facts. You've made your report to me, Ogilvie, and there your duty ends."

The Major-General rode off towards the van of the column. Ogilvie, saluting the rigid back, followed in dismay and foreboding: it was a terrible decision and would lead to much trouble if anything should become known to Lord Dornoch or the rank-and-file whose families were now in mortal danger; yet it was a sensible one in the circumstances and inevitable, always supposing the Major-General was right about the Czar's army in the north. It was Ogilvie's task, and he knew it, to maintain the secrecy that he had himself desired. But when speaking to the Colonel, and later to the Regimental Sergeant-Major and other married men, he was ill-at-ease, seeing himself in the role of the snake-in-the-grass, as the officer who had failed in the first regimental duty of succouring his men.

# 13

BEFORE THE ORDER could be passed for the column to move out, a delay had to be accepted: something curious had happened to the Supply and Transport, whose animals and wagons seemed to be receiving close attention from the priests of His Highness's entourage. Ogilvie came upon the Regimental Sergeant-Major fizzing like a fuse.

"What is it, Mr Cunningham?"

"Sir! It is more shriving and blessing, this time of the elephants, mules, horses and carts, sir. Each day has its proper shriving detail, I'm told."

"Will it take long?"

"I can't say, sir." Cunningham was red-faced and sweating. "The high priest is at it now, sir, all apricot silk and gold crown, standing in for His Highness."

Ogilvie grinned. "The customary language of the Supply and Transport hardly tallies with blessing, Sar'nt-Major, does it?"

"It does not, sir, but thanks be, it's not our worry. And now if you'll excuse me, Captain Ogilvie, I'll be away to stop any of our lads drifting to the rear for a look-see."

Cunningham marched away; Ogilvie stared down the line towards the Supply and Transport sector of the column, smiling to himself as the priests and acolytes milled about the mules and commissariat carts: the elephants, brought down to join the other animals for the ceremony, looked bored and superior. Ogilvie turned away, reflecting upon the native mind that knew not the word hurry: no doubt to the priests of Chamundi there had seemed no reason not to take advantage of an unexpected halt in the march! He went to make his tongue-in-cheek report to

Lord Dornoch, indicating that he had escaped from the Mullah's men under cover of the night after overpowering the guard. This the Colonel accepted, but during the morning, after the blessing of the transport had been concluded and the bugles had at last sounded the advance, Ogilvie was approached by the Adjutant. As, to the shouts of the colour-sergeants marching beside the ranks with their crimson sashes and their sloped rifles, the rise and fall of boot-leather began again, Black, riding up the marching files of the Royal Strathspey, joined Ogilvie at the head of his company, a sardonic look in his eye.

"You were lucky, James."

"Lucky?"

"To be the sole survivor of a holocaust." Black shook his head sadly. "A pity about the guns."

"Yes."

"Oh, not your fault, of course... Captain Quentin being in command—poor Quentin, a tragedy. The whole lot wiped out to a man, gunners and *sowars* all." There was another headshake and Black's voice took on a brooding tone. "Strange, James, strange indeed, is it not?"

"What do you mean by that?" Ogilvie asked sharply.

"Why, that you alone should be spared, you alone taken prisoner! Is it not strange—have you not thought about this?"

"Yes, I have."

"And you've come to no conclusion?"

"No," Ogilvie snapped back. "No conclusion other than as you yourself suggested—luck."

"Well, perhaps, perhaps. Perhaps there are other aspects, however."

"What aspects, Andrew?"

Black shrugged. "Oh, it just occurs to me that the world is a small place, James, even here on the North-West Frontier—possibly even smaller here. And the name of Ogilvie—"

"They wouldn't have known the name. Are you saying—"

"They could have known the face, James. Even in the thick of the fighting... yes, indeed, I am saying that you could have been taken with intent—intent to make use of your family connection with the high command." The Adjutant looked at him from the corner of his eye. "This did not occur to you at all, then?"

"It occurred to me, yes."

"And?"

"And nothing, Andrew. I was wrong, that's all!"

"The Mullah made no overtures?"

"None."

"And uttered no threats?"

Ogilvie stared; Black looked away. "What threats have you in mind, Andrew?"

"Oh, I can't be specific. It was just a thought, just a thought, nothing more. No doubt I was wrong and they had no knowledge as to who you were...but I would have thought the enquiry would have been made all the same, and you could not have been blamed for giving your name when asked. It would be perfectly proper, providing of course you gave no other information."

Ogilvie checked an angry reply: it would not do to have a scene upon the march, and in front of his company. In any case Black waited for no reply: he touched spurs to his horse and rode ahead towards the Colonel and Major Hay, leaving Ogilvie to seethe. He might have known that Black would make trouble— Black with his terrible sense of inferiority and his out-of-joint nose ever on the twitch to smell out nepotism descending from the Northern Army Commander to a regimental son. God alone could tell what worms were now wriggling in the Adjutant's brain! In Black's eyes, perhaps, Ogilvie could have made a deal with the Mullah in exchange for his life in the attack, for his freedom afterwards. Ogilvie scowled ahead along the pass, brightening to brilliance as the sun climbed towards noon. Certainly Black's inner thoughts didn't matter so long as they remained inner ones, but there was no doubt that the Adjutant had come close to some of the truth, and a busy mind, nagging away over the dusty miles to the valley of the Jhelum, might well come closer.

*     *     *

Later that morning Ogilvie was sent for to attend upon the Army Commander: his father, to whom nepotism would have been utterly foreign, and who in any case had not the executive command or responsibility for the column, had allowed a decent time to elapse before having a few unofficial words with the sole survivor, as Black had had it, of a holocaust. Approaching

126

Ogilvie senior as he sat with Sir Thomas Lee at a pre-luncheon *chota-peg* during the mid-day rest, Ogilvie saluted and remained at attention as his father's blue-eyed gaze swept him from head to foot, critically.

"I'm told you met the Mullah—for the second time. And got away intact."

"Yes, sir."

"A terrible thing, all those losses. A terrible sight to find. I'm deeply sorry." The eyes remained roundly staring. "How did you come to preserve your own life—hey?"

"A little luck, sir."

"A *little*? Damn it, I'd call it a hell of a lot, buggered if I wouldn't!" Sir Iain gave a short, dry laugh and slid a finger round the inside of his sweat-soaked tunic neckband. "However, you seem to have satisfied Sir Thomas that you kept your end up by some good fighting as well."

"Thank you, sir."

"And the Mullah. Have you anything else to report?"

"Nothing beyond what I've reported to Sir Thomas, sir."

"I see. This Mullah...he didn't try to get at you on my account, did he?"

Ogilvie hesitated fractionally, felt the eye of the Major-General upon him, but kept his own gaze upon his father's square, red-brown face. "No, sir."

"H'm. Well—I'm glad to see you back." Sir Iain paused, coughed, and said abruptly, "That's all, then. Off you go."

"Thank you, sir." Ogilvie saluted again and turned about smartly. Making his way back to where the officers of the Royal Strathspey awaited the laying of the trestle tables for luncheon, Ogilvie encountered the Regimental Sergeant-Major and received a swinging salute.

"Captain Ogilvie, sir."

"Yes, Mr Cunningham, what is it?"

"May I have a word, sir?"

"Of course!" Ogilvie smiled, looking sideways as he went on in step with the RSM. "Still troubled about Dasara and His Highness' thunderbox?"

"No, Captain Ogilvie, the thunderbox has been satisfactorily constructed, also the screens. It is not that, sir." Cunningham lifted a massive hand and twirled at the ends of the moustache, rigidly waxed as ever by some mysterious process that withstood the sun's heat. "It is the junior NCOs, sir, many of whom are married on the strength."

"Well?" Ogilvie felt a twinge of alarm.

"Their minds, sir, are not wholly here. They're in Peshawar, somewhat naturally."

"Yes, natural indeed, Sar'nt-Major."

"But not good, sir, not on active service. The men depend upon their NCOs, sir, for their lives. If the discipline should go—"

"Do you believe it will?"

"Not go entirely, sir. Never that, I hope. But even a slackening ...do you understand me, Captain Ogilvie?"

"Yes, I do, but surely you can cope with that, Sar'nt-Major?"

"Up to a point, sir, and indeed I have done so. But there comes a time when an officer is needed to back me up."

"Then what do you suggest?"

"A word with them, sir. Individually or in a group. Some reassurance."

"But why me, Mr Cunningham?"

"Beyond all the officers bar the Colonel, sir, the men trust you and respect you."

"Kind words, Mr Cunningham—"

"True ones, sir, with the greatest respect to the other officers. The name of Ogilvie means very much to the regiment, sir." There was a curious urgency in the Regimental Sergeant-Major's voice, almost an entreaty. "If you would tell them yourself, sir, that the wives and children are safe in Peshawar, then I believe there would be a settling down, if you follow me."

Ogilvie nodded. "Perhaps. But I can speak to my own company only, you know that. Properly, it would be the Adjutant's concern."

Cunningham pursed his lips and gave no answer: his silence was eloquent. "A point could perhaps be stretched, Captain Ogilvie." They walked on. As if going off at a tangent, Cunningham said, "I've not much longer with the colours, Captain Ogilvie. The years creep up on a man, more's the pity. I have no yearning at all for the reserve."

"I know that."

"And even less if—" Cunningham broke off. "Mrs Cunningham and me, we've been married for twenty years and a little more."

"I know that too. But don't you start worrying, Sar'nt-Major, or we're all done for!" Ogilvie gave the old soldier a keen look. "Don't look on the black side. We're all going to come through this."

"That's what I'm asking you to tell the men, sir." All at once Cunningham's voice broke a little and he went on in a low and somehow haunting tone, "Captain Ogilvie, I'm a highlandman born and bred. My family on both sides have been crofters for many generations—my father's people even survived the clearances. Not all were from the mainland. Some came from Skye, others from Orkney. In the highlands and islands, as you know well, sir, there are things that cannot be explained away, things that are of the mind. The Sassenachs laugh at it, but it's there." Cunningham put a hand across his heart. "I see much sorrow, Captain Ogilvie."

Ogilvie understood, and said so: the quality of feyness was nothing to scoff at; to those who possessed it, it was real enough, and it came to the unlikeliest of men. But it was not welcome in the Kashmiri mountain passes, especially under the current circumstances, and it brought a leaden feeling to Ogilvie. "Try not to see sorrow, Mr Cunningham," he said. "We're still in full control of the Raj, and we're far from forgotten at home. We'll never be let down—"

"It's a long way from Portsmouth hard to Bombay, sir, and a long way from Bombay to the Frontier too. It's now we need the strength, not in three months' time when it'll be too late."

"Look on the bright side," was all Ogilvie could find, so inadequately, to say; he could find no words to give comfort in regard to the women and children. To have done so would have been in his eyes a betrayal, a rendering of false hopes that would forever damn him in the eyes of the regiment afterwards. For the same reason he knew that he could not accede to the Regimental Sergeant-Major's request to speak to the NCOs. He repeated what he had said earlier, that such was the concern of Captain Black and he was not able to usurp the functions of the Adjutant; but that he would have words with the Colonel, who was better equipped than he to reassure the married men since he, too, had a wife in Peshawar. As Cunningham gave a stiff salute and marched away Ogilvie was aware, ruefully, that he had disappointed. Cunningham felt let down with a thump. Walking with somewhat dragging footsteps to join his brother officers at luncheon, Ogilvie found himself pondering on highland prophecies, on the curious awareness that could be called second sight. Cunningham, by means very different from those that might activate Andrew Black, could also come close to the truth. When, after the clutter of the mid-day meal was cleared away and the plates and mess-tins washed in a clear-flowing stream, the interminable march was resumed, Ogilvie had much on his mind. All too vividly he saw in his imagination the ordeal that would be taking place back in the Mullah's strongpoint, the misery and the terror, the indignities, the appalling lack of hope. It seemed a sheerly criminal act for the column, for British power, to be marching away into the great distances of Kashmir, lending no support or comfort to the helpless; but he knew that there was no alternative. Jarring his wretched thoughts came the native sounds, the continuing sounds of Dasara: the thin, reedy pipes, the drums, the low-sung dirges, the comings and goings of the priests in their robes as they attended upon the much-shriven Maharajah of Mysore in his enshrouded, mysterious howdah lurching like a ship in a choppy sea along the pass behind the Viceroy. So much power, so much pomp and splendour, so many useless prayers ascending to God in the skies above! It was all of no avail to the prisoners in the hill-bound cavern to the south and west, and might well be equally of no avail to the Raj if and when the great armies of the Czar of All The Russias pincered down from the Afghan passes to grip and decimate the whole of the Northern Command. The British regiments could be marching to their Waterloo; the Czar would know their strength and composition, and would certainly be very well prepared to meet and beat... Ogilvie shook his head free of his thoughts, turned his horse out of the column and rode down the line to the rear. Passing the Regimental Sergeant-Major he was somewhat pointedly ignored: Cunningham kept his eyes front, his face stony as he marched along straight-backed and formidable, his kilt swinging around sun-browned knees, his pace-stick rigid beneath his arm, every inch a fighting soldier of the Queen, not by his physical looks a man in the smallest degree prone to visions and prophecies and least of all to fear. Ogilvie rode on, coming up in rear of the battalion. Once again, he found the Adjutant, hawk-eyed for detail as usual, on the watch for slovenly marching, for loosened neckbands, for helmets pushed to the backs of heads, ears cocked for whistling, for vulgar comment, very conscious of Dasara and the displeasure that might be handed down to him from the priesthood via His Excellency, Sir Thomas Lee, the Brigadier-General and the Colonel. He was now passing on, as it were, adverse comment in advance.

"Ah, Captain Ogilvie." Gone the morning's camaraderie that had been implicit in the use of the Christian name. "I am glad enough to see keenness in you, but your company leaves much to be desired."

"Really? In what respect, Captain Black?"

"Their marching is what I refer to, man! And some belts are not decently pipe-clayed—"

"Pipe-clay needs water."

"Of which we are not noticeably short. The Colonel spoke in cantonments of the need to smarten-up for these people's religious festival, Captain Ogilvie. If this were an ordinary march, I would naturally permit more latitude, but it is not." Black rode closer and lowered his voice; a smirk hung round his thin lips. "I noticed you had an audience of the Army Commander, James. Do I take it that he also is...curious?"

"Take it how you wish," Ogilvie answered shortly. "Or if you want a word by word account, then I suggest you refer to Sir Thomas, who was present throughout."

Black gave him a cold look. "I dislike impertinence," he snapped. "I asked a perfectly simple question—"

"Then here's a simple answer: it was a private conversation with my father, nothing more." Ogilvie rode ahead, leaving the Adjutant to fume in his wake, and then vent his temper on the colour-sergeants. Relentlessly the march continued throughout the afternoon with the men, unable to march properly at ease and to help their feet along with singing, growing more sullen. The details provided by the various battalions to chivvy the long straggle of natives and their untidy commissariat into some semblance of a line became more acid in their comments, rougher in their actions. A few minor scuffles broke out as guiding hands became fists and blows were struck: soldiers sweating into neckbands and carrying heavy Slade-Wallace equipment were becoming short-tempered with scruffy natives and inflamed by the never-ending dirge of their music. The one completely imperturbable unit lay in the rear of the column's first half—the Viceroy's personal mounted bodyguard in their full-dress uniforms of scarlet and gold and striped puggarees, bearing their

131

lances as straight as a guardsman's back, protective and loyal warriors on the flanks of the viceregal elephant. As once again the daylight faded from the sky, the bugles sounded the halt, repeating down the line, and the company officers fell their men out to make camp and prepare the field kitchens for supper. Welcome cooking smells rose on the still air as the various guards were set and the rosters for picket duty in hastily-constructed sangars read out by the section sergeants. Ogilvie, smoking a pipe when his company had been settled into their bivouacs, watched as a white-robed acolyte hastened up from the Maharajah's retinue and approached the Regimental Sergeant-Major, who listened, nodded, looked peeved and caught Ogilvie's eye.

Ogilvie sauntered across towards him, jerked his pipe-stem in the direction of the waiting native. "What does he want, Mr Cunningham?"

"Sir! It's time for thunderbox duty."

"*What?*"

"His Highness—"

"Yes, I understand. But why you of all people?"

"I have asked myself the same question, sir, many times. The fact is that the 114th provided the bloody thunderbox, begging your pardon, sir, and I was myself the intermediary in its construction—"

"So they trust you to—er—operate it, Sar'nt-Major, is that it?" Ogilvie kept a straight face with difficulty.

"Not operate it, sir, thank God. *Guard* it."

Ogilvie nodded. "I see. Well, I'll not detain you, Sar'nt-Major. Please carry on."

"Sir!" Cunningham swung a hand to the salute, stamped his feet in an about-turn, and began calling for the Orderly Sergeant, one Corporal Baxter. A guard of twenty men was fallen-in with rifles and was addressed by the Regimental Sergeant-Major: "Those of you who have not done thunderbox parade before, listen carefully. You are to provide the latrine guard for His Highness the Maharajah of Mysore, and you will provide it smartly and you will not *snigger*. You will be marched to the vicinity of His Highness's elephant. You will be turned about face whilst His Highness is disembarked and conveyed by hand of native behind screens to his thunderbox...you will march to the vicinity of the thunderbox with faces averted decently and when halted will form hollow square about the article facing outwards. Is that clear? Very well. Carry on, Corporal Baxter."

"Sir!" Baxter's voice roared out along the pass. "Thunderbox party, atten...*shun*! Fix...*bayonets*! Into file, right...turn! Quick ...march! Left...left...left, right, left...." His face stolid and unsmiling Corporal Baxter marched his detail towards the rear and the Regimental Sergeant-Major, picking up the step, proceeded to do his duty smartly. All the occasion lacked, Ogilvie reflected, was the pipes and drums.

\*    \*    \*

That night after Last Post it was Pipe-Major Ross himself who played the battalion to bed with 'The Flowers of the Forest', standing on a rock ledge half-way up the western side of the pass and silhouetted against a climbing moon, his kilt and his tartan plaid blown about by a cold night breeze, the hackle of the Royal Strathspey rising proudly from the regimental bonnet that Ross now wore in place of the daytime Wolseley helmet. Ogilvie, wakeful and not yet turned into the tent set up by his bearer, watched and listened to the haunting notes of the pipes sounding out over the weird, jagged landscape. Along the pass he saw Lord Dornoch, also watching and listening, a cane tapping gently against his trews. That night Ogilvie heard the pipes with much sadness and foreboding: the tune had the sound of a lament in a very special sense, a lament for the non-combatants seized from the Peshawar cantonment, a lament for the hopes of so many of the Royal Strathspeys spread out in the bivouacs along the pass. The tune ending, Ogilvie saw Pipe-Major Ross lift the chanter from his lips and stand motionless, rigid at attention as though unwilling to break off, held as it were by the magic of his own making. Ross was still standing there when the sound of a rifle-shot broke over the pass, shattering the curious silence into a thousand fragments, and Ross got on the move, leaping down the hillside as nimbly as a mountain goat. Hard upon the heels of the shot there came a wild scream, a scream of pain and terror, and a kilted body fell from the heights, arms and legs spread wide, bouncing off the hillside to land in the floor of the pass and lie still. More firing came from the remaining pickets, and the whole column came alive with sound and moving men, the bugles sounding the alarm from the

Major-General's headquarters tent and the sergeants mustering their sections as the orders were passed down to clear the pass and scatter up the hillsides to the crests.

# 14

AT THE HEAD of a mixed bag of Scots from several companies Ogilvie reached the western crest from where the firing had come. He looked around: away to his right he saw Alastair Fergusson of D Company.

"See anything?" he called.

"Not a damn thing..." There was a pause, then a muffled cry from Fergusson. From his very feet, as it seemed, a man had sprung upon him, a tall native in flowing, ragged garments. Ogilvie and half-a-dozen Scots ran across, leaping like goats, but were too late to save Fergusson: as they came up and fell upon the native, Ogilvie saw the haft of the knife protruding from the back between the shoulder-blades and angled downwards for the heart, a well-placed penetration. The killer, held by the Scots, struggled furiously until a lance-corporal smashed a fist into his mouth. The struggles stopped, but, as Ogilvie approached, a stream of bloodied saliva shot towards him, followed by much abuse in rapid Pushtu.

"Will I stop the bugger again, sir?" the lance-corporal asked, bunching a ready fist.

"No, leave him. Take him down to the pass while I look around up here. Take him to the Colonel for questioning, Corporal MacKechnie."

"Aye, sir." Ogilvie watched as the man was dragged away roughly, then, calling up some more men, he started on a reconnaissance of the hillside. That hillside was now swarming with men, Scots and English, but there were no more natives to be seen. After an exhaustive search along the crags and declivities, the order came for the men to withdraw down into the pass, leaving doubled pickets plus one company to reinforce the guard by spreading out along the heights. Ogilvie scrambled down the rocky sides and went to the Colonel's tent. He found the captured Pathan being questioned by Black in the presence of Lord Dornoch and Sir Thomas Lee, who was attended by his Chief of Staff, and the Brigadier-General commanding the Royal Strathspeys' brigade. And Captain Black appeared to be having little success in his task of questioning.

Lord Dornoch looked round as Ogilvie came up. "Ah, Captain Ogilvie. You have a good command of Pushtu, have you not? Captain Black, I think perhaps—"

"I am quite able to cope, Colonel."

"No doubt, given time." Dornoch's voice was cold. "Time may be short, if an attack is planned. Ogilvie, I'd be obliged if you'd make this fellow talk, and quickly."

"Yes, Colonel." Ogilvie faced the Pathan, saw the flicker in the eyes shown up in the light of a storm lantern held by a corporal. It was almost a flicker of recognition: but in a physical sense this was highly to be doubted. Ogilvie felt a prickle of apprehension, a feeling of danger in the air: it was possible, indeed likely, that this Pathan was one of the Mullah's widely-spread observers, one of those whose task it was to ensure that the Mullah's demands were met, and to be seen to be met by the halting of the column outside the pass in the Jhelum valley... and if so, then it was equally likely that he knew the name Ogilvie and had recognised it as the Colonel had spoken. Ogilvie caught the eye of the Major-General, held it for a moment, and saw Sir Thomas register. Ogilvie turned to Lord Dornoch.

"Colonel, I believe I may have more success if I question the man alone."

"Why so?" Dornoch asked testily.

"I believe he may be put off, Colonel, by the presence of so many high-ranking officers."

From the corner of his eye Ogilvie saw the Major-General moving in with his support for the suggestion. Sir Thomas, however, was too late. A stream of Pushtu came from the man, and he kept gesturing with nods of his head towards Ogilvie, speaking of him by name. Ogilvie glanced at Black: the Adjutant, whose command of Pushtu was in fact reasonably good, was listening in consternation mixed with malice and staring back at Ogilvie as though his eyes were about to leap from his head.

Before Ogilvie could speak, the Adjutant had clutched excitedly at Dornoch's arm.

"Colonel, the man speaks of the women and children—*ours*, from Peshawar!"

"What about them?"

"A number have been cut out, and taken into the Mullah's custody! And this, as I gather, was known to Captain Ogilvie, Colonel!"

In the light of the storm lantern, Dornoch's face looked suddenly drained of blood, an old and faded face that stared at Ogilvie with accusation and a tremendous surprise, but as yet wordlessly. Into the acute and embarrassed discomfiture of the group came the voice of Sir Thomas Lee. "Dornoch, my dear fellow, the blame is not Captain Ogilvie's but—if blame there is—it is mine. And I have this to say first: there is to be no mention of what has been said outside this group, from my Chief of Staff down to your corporal. This is of over-riding importance, and any breach of my orders will lead to Court Martial proceedings the moment this force returns to cantonments. I trust that is clear. Now, Dornoch, a word in your private ear, if you please."

\* \* \*

"I accept Sir Thomas's explanation, James," the Colonel said half an hour later, "and, through him, yours."

"Thank you, Colonel."

"I fancy you did right to speak to the Major-General first, though as your Colonel...however, no more about that." Dornoch paused; when he went on his voice was heavy and weary. "Yes, I repeat, you were right. My own reaction would have been the same as your father's without a doubt. Frankly, it still is, but I realise the Major-General's order, that is to say his decision to continue, was correct and unavoidable. Meanwhile, however, our women and children are in the hands of that damned Mullah, and I do not propose that they shall remain there." Thinly, without humour, Dornoch smiled. "I have so convinced Sir Thomas, by threatening to make a report to your father! If Sir Iain should get wind of this, the whole column would be put in uproar—as I understand you realised very well yourself. I have persuaded Sir Thomas that the better way is to keep this within the regiment. D'you follow me?"

"Not entirely, Colonel—"

"The women and children are to be cut out," Dornoch said savagely. "As Colonel, I cannot for one moment accept that we must leave them there."

Ogilvie said, "If there's any attack on the cavern, the Mullah will have them all killed, Colonel. He was specific on the point. Had he not been, I would have suggested a cutting-out expedition to the Major-General as soon as I rejoined the column."

"I know that, James." Dornoch's voice was hard, his face implacable. "In my view the Mullah's likely to kill them anyway, win or lose. Indeed, given the time, he's more likely to use torture than if he's suddenly faced with an attack in reasonable strength."

"Colonel, I believe the risk is far too great—"

"And I do not. I believe we have no option but to take it. Are we men or mice, James?"

"It's the women and children who are at risk, rather than us, Colonel."

Dornoch slammed a fist into his palm. "I repeat, we can make it no worse for them. We have to do what we can. Do you not see? Do you not think, if they're going to die, they'd not rather do so in the knowledge that the regiment is at hand?"

"For revenge afterwards, Colonel?"

Dornoch's eyes flashed. "Even that would help. Our women are as…as *loyal*, as patriotic as we are ourselves. I will not let them down!"

"Colonel, I resent—"

"No, James." Dornoch laid a hand on Ogilvie's arm. "I do not criticise anything of what you did. You were right to consider the column and Their Excellencies above all else—very right, and right also to keep this from your father. What I'm ordering now is on a domestic scale—wholly within the regiment."

"You say ordering, Colonel?"

Dornoch nodded. "It's an order indeed. You shall go in command of the cutting-out force, taking your own company. I repeat, I have convinced Sir Thomas Lee, if only reluctantly and under a kind of duress! You'll have his sanction now. Well?"

Ogilvie answered stiffly. "There is no question of my refusing an order, Colonel—"

"And in your heart you're glad enough of a chance to do something, I know." Looking into Ogilvie's eyes, Dornoch saw the responses: worry and doubt had nagged at Ogilvie's mind and he, as much as the Colonel himself, had detested the thought of leaving women and children in the Mullah's bloody hands; action would be welcome enough, and revenge was in fact good. Dornoch went on, "Now—you may take that Pathan for a guide if you need him. Do you?"

Ogilvie shook his head. "There'll be no difficulty in finding the way back, Colonel. In any case, the Pathan'll be no more than one of the extended watchers, and—"

"And won't necessarily know where his HQ is? I take your point, James. Now, you'll prepare your company for the march back, see them well provided with food, water and ammunition, and you'll detach from the column when you're ready, as quietly as possible, taking care that neither His Excellency nor your father is made aware of the movement—I'll account for your absence when the march resumes at dawn." Lord Dornoch paused, looked searchingly into Ogilvie's face. "You must tell your company the facts, but not until you are well clear of the column."

"Yes, Colonel." Ogilvie hesitated. "Colonel, may I take Mr Cunningham?"

Dornoch frowned. "For one company, leaving me all the others without a sar'nt-major?" Then he added, "Is this on account of the truth having to come out, James? You wish his support?"

"He's a steady man," Ogilvie said. "I think it would help, Colonel."

"Very well, you may take Cunningham," Dornoch said briskly. "Off you go and make ready. March out as soon as you are— don't report back to me. Good luck, James." Dornoch reached out his hand and took Ogilvie's in a hard grip. "Make a success of it. And when it's done, force-march for all you're worth to overtake the column. I'll put a few delaying tactics of my own in hand for you!"

*　　　*　　　*

It was quietly done and efficiently: Ogilvie sought out the Regimental Sergeant-Major with orders to prepare B Company for detachment at once. For the present he indicated its purpose as being simply to attempt to take the Mullah's person following upon revelations made as to his whereabouts by the captured Pathan. Cunningham went about his business assisted by the colour-sergeants and when Ogilvie's senior subaltern, Neil Baird, reported the company ready to move out, the order was given to detach to the rear. With a piper and two drummers and two ammunition and commissariat wagons they marched down the line of bivouacs, past men already back to sleep, past the tents of His Excellency and Sir Iain Ogilvie, past the now silent native contingent and the splendid tent of the Maharajah of Mysore, past the tethered elephants and the mule-train, the remaining guns and the squalid groups of camp followers, men and women bunched close together for mutual warmth. By Ogilvie's estimate it would be two days' forced-march back to the Mullah's hillside cavern: the rests would be the minimum and already, with his ride through the passes the night before still unobliterated by such snatched sleep as he had been able to find in a commissariat wagon on that day's march, Ogilvie felt his eyelids droop with tiredness. To keep awake he talked with his subaltern. Baird, so far only given the same story as had been given to the men before moving out, expressed his fears.

"We'll be reported ahead, surely?"

Ogilvie shrugged. "The Mullah will have his observers, of course. That's not unusual in these parts, is it?"

"No..."

They rode on. Ogilvie, though still largely doubtful of Dornoch's wisdom, recognised that some sort of success was perhaps not too impossible... Dornoch had spoken of the likelihood of the hostages being killed whatever happened, but there was another side to that particular coin: hostages were hostages, and were for use as such, and once they died, their value was gone. It was possible that the Mullah would not be panicked into a precipitate slaughter. Ogilvie kept the Scots marching through the night with no more than one short rest, and halted again just after the dawn for breakfast. When the meal was finished, Ogilvie put the facts about the hostages to his sub-alterns, baldly and abruptly, not inviting comment. Then he took the Regimental Sergeant-Major aside.

"There's something I must tell the men," he said, "but I shall tell you first, Sar'nt-Major, and I'll make it short. Some of the wives and children are at risk."

Cunningham gave a start, his eyes widening. "Sir? I don't understand."

"Then listen, Sar'nt-Major." Briefly, Ogilvie explained the situation and the reasons why Sir Thomas Lee had decided to keep the facts to himself for as long as possible: the security of the Raj, Ogilvie said flatly, had of over-riding necessity to come first. But now he and his company had been ordered to redress the balance.

Cunningham stared at him, his face working with surprise, anger, bewilderment, anxiety. He said, "I'm flabbergasted, Captain Ogilvie! I'd never have believed it possible that any officer would leave the women—"

"Steps would have been taken as soon as possible," Ogilvie interrupted, realising how empty the words must sound. "It was a matter of priorities and a wicked decision for any officer to have to make. You must remember Sir Thomas was, and is, directly responsible for the life of the Viceroy, Mr Cunningham."

"Aye..." Cunningham swung round on his heel, away from Ogilvie, staring into the long distance, the vista of the mountain pass. "You must give me a moment," he said. There was a silence between the two men. Then Cunningham turned back to face the officer once more. His face was set hard, his eye was bleak: something had been fought down, some inner victory won. He said, "Very good, Captain Ogilvie, sir. The facts must be accepted and the best must be done now. I shall talk to the men, sir."

"That's my job, Sar'nt-Major—"

"No, sir. I shall do that. I shall do it better, and well you know that, sir. I am a married man and you are not. And I know now why you would not reassure the men earlier, Captain Ogilvie. Sir!" Giving a salute, the Regimental Sergeant-Major turned about with a crash of boots and, his pace-stick firm beneath his arm, marched off towards the men who were clearing away the impedimenta of breakfast. Ogilvie's feelings were mixed: Cunningham's reaction had been censorious and there was no denying it, but time would bring him a realisation of the inevitability of the facts he had accepted; and in the meantime Ogilvie was glad enough not to have to address the men.

\* \* \*

141

In Peshawar there was the greatest consternation: in the Royal Strathspeys' cantonment two nights before, the barrack guard and gate sentries, attacked with the silent knives by mere shadows with oiled skins, had been slaughtered to a man even before there had been time to give the alarm. Fifteen wives and twelve children, boys and girls in no case more than six years old, had been taken and spirited away. The remaining wives had spoken tearfully of the sound of horses' hooves afterwards, fading fast into the night. Set as they were two miles from the city, the cantonments gave easy access straight into the wild hills, and the pursuit, mounted as speedily as possible but not speedily enough from the reduced garrison, had found nothing. In the early morning Bloody Francis Fettleworth had arrived in person from his headquarters in Nowshera, with his Chief of Staff and ADC and Major Blaise-Willoughby in attendance. He was horror-struck, a shaking plum-pudding on horseback.

"Terrible," he said, mopping at his face with a handkerchief as the Scots women surrounded his horse. "A tragedy—but never fear, they shall be found. They shall be found, I say!" He shook a fist in the air.

"They'll be found dead, sir," one of the women, a tall, gaunt woman with flashing eyes, shouted up at him. "As God's ma judge, General, yon bastards'll kill them long before you can get at them with your fine words!"

"Madam, I give you my promise—"

"It's no' promises we want! It's action!" The gaunt woman's words were taken up by the others; there was much shouting, with an underlying menace. Fettleworth looked nervous: the situation had suddenly become ugly, and he knew Scots women by reputation. They had scant respect for rank when they were roused, and they were mostly physically strong, big-boned fish-wives, weavers and the like, who minced no words and didn't mind using their fists. Fettleworth looked round and backed his horse a little way, its hooves sending up spurts of sand from the parade-ground. There was a rising cloud of anger from the women, one of whom clutched at the General's stirrup-leather and shouted up into his startled face in broad Scots which, fortunately, Bloody Francis was unable to interpret. Becoming angry himself, he was about to lash at the woman's arm with his riding-crop when he saw the sergeant of the guard coming across at the double with a party of soldiers carrying their rifles at the short trail. Trembling slightly, Fettleworth held his hand. Unceremoniously the guard pushed into the throng of women, thrusting them aside, speaking to them roughly in their own tongue, putting a strong line of khaki and arms between them and the Divisional Commander. Fettleworth, scarlet in the face now, safe but keenly aware of the indignity of virtual rescue from females, spoke loudly.

"I understand your concern, naturally. However, there is never an excuse for bad manners and poor behaviour..." He lifted his voice even higher over the jeers that this brought forth. "I have come to help...to see to it that you who remain are kept safe. You must trust me. The women and children will be brought back, you have my guarantee..."

His voice was lost in the hubbub. Flushing angrily, he turned to his Chief of Staff. "By God, Lakenham, they're a damn rabble! What's the use of my saying anything more?" He turned his horse and rode away, followed by his staff, his head in the air and nostrils wide. He made for Brigade; here he found a skeleton staff headed by a major with whom he had already been in contact by means of the telegraph line from Nowshera.

"Well?" he demanded rudely.

"All available men are out searching, sir. I've pressed all sorts of odds and ends into service—"

"With what result, may I ask?"

The Major spread his hands. "So far, sir, none."

"And the units extended towards the Khyber—they've sent out parties, have they not?"

"They have, sir, but again with no result. With your orders in mind to contain any probe from the Khyber, they've not depleted their strength too far."

Fettleworth nodded. "They've done right. God, what a situation this is—Calcutta will be onto me like a bloody avenging angel! I can only wish God-speed to the troop trains from Ootacamund!" He paused, rhetorically asked for the hundredth time, "What's the *reason* behind it? Hostages of a sort, no doubt—"

"Quite, sir—"

"But with what precise point in mind? I dare say we shall be enlightened shortly. In the meantime we shall need a nominal roll of those missing...did I understand you to say that Lady Dornoch was not among them?"

"She was not, sir. She had been accommodated temporarily

here at Brigade, and—"

"How is she?"

"Upset, sir. She went at once to talk to the wives and women, and I gather was further upset. She's been put to bed by the Medical Officer."

Fettleworth nodded again. "A brave lady, Major, the very best."

"Indeed she is, sir. I'm afraid it's hit her badly that Mrs Cunningham was taken—"

"Cunningham, Cunningham?"

"The Regimental Sergeant-Major of the 114th, sir."

"I see. I'm very sorry." Fettleworth blew through his drooping moustache in something like despair. "I'll remain here until there's some further word," he said. "You'll keep me informed minute by minute, if you please. Lakenham, I'm undecided as to whether or not we should let Dornoch know the facts. What d'you think?"

"How, sir?"

Fettleworth's answer was impatient. "What the devil d'you mean, *how*?"

"The field telegraph line remains cut, sir."

"Oh—yes, yes. Of course! Oh, damnation." Another of Fettleworth's many worries reared its head before him: word had come through from Rawalpindi that the sappers sent out to repair the field telegraph line had overtaken the despatch riders who had headed north on the General's earlier order. They had overtaken them because they were dead, little more than heaps of bones being picked at still by the vultures under a metallic sky. After making this discovery the sappers and their infantry escort had been savagely attacked by tribesmen who had swarmed like bees out of the wild hills. The British force had been wiped out to one signaller, the man who had sent the message back, himself badly wounded. The message had ended abruptly and there had been nothing further...Fettleworth shook his head and said, "Well, there's no point in giving Dornoch depressing news, I suppose." He rubbed his hands together, quite glad to be relieved of at any rate one decision. "Major, we've not breakfasted yet. No doubt you can have something prepared? Porridge, kedgeree, liver, eggs—two—and bacon. Fruit. Hot buttered toast and marmalade, and coffee. Nothing elaborate, don't you know. My taste is simple enough and I'm too bloody worried to eat much." He stalked towards the Brigade Mess, clanking his spurs

and loosening the neck of his tunic, ruining his appetite still
further by searing thoughts of the despatch he must shortly
draft for Calcutta. On his way, he stopped and listened: there
had been a bugle call, followed by the clamour of a brass band.
His face solemn, he moved to a window and looked out across
the parade-ground to the flagstaff: Brigade's standard was creeping up to the truck, and the brass was thundering out 'God Save
the Queen' over the heads of an immaculate guard, all starch
and pipeclay and arms at the present, the personification of an
embattled Raj. Bloody Francis's chest swelled out against his
Sam Browne belt and a hand refastened the tunic's neckband
before dropping smartly to his side. As the last notes of 'God
Save the Queen' faded into the empty air of a sadly bare parade-
ground, a small but distinct sound came from close by and
Fettleworth swung sharply round, eyes bulging.

"Blaise-Willoughby, confound it, can't you—"

"It was Wolseley, sir."

"That bloody monkey! Oh, *blast* you!" Fettleworth stalked
away in a huff, simmering. Political Officers were all the same,
no reverence, a damn republican crew of too-clever-by-halves,
though to his knowledge only one kept a bloody monkey...In
the Mess, Fettleworth came face to face with the inevitable
portrait of Her Majesty, looking down her nose in profile and
seated upon a sofa, in essence bestriding her Empire. Emotion
swelled again in the Divisional Commander's breast: in this
terrible affair of kidnap and possible mutiny, much depended
upon himself, not least the well-being and the peace of mind of the
old Queen in Windsor Castle: he must not let her down.

\*     \*     \*

Ogilvie had felt the questions in the air as his company moved
out south for the connecting pass, the questions that cried out
to be answered but by order of the RSM were not to be given
voice. Cunningham had told the men all they needed to know,
adding that there was no positive news that in fact any of the
women and children had been taken by the Mullah: this could
turn out to be a fool's errand, but at the least they might well
find the Mullah himself, or clues to his whereabouts if, as was
likely, he had moved on by now—and if they caught him, the
threat of mutiny could be considered more than half over, though

145

there might remain the interwoven threat from the armies of the Czar, already on the march from Afghanistan. To Ogilvie, Cunningham broached his fears on this point. "They'll not carry out an ignominious retreat from conquest so easily, sir."

"I don't agree, Sar'nt Major. Mutiny is to be their pivot! Remove the native support, and the situation changes somewhat drastically for them."

"Aye, maybe so, sir. But they'll lose face—"

"Better to lose face than to lose a war almost before it's begun. With the Mullah gone, we'll have India back on our side, fighting for the Raj and united against outside threats." Ogilvie turned to look back at the company. "The men, Sar'nt-Major. What's the mood? What's the spirit?"

"The spirit, Captain Ogilvie?" Cunningham gave a hard, savage laugh. "You don't need to ask that, sir. When they get their hands on the Mullah, sir, there'll not be an inch of flesh left on the bone!"

Ogilvie made no response to that for the moment, but later, when a halt was called for rest and refreshment, he took the opportunity to speak to all ranks. "You know the orders," he said, "and you know the objective. Now you must know the tactics. You'll all be aware, I take it, that we can't hope to surprise the Mullah's men. The reports will already be going back from his observers. In that, there lies an obvious risk which we must accept." He explained why he did not in fact consider the risk to the hostages to be too great. "A lot will depend upon the situation as we find it when we engage the enemy, but here's part one of my tactical plan." He turned to his senior subaltern. "Mr Baird?"

"Sir?"

"I propose to time our arrival tomorrow for the night hours, and I expect to be in the westward pass by first dark. On my way from the Mullah's hide-out to rejoin, I saw a narrow defile beside the pass...some ground separated from the pass itself by a high spur of rock and forming a cul-de-sac. As we approach this spur, your half-company will detach without further orders and march quietly into the defile, where they will wait. The second half-company under myself and Mr Cunningham will advance on the Mullah behind the pipes and drums. It will be to some extent a case of sleight-of-hand, and we shall have to hope the Mullah does not give too much credence to his observers' estimates of our real strength. The defile is no more than some half-mile from the cavern, and when you hear the first shots fired, Mr Baird, you'll lead your half-company out into the pass and up the western side. When you reach the top, you'll turn south and come up as silently as you can, closing an expanse of flat ground which you'll find is immediately above the entrance to the cavern itself. Having cleared the flat ground, you'll descend the hillside to the cavern, and take it and its occupants over." He looked along the ranks. "Are there any questions?"

"Do you expect the women and children to be found in the cavern, sir?" Colour-Sergeant MacTrease asked.

"Either there or on the flat shelf above, Colour MacTrease." Ogilvie, who had said nothing of the grisly death of the Mullah's disloyal follower, shivered suddenly. If things should go sadly wrong, then that flat ground could well be a sight of the most appalling horror...

# 15

PRESSING WEST NEXT day along the connecting pass, Ogilvie worried about time: after releasing the hostages, he would have all this desolate mountain country, and more, to traverse again. The Colonel had spoken of delaying tactics: such could be employed easily enough, certainly, but could not be carried too far. Sir Thomas Lee had been adamant that the column, with His Excellency and His Highness, must reach Srinagar before the Russian armies could strike down from the north. Srinagar would be defensible and the mutineers and the Russians could be held outside the city while the Raj mustered its full strength for the relief. Lord Dornoch would need to have this well in mind. Riding along, Ogilvie discussed his worries with Baird.

"The hills will be alive afterwards, Neil."

"Not if we make a clean sweep."

"Kill the lot? We can't guarantee that. One or two will try to slip away at the start, to pass the word on."

"The bush telegraph!" Baird eased the helmet on his head; sweat poured from the leather band inside. "We may meet a probe from Peshawar, James, if we're lucky—"

"Very lucky!"

"But Fettleworth's bound to send out patrols."

"Of course, but he can't spare many men just now. We know that, so does the Mullah. Besides, there's a strong element of the needle in the haystack out here, isn't there?"

Baird nodded. "What about Sir Iain, James?"

"My father? What about him?"

"Well, I know I've raised this before, but—"

"It's out of our control in any case," Ogilvie said abruptly,

148

squashingly. His father would have known long since that Lord Dornoch had detached a company: unless Dornoch and Sir Thomas Lee between them had managed to dream up a sufficiently convincing story, his reaction was predictable enough: he would fly into a fury, take over the command of the column, detach the rest of the regiment to the rear to assist the lone company, and hold the column in the pass until they all rejoined. Of course, His Excellency would for a certainty over-rule the Northern Army Commander—but, as James Ogilvie knew well, his father was entirely capable of disregarding even the Viceroy when his temper was up, and there could be the most undignified public brawl...

\*     \*     \*

Nightfall was not far off now: they marched in silence, not in any useless attempt to preserve secrecy but because they were weary and tense, expecting attack at any moment as they began to approach the Mullah's stronghold. During the day one incautious native head had been seen on the peaks: the second time it showed, two marksmen had opened fire, and the head had disappeared. The pickets had investigated, and had found a body with a shattered skull. Possibly a link in the chain had been broken, but this gave no particular comfort to the Scots as they began to approach action, half expectant that the Mullah's advanced scouts would open on them from the peaks before the last of the day's light went. Out now from the side pass, they made their way along the track that would lead them directly below the cavern and its arms and explosive. Ogilvie, in the lead with the Regimental Sergeant-Major and a subaltern, lifted a hand as they began to approach the rock-sheltered defile: his signal was passed down the ranks of Scots until it was repeated in the fading light by Baird in the lead of his half-company. A halt was called until twilight had faded into full darkness, with as yet no moon. Ten more minutes and the word was passed, quietly, for the march to resume. As Ogilvie came abreast of the defile he called to the solitary piper.

"Now, Piper MacAdam."

"Sir!" A single beat came from a drummer like a knell in the night, and at the same moment Piper MacAdam blew air into the pipes ready beneath his arm. The leading half-company moved on openly behind the pipes and the drummers' tattoo—and in rear and in silence Baird doubled his two sections out of sight into the defile. Ogilvie felt a cold sweat start down inside his tunic. Dismounting, he handed his horse over to a man detailed by Cunningham: soon now the climb would start, the rush up the hillside to their right if they were given the chance. Bravely the pipes sounded out, savage in the night, playing the action tune of the Royal Strathspey, 'Cock o' the North'. Every man marched with his rifle at the ready, all his senses on the alert to fire back at the first bullet from the heights. As none came hopes began to rise, but were cast down by the implication of possible flight on the part of the Mullah: the hostages would not have been left behind. Ogilvie's face hardened as they advanced into stillness and silence broken only by the pipes and dreams themselves, and the footfalls of their advance over the rocky, uncertain ground of the enclosed pass. When the fusillade opened from above, Ogilvie was taken by surprise. A bullet whistled past nicking his left ear: by his side his subaltern, MacIver, fell and was caught by Cunningham and carried aside. Ogilvie shouted the Scots off the floor of the pass as the bullets sang and buzzed in amongst them and boulders began to come down.

"Spread out and climb!" he shouted above the sound of the rifles, those of the maddened Scots now replying to the native jezails. He flung himself up the steep hillside, keeping in the lead, and was aware of the Regimental Sergeant-Major, free now of his burden, coming up behind, running like the wind and puffing hard, a revolver firing upwards at the pin-points of flame that gave away the positions of the enemy. Within moments Cunningham was by his side.

Ogilvie asked, "Mr MacIver?"

"Dead, sir."

Ogilvie fired point-blank as a Pathan rose up right in front of him with a bayoneted jezail aimed at his stomach. His bullet took the man between the eyes. Ogilvie and the RSM plunged on, treading the body against rock. Now they were in the thick of it and there was no holding back on the part of Cunningham. Firing, now and again using his revolver as a club to smash the heads of the Pathans, he stormed on, caring nothing for his life, determined only to kill and to reach the hostages and possibly, for all he knew, his own wife. Behind them, and spread widely along the hillside, the Royal Strathspey came on ferociously, shouting highland war-cries and given heart once again by the skirl of the pipes, sounding out loud and clear to the tune of 'The Campbells Are Coming'. Before they reached the crest, however, they came into increased fire from the jezails, a barrage of lead that forced Ogilvie to discontinue the climb.

"Sar'nt-Major, they must get their heads down into cover!"

"Aye, sir." Reluctant, but seeing the good sense, Cunningham bellowed the order. Settling himself down beside Ogilvie he said, "It'll not be long before Mr Baird comes up, sir."

"Exactly. Until he does, we'll hold the ground we've gained. We don't want unnecessary casualties—" Ogilvie broke off: a lull had come in the shooting, and clearly he had heard a woman's cry, a cry of pain and terror. "Did you hear that, Sar'nt-Major?"

"I did, sir." Cunningham's tone was ugly. "There's not much time left. And I'm going in—"

"Not with my permission."

"Then without it, Captain Ogilvie." Cunningham scrambled up; Ogilvie grabbed his forearm and held it fast. "Let me go, sir!" The RSM pulled, dragging Ogilvie up alongside him.

"You're staying here, Mr Cunningham. That's an order. Do you want to face Court Martial?"

"My wife's more important to me than—"

"You don't know she's here. If she is, you'll be no use to her dead. See sense, for God's sake, Sar'nt-Major! I'm saying to you just what you'd say to any NCO or man in similar circumstances."

Cunningham seemed about to jerk free of Ogilvie's grip when a voice was heard, a loud voice, a native but not the Mullah, speaking in English. "British soldiers, listen," it said. Ogilvie whispered to Cunningham to get down; this time the RSM obeyed. The pipes and drums broke off. The speaker could not be seen: the moon was still not up and the hillside was virtually pitch black, only the summit visible as a darker line of jags against the night sky. The voice went on, breaking into a death-like stillness. "British soldiers, we have your women and children under guard and helpless. You cannot help them. If you advance, they die and so do you." There was a pause. "Where is your officer sahib?"

Ogilvie stirred: he felt the heavy pressure of Cunningham's hand on his shoulder, his voice close to his ear. "Keep quiet, Captain Ogilvie, and don't tell them!"

"Why not?"

"Because I have a feeling they'll pin-point you, and shoot you. And that won't help the men. Do as I say, sir."

Ogilvie remained quiet and the speaker went on, the voice sounding harsher. "Your officer sahib fears to reveal himself, and I shall speak to you directly. I am asking you to throw down your weapons and show yourselves in peace. If you do this, you will not be harmed, nor will the hostages. If you do not, the hostages are lost, and for you, British soldiers, you will be blown to little pieces by canisters of high explosive that are ready to be cast down upon you. I shall light a lamp, containing no oil beyond what has soaked into its wick. When the flame dies, no time will be left to you."

A small yellow flame appeared, feebly flickering from the crest. There was extreme tension on the hillside, and the angry voices of the rank-and-file floated up to Ogilvie: it was all too clear. Some were for fighting on, others for taking a chance on the native's words. Not many, but enough to spread the rot. Ogilvie could remain silent no longer. In a loud voice he called, "Any man who lays down his arms will face Court Martial for cowardice unless I use my prerogative and shoot him first."

There was a startled silence: this was broken within seconds by a report from a jezail above, and fragments of rock flew around Ogilvie. He wriggled further into cover and kept quiet. As the flame began to die, he saw two kilted shadows moving out from behind the boulders on the hillside, scarcely visible were it not for their movement. He was about to fire a shot over their heads when a sustained burst of rifle-fire came from behind the summit and the air seemed suddenly filled with the shouts and cries of the Pathans.

Ogilvie came to his feet with a jump. "It's Mr Baird!" he called out. "Mr Cunningham, sound the Advance!"

"Aye, sir!" Exultantly Cunningham shouted to the bugler, and the notes of the Advance rang out. As one man the Royal Strathspey surged from cover and pounded full pelt up the hillside to the jagged peaks, firing blind as they ran, lunging with their fixed bayonets as they found solid shadows as targets, penetrating, twisting and withdrawing the bloodied blades again and again. The tribesmen, utterly surprised from the rear with all their attention on the hill-face, were caught like rats in a trap, and like rats in a trap they fought and twisted and tore. But the Scots were maddened, terrified for the womenfolk and the children, and they fought with a savage ferocity that carried all before them, urged on by the wild notes of the pipes. As the moon began its slow climb up the sky a terrible scene of blood and carnage lay revealed, with bodies everywhere, shockingly hacked, many with severed heads and limbs and, openly upon a spur of rock high above, the tartan of the Royal Strathspey blowing on the night wind around the knees of Piper MacAdam. Neither Ogilvie nor Baird, nor the Regimental Sergeant-Major, were able to stop the massive slaughter. Their voices rose but were unheard in the fighting and the wild Highland cries, in the screams of the Pathans as they died with the bayonets in their throats, chests or stomachs. Apart from any who might have run from the fight, not one of the Mullah's bandits remained alive when it was over. Twenty-three Scots lay dead or wounded; and of the Mullah, alive or dead, there was no sign. The women and children were found safe in the cave store-house, along with all the arms, ammunition and high explosive. Most were crying, all were smiling: Cunningham clasped his wife as though he would never let her go, and it was she who gently pushed him away as Ogilvie entered the cave, streaming blood from a gash on his right thigh from the rip of a bayonet through the heavy cloth of his trews. In the light of flares Cunningham's eyes were moist.

"Now let me be," Mrs Cunningham said, smiling at her husband. "It's no' seemly before the men, and here's Captain Ogilvie now, Donald."

Ogilvie was conscious of a minor shock: had he been asked, he could not easily have come up with the Regimental Sergeant-Major's Christian name and it seemed odd to hear that formidable Warrant Officer referred to in tones of mild reproof and by his first name...to all ranks of the Royal Strathspey he had been known, it seemed from time immemorial, by the sobriquet of 'Bosom'.

* * *

"It's a fair shambles, Captain Ogilvie, sir." Cunningham gazed round at the dead in their stiff, grotesque attitudes. The wounded had been carried into the cave and were being tended by the women, with the aid of the primitive medical stores that had accompanied the march in the commissariat wagon. "You'll stop to bury them, I take it?"

"We'll build cairns, Sar'nt-Major," Ogilvie answered shortly, already hearing the slow flap of the vultures' wings. "And quickly, too," he added. "We'll not linger here. We have to overtake the column and that'll mean forced marching. What was the count of the hostages?"

"Twenty-seven all told, sir, women and children, and all correct, thank the Lord, sir."

"Yes. Well, they'll have to take their turn in the wagons, and my horse'll be available too. We'll march as soon as the burial details have finished."

"I'll sort them out at once, sir. And the Mullah, sir?"

Ogilvie shrugged. "I hardly expected he'd stay, somehow! Our job was the hostages, and that we've done. All the same, there is something else before we leave, Mr Cunningham."

"Sir?"

Ogilvie swung an arm around the packed arsenal. "We won't leave them all this."

"You'll blow it up, sir?"

"Right, Sar'nt-Major! It won't be the first of their ammunition dumps I'll have deprived them of."

"And the racket, Captain Ogilvie?"

"Will be heard for miles around—I know! And I'm not forgetting the women and children. But I can't leave this lot intact to be used against us. In any case, we're going to be shadowed right along, and attacked. That's inevitable. See that powder fuses are run out, if you please, Sar'nt-Major."

"Very good, sir." Cunningham saluted, turned about and called for Colour-Sergeant MacTrease. A fuse detail was ordered, and men got to work on splitting open the barrels of powder, heaping the contents in the middle of the cave and moving some of the cases of high explosive close to the heap. Three separate trails were laid from the loose powder, out through the mouth of the cavern, past the guarding ridge of rock outside, and out to the open hillside beyond. When this was done the dead and wounded were carried down into the pass, bright now beneath the moon. The women and children were assisted down and mustered in the centre of the company with the wounded men, and escorted the short distance to the defile where the commissariat and ammunition wagons were hidden. Ogilvie retained one section and sent them back into the cavern to remove as many as possible of the more modern rifles, together with cases of cartridges, and a Maxim with its spare ammunition-belts. These were carried down the hillside and the last of the Scots were marched away to pick up the wagons, with orders to enter the defile and flatten to the ground behind its solid rock wall. Ogilvie remained behind with flares and matches, looked down and saw the Regimental Sergeant-Major climbing back up the side of the pass towards him.

"All right, Sar'nt-Major," he called. "I'll manage on my own."

"You're exposed up there, sir. You'll need cover. There may be some of those buggers still—"

"Two of us make two targets, Sar'nt-Major. Go back and see to your good lady."

"Sir, I—"

"An order, Sar'nt-Major. Stand away now." Ogilvie knelt, struck a match and lit his flare. He held it until the flame had a grip; yellow light flickered off the rock and scrub of the hillside. Seeing Cunningham make his way slowly down again to the pass, he put the flame to the first of the three trails of powder, watched the running, fizzling spark, and then, when the first trail had burned for some four feet of its length, lit the second. Fading away along the pass he heard the tramp of marching feet as the Scots made for safe cover. He had just lit the last of the powder trails when he heard a single rifle shot, closely followed by a sharp cry from the lower slope of the hillside, and he saw Cunningham roll down to the pass. As he leapt to his feet something took him like a sledgehammer on the side of his skull and he fell unconscious, his body dropping across the blackened ends of the trails as the three lines of sparkling fire flowed on smoothly towards the cave-mouth.

# 16

THE NORTHERN ARMY Commander stared bleakly from the Viceregal howdah across the interminable ridges of the Kashmiri hills, extending on all sides as far as the eye could see. They were in a high sector of the pass, and after a stiff climb the cooler air was welcome to the marching men and the horses and mules of the ammunition and commissariat trains, though the more rarified atmosphere tended towards some shortness of breath. Nevertheless, Sir Iain Ogilvie felt some envy for the cavalry and infantry and gunners, even for the lowly Supply and Transport: he was not fond of elephants. Had he wished to be heaved around like a ship in a seaway, he would, he reflected dourly, have joined the Navy. But His Excellency the Earl of Elgin, Viceroy of India, had expressed a wish to be joined by the Northern Army Commander, and the Viceregal wish, like the Royal wish itself, was to be taken as a command. Hence the discomfort, and hence too the furious thoughts that nagged at Sir Iain Ogilvie's mind, indeed pronged into him like red-hot lances. Earlier there had been a right royal row with His Excellency, since when His Excellency had been icily polite but had seemed disinclined to let Sir Iain out of his sight. It had blown up when Sir Iain's eagle and jealous eye had noted his old regiment marching one company under strength. He had approached the column commander for an explanation, which had been given readily enough—something about information having come to hand of the Mullah's whereabouts—but Sir Iain had detected some reserve in Sir Thomas's manner; and had found a similar reaction from the Royal Strathspeys' colonel: a stiffness, and a disinclination to elaborate. This had aroused

Sir Iain's curiosity and alarm and he had grown angry.

"You tell me it's my son's company, Dornoch. I wish to know more."

"I can add nothing more, Sir Iain. You have such facts as I know."

"Have I, by God! Something tells me I have not! What's my son been up to, hey?"

"Nothing beyond his duty, sir. He acquitted himself well enough whilst detached earlier, as you know."

"H'm." For some moments Sir Iain rode on in silence, frowning. Then he uttered again, sharply. "My son's young still. If the Mullah himself is at the end of this probe of yours, Dornoch, then you have more experienced officers at your service, have you not?"

"No," Dornoch answered baldly. "Captain Ogilvie, sir, is an officer of very great experience as it happens, and—"

"Dammit, I know my own son's record—"

"Perhaps, sir. I, as his Colonel, know the man himself, and know him better than you do, with respect. I have every trust and confidence in him and his judgment."

"More than I have, then!"

Dornoch smiled icily. "A failing of fathers, I fancy."

"Don't be impertinent!"

"I apologise, sir."

"Like hell you do!" Sir Iain swung round on the column commander. "Sir Thomas, I feel I have not been given the facts, the whole of the facts. I want them and I want them now. I'm aware I do not command the column, but it was my own decision that I did not do so—since I wished to have full freedom of action in my wider responsibilities whilst His Excellency is in my care. I must remind you that I still command at Murree, and I speak now as the Lieutenant-General Commanding, Northern Army. Well?"

"Sir, there is nothing I am able to add."

"Then remain silent at your peril, Sir Thomas. In due time the facts must emerge—and I shall still command at Murree! Must I be more explicit?"

Again there was a silence: Lord Dornoch met Sir Thomas Lee's eye, and gave a fractional nod accompanied by an unheard sigh and a heartfelt prayer that, at this very nasty moment, some action by the invisible enemy in the hills around them might cause a most welcome diversion. But the enemy did not oblige and Sir Thomas said, "Very well, sir, you shall be told the facts, but I beg of you not to be precipitate—"

"Precipitate my damn backside."

"Yes, sir." Crisply, in a few words, Sir Thomas passed on the story. The expected explosion did not come: Sir Iain's face whitened and he remained deadly calm and icy. The equally expected reaction, however, did come in full: Sir Iain, swinging his horse round to make towards the Viceroy, said, "The previous orders are countermanded. You are relieved of command of the column, Sir Thomas. I am taking over personally and at once."

He rode to the rear, pushing arrogantly past marching officers and men, leaving consternation in the van of the advance. Turning alongside the Viceroy's elephant, he called up to the howdah. "Your Excellency, I request an audience immediately."

"Upon what matters, Sir Iain?"

"The conduct of the advance, Your Excellency, and it'll not wait. I think we should speak more privately than shouting from the pass allows."

The Viceroy leaned across for a word with his Military Secretary and a highly-placed Civilian from Calcutta, a prim man with pince-nez and a white tussore suit. Then he spoke again to Sir Iain, abruptly. "Very well, General. You may join us if you wish."

"Thank you, sir."

The mahout was given his orders: the elephant was drawn a little aside, and halted. There was a sickening lurch and whilst the Viceregal party held on tight, the animal sank onto its fore knees, then let down its immense rump. Sir Iain handed his horse over to a *syce* from the Viceroy's entourage and scrambled with some difficulty into the ornate howdah, managing to salute the Viceroy and Vicereine as he did so. Addressing the latter he said, "My apologies for the intrusion, Ma'am. This will not take long." He shifted target to Lord Elgin. "Your Excellency, I have taken over command of the column—"

"Why, Sir Iain?"

Sir Iain explained, rapidly and angrily giving the full story of the hostages. The Viceroy was shocked, and said so: there was genuine concern and consternation in the howdah, and Sir Iain was asked what he proposed to do. He proposed, he announced, to halt the column and hold it in the pass whilst a strong force was sent to back up the one company that had been sent so far: the Royal Strathspey, he said, would march as a regiment with two more battalions and two mountain batteries, plus cavalry. To this the Civilian from Calcutta made strong objections: Whitehall, he said, would come down like a descending sword of Damocles. Their Excellencies could not be held in danger in the pass; it was very unfortunate but women and children must not be allowed to weaken the Raj or the determination of its generals. Sir Iain became almost speechless, but not quite: furious, he had a good deal to say about damn Civilians interfering in military matters upon which they had no right to pronounce. Thus the row developed, with poor Lady Elgin doing her best to make out she was not listening...and in the upshot Sir Iain was ordered to hand back the command of the column to Sir Thomas Lee and to allow the column to proceed.

"I'm damned if I will, sir!" he said in a grating voice. "My regiment—"

"We all appreciate your feelings, General, but I am adamant—though at the same time extremely sorry. I have nothing further to say, and if you are wise, neither have you."

"I shall—"

"Meanwhile I ask you to be good enough to ride with me in my howdah, General. There are matters that can profitably be discussed, I think...and it will serve as a reason for Sir Thomas resuming the command."

Sir Iain glowered: it was a tactful enough move, and it was being tactfully put, but Sir Iain was quite experienced enough to assess the facts: the Lieutenant-General Commanding at Murree could scarcely be placed in arrest in order to prevent his impetuosity leading to disregard of orders, but a Viceregal wish for him to share the howdah came to precisely the same thing...

\*       \*       \*

There was a sharp pain in Ogilvie's skull and a dull, spreading pain inside the head itself, a raw feeling allied to a regular throb that left him sick and drained. His limbs felt cold as ice, and immovable. His face was pressed against rock, and there was a stickiness drooling down from his hair. As from a far distance he heard firing, and then shouts, and then footsteps, running footsteps growing louder. There was also a fizzling sound and pinpoints of light danced, flickering against his closed eyelids, but he didn't know what these might be. Then he felt himself seized, and dragged backwards over the rock before being lifted and carried. There was a great confusion in his mind, but the mists were starting to clear just a little, and he was aware, as he opened his eyes briefly, of being taken down a hillside, very fast. Then the progress levelled out and the pace increased. There was heavy breathing around him, and he was being roughly handled: close to him he heard what sounded like a prayer, fervently uttered aloud. The journey seemed long and the sick feeling worsened: at last, however, he was laid flat on the ground and as somebody bent over him the words of the prophets appeared to come true and the world to end. He was conscious of a vast light, a huge roar of sound, and a tremendous buffet from the very air. One after another explosions came to him in bursts of unimaginable sound and fury, and everywhere things dropped, pieces of rock large and small clanking down like a rainstorm of solid matter, and over all a familiar enough stench of burning gunpowder and high explosive.

He heard a voice in his ear, asking if he was all right: the voice, like the smell of battle, was familiar; and, recognising it, he found memory and awareness returning. He opened his eyes again. "I'll do," he said. "I was knocked out, that's all..."

"You were shot at, sir, by a Pathan in hiding. The bullet grazed your head. Another hit me, but I'm all right too."

"I saw you fall...didn't I?"

Cunningham said, "Maybe you did, sir. I was no more than sent off balance to be honest. I was struck in the rear, Captain Ogilvie, the fleshy part, an awkward place but far from serious." He paused. "The powder trails worked, sir."

"I gathered that." Ogilvie tried to sit up, but the pain in his head stabbed like many daggers, and he fell back again. "Who got me clear, Sar'nt-Major? You?"

"No, sir. Not me. A patrol of the 1st Dorsets, sir. They'd come up from Rawalpindi after word got through from General Fettleworth. They'd heard the first rifle-fire, and it drew them on."

"*Primus in Indis*, Sar'nt-Major..."

"Sir?"

"The Dorsets' motto...they were the first British regiment to serve in India." Ogilvie gave a faint smile. "Thank God they're back again!"

There was a chuckle from Cunningham. "I think you're getting better, Captain Ogilvie, and amen to what you just said." He paused. "Do you wish to move out now, sir?"

"Yes, as soon as the dead are buried, Sar'nt-Major. I—"

"You'll travel in a commissariat wagon for a while at least, sir. I'll take charge until you're fit again."

"You?"

Cunningham said, "Mr Baird is sorely wounded, sir, by the same bugger that fired at us, and is in a much worse way than yourself. I'm no doctor, but I'll be surprised if he lives to reach the column—if any of us do at all!"

"What about the Dorsets' patrol? Have they no officer?"

"No, sir, he was lost some way back towards Rawalpindi, shot in the head." Cunningham got to his feet and called for a bearer party. Ogilvie was lifted and carried to one of the wagons where he was made as comfortable as possible on a pile of canvas and sacking. In the cart with him were three of the women, one of them being Mrs Cunningham, stout, motherly and straight-backed. When the burial parties had done their work, the company formed up in two files for the long march to overtake the Viceroy's column. Mrs Cunningham tended Ogilvie's scalp wound and cut thigh, bandaging them with dressings from the field medical supplies after cleaning up the skin with some astringent bottled fluid that stung like a million angry bees. By the dawn Ogilvie was feeling fit enough to ride, taking over his horse from a corporal's wife, grotesque on horseback with her full skirt drawn up to her waist and long white pantaloons reaching down widespread and ample legs. They were moving now through the joining pass, easterly to cross the track of the main column, and so far there had been no attack. Strengthened now by the 1st Dorsets, Cunningham had double-banked the pickets for greater protection on the flanks of their advance and they marched with the pipes playing and the drummers beating out the step. During the afternoon Baird died. After the brief halt when the body was protected against the vultures by cairns of piled stones, they marched on beneath a cloud of depression, scarcely any man speaking as the wail of the pipes sounded out along the pass. In the carts the women were silent also: neither Baird nor the subaltern killed in the first assault had been long with the Royal Strathspey, but the sense of family was strong even so. It was especially so, Ogilvie thought, out here on Indian service where men were exiles from home for many years at a stretch and the ties one to another were of great importance, surrounded and outnumbered as they were by an alien race; however humble and polite that race could be, and normally was, there was always death and danger hanging over the British soldier and his dependants. Scotland and familiar faces meant much, and losses were always diminishing to a regiment out of proportion to the actual numbers of the casualties. As they marched away and left the dead officer behind them, the rough cairn marking another milestone in the military story of the Raj, Ogilvie's thoughts turned inwards to the way of the soldier: his was in many respects a curious life when one took time to examine it and make the comparison with that of the civilian. Though perhaps in not quite so total a sense as life at sea, life in the British Army was a thing apart, and those comparatively few men who served in it tended to think of themselves as apart also, and much superior to those who had never taken the Queen's shilling. In the British Army life was hard and dangerous, a man's life. The discomforts of the barrack-room, the often torturous drilling on the square, the cruelties of punishment, the harsh discipline and the insistence on smartness, as well as the pride of regiment and battle honours—these were some of the things that set them on a pedestal above their easier-living fellows. The uniforms accounted for much of the rest: there was scarcely an under-housemaid in the British Isles who would not be thrilled to rest her hand upon the arm of a private soldier in scarlet and blue, kilt and doublet, or trews—men in infantry helmets, bonneted highlanders, Household Cavalry in pill-box caps, riflemen in busbees and green jackets, all of them soldiers of the Queen. Listening now to the pipes and feeling the immense heat of the afternoon sun burning his face, Ogilvie thought of the civilian: civilians, except for those fortunate enough to be countrymen, found their lot mostly behind office desks or at menial and repetitive tasks in factories and such; a strange race indeed! One, too of which he had had little experience: his upbringing had been military, with his father and both grandfathers in the army. That early life, followed by the Royal Military College at Sandhurst, and then the regiment in India... there was nothing unusual about it for his class, of course, since the sons of great families were expected, if they did not choose the church or the law, to enter the Queen's service—but it did mean early divorce from the life of the civilian. One grew up as a soldier, one thought as a soldier, one became a soldier, a simple progression. One grew apart from the lesser mortals...

"Captain Ogilvie, sir."

Ogilvie started. "Yes, Mr Cunningham, what is it?"

"You seemed preoccupied, sir."

"I was thinking..."

"I knew that, sir." Cunningham tweaked at his moustache, looking up at Ogilvie as he marched beside the officer's horse. "I'd not think too much, sir. It's all part of the life. We knew that when we joined."

"Of course. I wasn't thinking specifically of the casualties, Sar'nt-Major. I was thinking of the army."

"I see, sir. Well, there's time and space for thought out here I will admit. What aspects of the army, sir, if I might ask?"

Ogilvie smiled. "Just comparisons. Sar'nt-Major, you've never known anything but the army, have you?"

"Not really, sir. There was the life on the croft on Speyside, when I was a wee lad, that's all. I remember happy days until my father and mother died, then I was away into the regiment as a drummer boy.'

"And the croft?"

Cunningham said, "All gone, sir. It was never re-occupied, and it fell derelict. There's a wall left...I went back for a look, the last time we were at Invermore, sir." He paused. "I didn't linger."

"Too many ghosts?"

"Sir?"

"Oh, never mind, Sar'nt-Major. What does the future hold? Another croft?"

"When I take my pension, you mean, sir?" Cunningham frowned. "That's hard to say, Captain Ogilvie. It's all plain sailing for you, sir, but not for me. You have Corriecraig and a life's work there when your time's expired, sir. I have nothing."

"Nothing—literally?"

"Well, there's the wife's mother alive as yet, with a wee cot in the Monadliaths, but I'd not be fancying that, not so long as the old lady's still there, that is. Oh, I'll no doubt find work to do."

"As a civilian, Sar'nt-Major?"

Cunningham's face darkened. "It's not a trade I like, sir, that of the civilian. It would be hard to fit in. I'll not take my pension till they throw me out, that's certain sure! Maybe the army will still find a use for me, who knows, sir."

"I'm sure they will, Sar'nt-Major. But if the Raj should go..."

"*Sir?*"

"If that happens, the army's area of operations becomes much smaller—"

"Good gracious me, Captain Ogilvie, what's this I hear?" Cunningham bristled. "The Raj will *not* go, sir! The Raj will *never* go!" Scandalised, he marched away. Ogilvie heard his voice a moment later, relieving his outraged feelings on Colour-Sergeant MacTrease. He grinned to himself: his words, an almost unconscious manifestation of his deep anxiety, had been indiscreet, thoughtless, and he was sorry to have upset Cunningham; but those words had brought out the customary reaction of all soldiers. Grumble they might, insubordinate they could be on occasions, bitter they could sometimes be about their officers; but whatever their standing as barrack-room lawyers might be, they did not ever see anything but victory in their sights. Which was just as well.

* * *

One attack, just one alone, disturbed the march: a burst of rifle fire from above, the expected sniping of any patrol through the passes. It was quickly dealt with, and Ogilvie believed it had no direct connection with the Mullah; rather it had the characteristics of a chance thing, an attack by a small and isolated bandit group. He forced the pace all the way, permitting no halts beyond the strict minimum necessary to prevent collapse from exhaustion. Nevertheless, it was a stroke of luck rather than speed that allowed them to overtake the column just as it had moved out into the valley of the Jhelum. Ogilvie's advanced scouts, reaching the end of the hills and the main pass two forenoons later, sent back the word by means of the heliograph. Ogilvie read off the message: *Column five miles ahead and halted.*

"Just where they shouldn't halt," Ogilvie remarked to Cunningham. "What the devil does that mean, I wonder?" He increased the pace, sending word down the marching line that the column was at last in sight. There was cheering, and men marched more smartly; the faces of the women relaxed into smiles of relief. To the pipes and the drum-beat they covered the five miles in good time, coming up into the straggle of the camp-followers and the commissariat train with its weary mules and drivers, out of the enclosing hills into the broad valley. From the native drivers they learned the reason for the halt: scarcely a military one. The previous night matters had gone sadly wrong for Dasara: the elephant of His Highness the Maharajah of Mysore had run amok. Two priests had been trampled to death, many wagons carrying women and stores had been overturned and smashed, and His Highness had been ejected from the howdah. Before he had been decently covered from prying eyes, he had been seen by heretics: the lead company of the rear half of the escort had had a most excellent view, as a result of which the 2nd Middlesex were in considerable disgrace, it being considered that the order to turn about should have been given instantly.

"But why the delay?" Ogilvie asked Cunningham in blank astonishment.

"I don't know for certain, sir, but I suspect extra shriving."

"Of the Middlesex Regiment?"

"No, sir, of another elephant, and possibly of the brevet priests."

"*Brevet priests*, Sar'nt-Major?"

"For want of a better term, sir. Owing to the casualties, there will have been, as it were, promotions in the field. The priests selected may not have the proper qualifications, sir, but of course all this is conjecture."

"It sounds like it!" Ogilvie snapped, and rode on through the throngs of natives, pushing ahead towards the van of the column. Reaching the sector where the Royal Strathspey was fallen out, he was met by Andrew Black.

"Ah, Captain Ogilvie! Welcome back—and thank God you have the hostages!" The Adjutant peered down the line, shielding his eyes from the high sun with his hand. "Is all well?"

"All's well with the women and children. I have casualties to report, I'm sorry to say." Ogilvie gave Black the details. "Where's the Colonel?"

"In his tent. He wishes to see you." Black paused. "And after that, I gather your father also wishes words."

"I'll bet he does," Ogilvie said, giving a short laugh, "if the truth's emerged, as I think from your face it has, Andrew!"

"You think right, but it has not reached the men—" Black broke off as a hubbub started behind him. The news had now reached the men in very physical form, and the hostages were being all but swept off their feet in the centre of a mob. "Captain Ogilvie, can you not control those women? They're your responsibility—"

"I'd leave them alone if I were you. It wouldn't be a good thing for the natives to see a British officer torn to ribbons, would it?" Ogilvie grinned into Black's furious face, and rode for the Colonel's tent to make his full report. Lord Dornoch came out to meet him, his face tight with worry. Ogilvie made his report, indicating the apparent disappearance of the Mullah and the unexpected advent, after the storming of the hide-out, of the Dorsets' patrol.

"Lucky for you!" Dornoch said. "Had they any fresh information from Rawalpindi?"

"None, Colonel, except that General Fettleworth is considerably upset about the taking of women and children."

"Of course. Well, I shall report the facts to Sir Thomas directly."

"Very good, Colonel. The current delay—"

"None of my doing," Dornoch said with a twisted smile. "I found a handful of excuses as promised, and had the connivance of Sir Thomas in the making thereof, in the interest of giving you time... but I can't be blamed for this one!"

"I understand it's to do with Dasara?"

"It is," Dornoch answered, and gave Ogilvie the story. It emerged that the RSM's conjectures had been to some extent correct. "The chief priest was one of the two that were trampled. Apparently his place can't be taken without full ceremony, that is by prayer that must be offered up from a place that has been decently prepared by proper blessing—at least, so I gather. It all means this: we can't march!"

"And the Middlesex, Colonel?"

"Yes, that hasn't helped. They have to... I don't know if I'm putting this properly... they have to obliterate what they saw last night, which was His Highness taking a header out of the howdah clad in a nightgown. Obliteration involves a good deal more prayer. They're at it now—all prostrate on the ground, surrounded by the priesthood. I gather their RSM objected to taking part himself, but having confessed he'd seen the unseeable, he was over-ruled. He's as flat as the rest of them, but I doubt if it's prayer he's uttering." Despite his overall anxieties, there was a gleam of humour in Lord Dornoch's eye. "It's no use our bellyaching, James, we have to wait and that's all there is to be said. His Excellency won't hear of offending the Maharajah."

"But the situation's changed now, Colonel! We have the women and children to consider—"

"Well, we knew we would have them once you'd been detached to cut them out, and that has been considered by persons with higher ranks than yours or mine. The orders stand, James; we'll be told by the priests when to march. In the meantime, the word's been passed for the pickets and sentries to be doubled up, and every man knows that as from now we must expect to see the Czar's army coming down from the north at any time."

# 17

"HALT! WHO GOES THERE?"

The sentry's shout in the night brought Ogilvie wide awake in his bivouac, and he sat up, reached for his revolver, and got on the move fast. All around men were stirring, and a guard under a corporal was doubling towards the sentry who had given the challenge. Ogilvie heard no response to that challenge, but heard the sentry's next order clear and loud: "Advance, friend, and be recognised."

With the corporal's guard, Ogilvie joined the sentry. They waited, looking around the camp's perimeter. All was quiet, the moonlight glinting now and then from the arms and equipment of the men in the strongly-guarded outposts and sangars. There was a crunch of footsteps coming closer, then Ogilvie saw a man in some kind of uniform, with a turban and high boots—a cavalryman, evidently. The man came closer, walking slowly and with a limp: the watchers heard heavy breathing, then the stranger came into a small circle of light thrown by the guard corporal's storm lantern.

The sentry spoke again: "Halt!"

The man halted; Ogilvie saw the watchful eyes reflecting the light from the lantern, held high now by the corporal. He stepped forward and asked, "Who are you, and where are you from?"

He had spoken in English, and the man answered in the same tongue, haltingly. "Sahib, I am Yuvraj Ghulam Sinha, a trooper of His Highness's army—"

"Which Highness?"

"His Highness of Jammu and Kashmir, Sahib. My squadron was patrolling to the north when it was attacked."

"By whom?"

"By a regiment of Cossacks, Sahib."

"Russians!"

"Yes, Sahib. I was the only one to escape them. All the others were hacked to pieces, but I feigned death, and so was left."

"How far away are these Cossacks?"

"Perhaps fifteen miles, Sahib. I believe them to be part of the great army of the Czar, of which we have heard rumours."

"You have done well to reach us," Ogilvie said, and turned to the corporal standing beside him. "See this man fed and his foot attended to, Corporal. And see that no-one talks about him or what he's said. I shall report at once to the column commander and any orders will come from him. Understand?"

"Yes, sir."

Ogilvie returned the salute and made haste towards Sir Thomas Lee's tent. The Major-General had been roused out already and met Ogilvie on the way. Ogilvie made his report, underlining the fact that if the man was to be believed the Russian army was now within a day's march of them. Lee nodded. "I'm going straight to His Excellency," he said. "You'd better come with me, Ogilvie." He paused, looking down towards the pool of light that still outlined the guard corporal. "And the man who brought the news." Ogilvie called the order, and the native trooper was sent along with an escort. The party, joined now by Lee's Chief of Staff, made their way quickly down the lines of bivouacs towards the Viceroy's tent. The guard came to attention, and Lee peremptorily demanded an audience of His Excellency.

"A matter of great urgency," he said.

They waited; within half a minute the Military Secretary appeared, pulling on his tunic, from a smaller tent beside the Viceroy's. "What is it, sir?" he asked.

Sir Thomas Lee passed the details. The Military Secretary vanished into Lord Elgin's tent, and with little delay the waiting officers and the trooper were bidden into the presence. The Viceroy emerged, half dressed, through the flap from the tent's sleeping quarters and stared at them in the light of a lantern. "I have your report, Sir Thomas," he said. "What d'you make of it?"

"I take it most seriously, Your Excellency."

"And they're how far away?"

"They could be upon us by dark tomorrow."

"You've no idea of their strength, I take it—no fresh

indication, that is, beyond what we know from the Political Service?"

"None, sir. But if the earlier reports were accurate—"

"Yes, yes. We would be greatly outnumbered."

"Very greatly outnumbered, Your Excellency. And we have women and children to think of now...there is only one thing to do, and that is to march at once. With forced marching, we can expect to enter Srinagar within thirty-six hours of moving out."

"Yes, I see. You're aware that I'm reluctant, most reluctant, to interfere in any way with Dasara and its ceremonies and proper observances." The Viceroy, frowning, paced the tent, up and down, then stopped in front of the native trooper. "What word have you," he asked, "of His Highness's army, and the escort that is to meet my column outside Srinagar?"

"Your Excellency, this I cannot tell. My regiment had been for some weeks upon an extended patrol."

"And thus out of touch with Srinagar..."

"That is so, Your Excellency. I am sorry."

"And the Cossacks. They were advanced before the main Russian army, an extended screen?"

"I believe this is also so, Your Excellency."

"There was no sign of other soldiers—of guns and infantry?"

"I saw none such, Your Excellency."

Lord Elgin nodded, and met the eye of Sir Thomas Lee. "We may well have longer than you suggest, Sir Thomas."

"I still advise no delay, sir."

"Well, we shall see. I wish words with Sir Iain Ogilvie, and with the Political Officer who joined us en route—Major Butler, was it not?" The Military Secretary left the tent at once to rouse out the two officers. Elgin continued his pacing: Lee sad no more. He had made his report and offered his advice, and now he could only wait. Ogilvie was aware of great tension in the atmosphere: Lee was impatient to be on the move, had no wish to have his column a sitting duck for Russian power, to go down in the history books as the general who lost the Raj and the Viceroy by acting too late. Lee's face was stiff, his mouth a hard, thin line, but a muscle twitched at its side revealingly. Soon footsteps outside announced the arrival back of the Military Secretary with Major Butler and the Northern Army Commander, and a moment later the robust figure of Sir Iain Ogilvie shouldered the tent-flap aside and entered with the Political Officer behind him.

"Ah, Sir Iain."

"Your Excellency." Sir Iain gave a stiff, formal bow. "I already have the facts from the Military Secretary, so we need waste no more time. I take it you'll approve an order to march immediately—"

"I have not yet—"

"*Immediately*, Your Excellency!" Sir Iain's voice was harsh, rough, domineering even. "We know the Russian strength—we wouldn't have a hope in hell! You must not be caught in the open field, sir. That's paramount. Once you're in Srinagar, we can and will withstand a siege while reinforcements are moved in."

"Sir Iain, there is still the question of Dasara—"

"Which must not be allowed to interfere!"

"I cannot ride rough-shod over Mysore, General. The princes of India are our friends and must be shown respect. Her Majesty herself, whose representative I am, is always insistent upon that very point. I do not propose to incur Her Majesty's displeasure—"

"My dear sir," Sir Iain snapped, "you'll incur a damn sight more of her displeasure by losing the Raj and getting yourself murdered like a common soldier! You have not the right to jeopardise the Viceroyalty, sir, nor the Raj either." He simmered. "You know very well I'm right! Sir Thomas?"

"Sir?"

"You support me, do you not?"

"I do, sir."

Sir Iain glanced at the Military Secretary. "Colonel Durand?"

"I also, sir."

"Major Butler?"

"I consider it vital, sir." The Political Officer turned to Lord Elgin. "Your Excellency, I've already made it clear to Sir Thomas that I'm concerned about *any* delay, Dasara or no Dasara. It's obvious now that the Russians are close. I urge you to march, Your Excellency, most strongly."

Sir Iain made a curious trumpeting sound of satisfaction. "Your Excellency? I think you are outnumbered."

"I think you are impertinent, General—"

"Sir, there is no time to stand upon our several dignities. In a military sense, I also represent Her Majesty, as commander of Her Majesty's Northern Army in India. In the absence of the

171

Commander-in-Chief, I am the sole military power, deriving my appointment not from you but from the Queen-Empress personally, and I happen to know Her Majesty's priorities." Sir Iain paused. "Your Excellency, are you prepared to give the order to march?"

"No, Sir Iain, at this moment I am not."

"I see, sir. Then in that case I shall give it myself, at the same time assuming the overall military command." While Lord Elgin stood speechless, Sir Iain, for the second time upon the march relieving himself of the passenger's passivity and this time adamant, swung round upon Lee. "Sir Thomas, the column itself remains yours until such time as we are required to mount action. Rouse out the men, if you please, and have them fallen in for the march."

\* \* \*

The recumbent and rebellious men of the 2nd Middlesex were back in their bivouacs, having completed their penance shortly after dark. They now turned out again with the rest as the strident bugles sounded down the line from the various Brigade Headquarters. Sir Iain Ogilvie had despatched his son to have words with the Maharajah's major-domo and senior priests, and the abandonment of prayer and blessing had been firmly requested. The susceptibilities of the native contingent having been thus hurt, urgent orders came down from the summit that no further hurt was to be inflicted: never mind the inconvenience, even the danger, all eyes were to be constantly averted from His Highness for the remainder of the march. Any disobedience would result in heavy punishment upon return to cantonments. As Cunningham remarked to Ogilvie as the Royal Strathspey was fallen in by companies, they were fortunate to be the leading battalion of the leading brigade.

"Often enough, sir, a man can't help the turn of his eyes."

"True, but I doubt if they need to worry too much, Sar'nt-Major."

"You mean the order's for the ears of His Highness, rather than the eyes of the men, sir. Well, there's truth in that I've no doubt, but on the other hand the priests will be on the sharp look-out." Cunningham gave a sigh as he watched the colour-sergeants hustling the men into the line of march, so many shadows in the moonlit night. "The priests, sir. How did they take the de-shriving order?"

Ogilvie grinned. "Oh, well enough! They were quite calm about it."

"That surprises me, sir."

"Why?"

"These religious observances are important to them, sir, as we know. Why, to stop them reaching full regimental acceptance—to use a handy term, sir—it's not unlike stopping a minister of the kirk in full pulpit-cry, I shouldn't wonder." Cunningham clicked his teeth and frowned. "There could be something more behind it, Captain Ogilvie, do you not think?"

"I don't see what it could be."

"Well, sir, the halt could have been contrived for the purpose of delaying His Excellency. If so, that would suggest a trojan horse in the Maharajah's entourage."

"Damn it, Sar'nt-Major, they're all good Hindus!"

"Aye, sir. Hindus do not like Muslims, I agree. It's still possible some of them like the Raj less. They could sink their differences in the common good as they see it."

Ogilvie nodded. "As a matter of fact, the possibility's been taken into account from the start, but I still don't follow your reasoning. I doubt if anyone would contrive being trampled by an elephant! And why not try to delay us further, if that's what they want, by continuing to insist on their full ritual?"

"Maybe they've delayed us long enough, sir."

"You mean the Russians are closer than we suspect?"

"Just that, sir, just that."

"We'll find out soon enough, I dare say." In the darkness Ogilvie made a grimace. "For my father's sake, I can't help hoping they aren't too far away, Sar'nt-Major!"

"Sir Iain's done the right and proper thing, Captain Ogilvie. I believe he had our women and children much upon his mind. And Sir Iain's more than capable of keeping his end up, as you know well. It may be dangerous to go against His Excellency... but I have a strong feeling Sir Iain will survive, sir."

"I hope you're right." Ogilvie turned aside as Andrew Black marched up, looking stiff and formal in the moonlight. Cunningham excused himself, saluted, and slammed his boots in a turn-about. "Do you want me, Andrew?"

"Yes, Captain Ogilvie, I do." The formality thus set by the

mode of address, the Adjutant, slapping a cane against his trewed thigh, continued. "There are orders from Brigade to all battalion commanders. The men will move out as silently as can be, with no talking whatsoever. Orders will be passed *quietly*. The horses will have their hooves muffled with canvas which is now being issued by the quartermasters."

"And the carts? Won't they give—"

"The carts are not your concern, Captain Ogilvie, but you may rest assured. Extra greasing of axles and all other moving parts is in hand at this moment." The Adjutant marched away, a thin, gaunt figure outlined now against a faint luminosity in the eastern sky over Srinagar: the dawn was not all that far off. Ogilvie found Colour-Sergeant MacTrease and passed the orders on. The preparations being quickly completed and the reports made, the column, with all its gear stowed, moved out on the word from the van, the men stumbling over stones and rubble strewn from the mouth of the pass behind them. As the dawn came up in brilliant colourings of red and green and purple and no signs were seen of any opposing army, the advance continued along the banks of the Jhelum. As the morning lightened they marched under a total relaxation of the silence order. From the rear the weird, tinny native music started up; in the van Sir Iain Ogilvie had words with Lee.

"By God, that's a fearful din! I propose to drown it. I'd be grateful if you'd be good enough to send word to Lord Dornoch with my compliments, and request the pipes and drums."

"Sir, His Excellency—"

"Is much concerned about Dasara—I know! So am I. But I'm also concerned about the men, Sir Thomas, none of whom to my knowledge are deaf but will certainly be dog tired. The pipes are the most wonderfully effective medicine."

"As to that, I agree—"

"Then see to it, man, at once!"

The order was passed: minutes later Ross and his pipers blew air into their instruments, the tartan-covered bags swelling beneath their arms, and as the drums beat out into the still atmosphere of the valley the Scots, at least, marched the better to the stirring and nostalgic strains of 'Loch Lomond'. Hearts swelled beneath the sweat-stained khaki-drill tunics like the bags of the pipes themselves; every man knew well what he might be marching to face, knew what was in the balance and shortly now to be weighed, and was given added spirit by the sounds of Scotland, sounds that had long echoed through war and history and had sparked the high courage of the Queen's soldiers. And from the ranks of the 114th Highlanders, The Queen's Own Royal Strathspey, the singing started, rose high and loud, and was not forbidden from the van of the advance as the words rolled out to the surrounding hills:

> "The wee birdies sing, and the wild flowers spring
> An' in sunshine the waters are sleepin'
> But the broken heart, it kens nae second spring
> Tho' the waefu' may cease frae their greetin'.
> Oh, you'll take the high road, an' I'll take the low road
> An' I'll be in Scotland afore ye;
> But I and my true love will never meet again,
> On the bonnie bonnie banks o' Loch Lomond..."

Even Andrew Black was caught by the moment: as the Adjutant rode by his company, Ogilvie saw the rapt look on the saturnine features. Seeing himself thus observed, Black flushed, looked away and rode ahead haughtily. Soon the singing stopped, but the pipes and drums continued, and the long, straggling column moved on, thus far unimpeded, towards the Happy Valley of Kashmir that was all too likely to turn out anything but happy for the British Raj.

*       *       *

"Bearer! Where's that bloody bearer?"

"Sahib." A dignified figure materialized from beyond the screen, advanced a little way into the Lieutenant-General Sahib's presence, halted, and bowed low.

"Oh, there you are. *Chota peg.*"

"At once, Sahib."

"Blast you, it had better be." With a sigh, General Fettleworth lay back in the reclining chair, enjoying the peace of his bungalow's verandah. A little way off, his wife sat with her sewing, and Fettleworth frowned. Her activity annoyed him, and he had said so many times, but, surprisingly for her, she had taken no notice. In Fettleworth's view, mem-sahibs should not be seen to work even at sewing. It was bad for the natives, and why anyone in their right minds should want to sew was beyond him, but no doubt—disliking her disobedience, he had never made the enquiry—the articles thus produced would be despatched back to various members of the family in England... angrily gazing at his wife, Fettleworth awaited his *chota peg* which he proposed to enjoy in the knowledge that all was going well so far for the Raj: a report had reached him via the telegraph line from the Residency in Srinagar to the effect that the Viceroy's column had been seen, marching in good order towards the capital, and was not far off safety. Safety was a word Bloody Francis, in the circumstances, was more than grateful to hear. The worst had not happened, and Fettleworth had managed to persuade himself that it was unlikely to happen in Srinagar, where the Viceroy would be much surrounded by the soldiers and trappings of a friendly state. The sheer nakedness of the long march was all but over...

A footstep broke into the General's reverie and it was not the bearer with the *chota peg*: it was his Chief of Staff.

"Oh—Lakenham. What is it?"

"Further word from the Resident in Srinagar, sir. Excellent news in part. Contact has now been made with the column, and they have the Scots women and children with them—"

"Good God!" Fettleworth stared. "Where did they find them, for heaven's sake, Lakenham?"

The Chief of Staff explained in full.

"By God, Lakenham! Well, thank heaven—I'm delighted—delighted, and much relieved." Fettleworth frowned, not liking the look upon the Brigadier-General's face. "I gather there is something else, something not good? Never mind my wife, you may speak freely."

"Yes, sir, that is what I intend to do." Lakenham took a deep breath. "I fear that the worst is about to happen—the signs at any rate are bad—"

"The devil take the signs." Fettleworth heaved himself from his comfortable chair, his belly wobbling like a scarlet jelly. "Tell me the news!"

"Sir, the Resident reports a Russian Army under the personal standard of the Grand Duke Alexis—"

"Where, for heaven's sake?"

"Advancing upon Srinagar some ten miles in rear of His Excellency's column. The Resident considers it likely that the

Russians intend to invest the city, with His Excellency in it. And there's something else, sir."

"Oh, God!"

"The Mullah has reached Srinagar. So much is known—but not his whereabouts. I fear the wheel is about to come full circle, sir."

"You mean—?"

"I mean mutiny, General Fettleworth, precisely as was anticipated. I believe we were right all along: it must come now, in Srinagar, with the death or capture of Their Excellencies and the Maharajahs of Mysore and Kashmir."

# 18

FETTLEWORTH WAS NOW in a deeply cleft stick: the most urgent action was vital and the immediate decision did not brook even the comparatively small delay that would be occasioned by making contact with the Commander-in-Chief in Calcutta. Something had to be done at once, and that something was plainly the despatch of an army to force-march towards Srinagar to relieve any siege of the ancient city and protect its illustrious prisoners. Hence the cleft stick: further to deplete the now meagre garrisons at Peshawar and Nowshera would be to invite attack from the second Russian army said to be assembled on the Afghan side of the Khyber Pass. Brigadier-General Lakenham had the essential facts at his finger-tips: the reinforcements on their way from Southern Command at Ootacamund would turn up too late to be of any assistance. They were at a far distance yet, still upon their long haul north by the train. Nevertheless, Fettleworth felt obliged to await their arrival. A cable was despatched to the Commander-in-Chief stating that in Fettleworth's opinion there were presently not enough troops available in Northern Command to be of proper use and that he proposed holding Peshawar, Nowshera and Rawalpindi with such resources as he had, and that a relieving column would be formed from Ootacamund's reinforcements as soon as they reached his command.

"We can do no more, my dear Lakenham," he said, and called again for his bearer: *chota pegs* existed to relieve tension and anxiety. Sinking into his chair Bloody Francis noted with irritation and astonishment that his wife was still sewing as though nothing had happened.

*       *       *

Marching by the banks of the Jhelum River, the column came within sight of the city of Srinagar: the cluster of old wooden buildings rose splendidly before them in fresh, clear air five thousand feet above the northern plains, a place of autumn colours filled with birdsong and bright with flowers growing from the very roofs themselves, a place, under normal circumstances, of enchantment. Currently Sir Iain Ogilvie was less concerned with enchantment than with the coming problems of defence: Srinagar would not be an easy city to fortify against strong attack. For one thing, it would burn easily; for another, it was bisected by the Jhelum itself, whose waters and the canals leading from them could well weaken any attempt to throw a ring of bayonets around the city.

"Very striking," Sir Thomas Lee remarked in tune with the Army Commander's thoughts, "but not the place for war. The whole feel is wrong."

"Exactly." Sir Iain gave a harsh laugh. "His Excellency expressed a wish to enter by the usual ceremonial route—by way of the river. The Maharajah customarily meets his important visitors just above the city, in his state galley—rowed by sixty men in full dress uniforms, poor buggers!"

"Picturesque," Lee murmured.

"No doubt. I put a stop to it, however. We have no time to waste now." The General lifted the field-glasses that hung on a leather strap about his neck, and swung them slowly around, studying the city and the surrounding Himalayan hills, his mouth set hard. The news brought to them a short while ago by riders sent out from the Residency had scarcely been unexpected; but it was certainly confirmation of the worst. Sir Iain had sent one of the horsemen back with word that he proposed to defend the city against all attack and that except for the promised escort the preparations that would have been made to welcome Their Excellencies were to be abandoned: the Mullah, he had advised, could strike more easily from out of a crowd. So far as possible the streets and waterways were to be cleared, and the remainder of the riders would remain with the column to guide it along the shortest route to the Maharajah's palace.

"I believe we're being met by the escort at last, sir," Lee said, bringing up his own glasses. "A sizeable turn-out, I fancy."

179

Sir Iain swung to look, stared intently at a colourful parade of uniformed men that had just come into view from the city—cavalry and infantry, surrounding a procession of nodding, lumbering howdahs. He swore. "More confounded elephants! Why the devil can they never cut the ceremonial!"

"India, sir. Panoply is part of the princes' way of life and they—"

"I know, I know! I didn't come out on the last damn troopship, Lee." Sir Iain went on staring through his field-glasses, then exploded angrily. "Good God above, it's the Maharajah himself, I swear! Two pisspots high, and obliterated under the biggest damn turban in India!"

"And much beloved of his people, I understand," Lee said drily. "I advise caution, Sir Iain, when he approaches. It would be fatal to upset his susceptibilities just now."

"I shall upset nothing!" the General snapped. "But I shall not halt the column." He slid his field-glasses into their leather case and called for his bugler. Then he turned to Lee. "I'm going back to report to His Excellency," he said. "In the meantime, you'll have to be ready for the niceties, I suppose. Extend the column to right and left, opening out so that the Maharajah can advance down the centre to meet His Excellency—and give him plenty of room to wheel his damn circus one hundred and eighty degrees—he can proceed back into the city alongside the Viceroy. All right?"

"Yes, sir—"

"And two squadrons of cavalry to ride ahead—a Captain's escort as a compliment to His Highness and that grandfather of all turbans!" Sir Iain swung his horse around and cantered down the line towards the Viceroy, his leather-sheathed sword bumping his horse's flank. Turning alongside the howdah, he saluted.

"Yes, Sir Iain?"

"Your Excellency, the Maharajah of Jammu and Kashmir is coming out to meet you. I have ordered such ceremonial as seems consistent with security."

Lord Elgin nodded. "Thank you, General."

"But I prefer not to halt the column, sir. I must impress upon Your Excellencies that there is a strong need for caution from now on. You must not expose yourselves to risks."

"That is noted, General."

"Very good, sir." The General saluted again and started to move away. He was stopped by Lord Elgin.

"General, a moment if you please. His Highness is a keen cricketer."

"Sir?"

Lord Elgin waved a hand, smiling. "I mention it only in case you find it handy as a conversation-piece."

"I see, sir. I fancy there'll be little time for conversation with the Russians upon our heels. As a matter of fact, I'm aware that His Highness plays cricket—in gold slippers, so I'm told." Saluting once more, Sir Iain spurred his horse towards the van.

*　　　*　　　*

To his annoyance but scarcely to his great surprise Sir Iain Ogilvie found his advice to the Resident disregarded: the loyal natives of Srinagar had turned out in their thousands to greet not only His Excellency the Viceroy and his Vicereine, and the Maharajah of Mysore, but also their own much loved Pertab Singh, Maharajah of Jammu and Kashmir. The townspeople crowded every houseboat, every rooftop, every window and balcony, every doorway and every narrow, twisting alley along the route through the age-old capital, waving and shouting and playing their various musical instruments so that the pipes and drums of the highlanders, and the fifes of the English battalions, were drowned in a sea of cacophonous noise. Sir Iain, riding at the head of the column as with difficulty it pushed through the throngs, was furious and a prey to anxiety: at any moment, if the Mullah should chose, a bullet could shatter the skull of the Viceroy of India and then there would be a bloodbath. Friend would go down with foe, and the Raj would slip over the brink. Sir Iain relieved his feelings upon Lee: "With all due respect to Pertab Singh, it's a miracle he's so damn popular with his Muslim people! Hindu priests are not economists."

"I beg your pardon?"

"He rates his Brahmin priesthood above his Prime Minister, and it fails to work. Kashmir's half bankrupt! His Highness is said to use thumbscrews to collect his tax...and he taxes grave-digging and prostitution amongst other things."

"India, sir—"

"Oh, not again, my dear fellow!" Sir Iain rode on, looking to

181

right and left, assessing the possibilities, coming to very definite conclusions as to his defence strategy: the city was plainly undefendable as such and they must fall back on the palace itself, turning it into a stronghold against the Russian advance. As he rode through the gateway, past the mounted native guard, and into the central courtyard, Sir Iain was not impressed with the impregnability of what could well prove the last fortress of the Raj; but knew that beggars could not be choosers.

\* \* \*

The Colonel called a muster of all officers and senior NCOs and put the position plainly and speedily. "We stand or fall upon this ground, gentlemen." He looked around at the palace walls, at the distant hills that frowned on all sides above, at the dark green of the poplars on their flanks reaching to where the tree-line ended in snow, now empurpled by the splendour of the Kashmiri sunset. "We as a battalion are under orders to provide the immediate palace guard. The other two brigaded battalions, and the other brigades, will man the walls and provide extra gate guards and mobile patrols for use as and where required if the attack comes. Yes, Captain Black?"

Black said, "Colonel, you say *if* the attack comes. Is it not positively expected?" He waved a hand towards the valley through which they had marched that day. "Certainly I see no Russians yet, but—"

"I fancy they're being held out of sight so far, but ready, Captain Black. The General believes, and so do I, that the Czar will not wish to precipitate anything of his own accord, and will wait until the Mullah shows his hand."

"But, Colonel, the Russians were said to be ready to attack as we left the pass, were they not?"

"I think that was an assumption rather than a known fact, Captain Black, but had they done so, it wouldn't have been difficult for them to have trumped up a story that we had gone first into the attack—that would not have been easy for us to disprove afterwards."

"But an attack on Srinagar—"

"Yes, they could scarcely make such a charge in that case! But once the Mullah has struck personally at His Excellency, the situation changes. The Russians will simply take advantage of a prepared position and come in to fill the vacuum left by a disintegrating Raj. From then on, it becomes open war."

"So the whole business still revolves around the Mullah?"

"Yes. That's the view of both Sir Thomas and Sir Iain and I share that view myself. In brief, once the Mullah lights the fuse as it were—which of course we're here to prevent—then in comes His Imperial Majesty's representative to pick up the pieces and turn them to his master's account." Lord Dornoch studied the set faces of his audience. "We shall all do our duty," he said simply, "and I stress that *our* particular concern is the personal safety of Their Excellencies and the two Maharajahs. Captain Black, you'll kindly see to the rosters for guard duty."

"Yes, Colonel."

"Two companies at a time will be required to mount the extra palace guard, and barrack accommodation has been provided for those not on duty—but all are to be available to turn out at a moment's notice. Is that understood? Then that's all, gentlemen." As the group began to disperse, he called them back. "One thing more to keep in your minds: we don't know what the Mullah's plans are, of course, nor what his timing may be. But he may well consider a suitably impressive moment to be the final act of Dasara. That act is due to take place at tomorrow's sunset."

The officers and NCOs moved away to their various duties, Black conferring with the Regimental Sergeant-Major on the subject of the guard rosters. Ogilvie reflected that the Colonel had made no mention of the city itself below the palace walls: the inference was that it would remain undefended and wide open to the Russian assault. Such was part of the fortunes of war, but it was an unpleasant decision for the inhabitants, loyal subjects of His Highness Pertab Singh and through him of the Raj. Ogilvie pondered on the Kashmiris and their warm welcome of the Viceroy that day. Srinagar, surely, must be hostile to the machinations of the Mullah...but, as ever, the virtue lay in the big battalions and right tended to follow might. If the Mullah could bring about a *fait accompli*, the multitude would equate their future wellbeing with his own. Ogilvie walked across the palace courtyard, sniffing the strange perfumes that seemed to pervade Srinagar, stealing subtly into every waft of air, fragrant with flowers and late fruits and spices. From the walls beyond the palace apartments he looked down into the valley, at the Jhelum River winding through the heart of Srinagar and out into the mountain-shrouded countryside. It was a beautiful place, perhaps the most beautiful and peaceful place he had ever seen outside the glens and islands of Scotland, not the place to suffer the shatter and blood of the Russian sabre and the bullet. As he stood and gazed at the fast-darkening landscape below the last rays of the setting sun he heard marching footsteps that stopped behind him, and as the boots crashed to a halt he turned to find a private of an English regiment saluting him.

"Captain Ogilvie, sir?"

"Yes?"

"Major Butler's compliments, sir—"

"Major Butler?"

"The Political Officer, sir, who fell in with the march."

"Oh—yes. Well?"

"He wishes to see you, sir. I will take you to him, sir."

"Very well—thank you."

Saluting again, the man turned about and marched away towards the palace building. Ogilvie followed, climbing a flight of marble steps and entering a great reception hall guarded by two dismounted troopers of the Maharajah's army, tall men who saluted with drawn sabres. Led by Butler's runner, Ogilvie crossed the marble floor of the hall, passing great pillars that lofted to a ceiling set with mosaic patterns of splendid colours. At the back of the hall there was a passageway lined with tiles of red and blue, purple and green, in intricate patterns depicting tigers, elephants and wild boar with immense tusks. At an apartment opening off the passage the runner halted, knocked at a door of burnished copper and announced Ogilvie.

"Enter."

Ogilvie went in; the door was shut behind him. The Political Officer was standing by a window, looking down upon the palace walls. He swung round; he was a tall man with a sallow skin and a dark moustache, more regimental-looking than Blaise-Willoughby and more incisive: from somewhere he had been provided with a suit of white tussore silk and was no longer recognizable as the weary supposed native who had joined the column on the march from Rawalpindi. "Ah—Ogilvie! Good of you to come. Sit down."

Ogilvie sat in a gilded chair not far short of being a throne. Butler remained standing by the window for a moment, then came across with a silver case of Turkish cigarettes which he handed to Ogilvie. Ogilvie took one, and Butler struck a match. He said, "You'll be wondering what this is about."

"Yes..."

"Well, I won't beat about the bush, Ogilvie. I want your help."

"You shall have it, Major."

Butler smiled, a sardonic twist of thin lips. "Hold your horses. You don't know what I want yet." He turned back to the window and once again looked down upon the walls and the higgledy-piggledy structure of the city below. The window was open; the scents of the night were creeping in insidiously. Butler waved a hand down into the darkness pin-pointed with yellow light from the bungalows and houseboats of the English community and the Residency. Abruptly he said, "There's just one order yet to give, and that is for the Resident and all Europeans to report for shelter to the palace—to this, His Highness has already agreed."

"When will the order come?"

"When your father sees the last hours approaching." Butler swung round. "I repeat—the last hours. You realise all that's at stake now?"

"For the Raj?"

"And the world—the whole damn world!" There was heat and bitterness in Butler's tone. "There will be an immense shift in the balance of power. India must not be lost." He paused. "Tell me, Ogilvie: do you understand why the Mullah has chosen Srinagar for his death blow at the Raj?"

Ogilvie shrugged. "The contingency of events. The meeting of His Excellency and the Maharajahs, and the Czar's—"

"Yes, yes. But there's something else. Currently it's of much greater importance—that is, in an *action* sense. I refer to the question of religion."

"Dasara?"

The Political Officer nodded. "Dasara will play its part, but there's a broader issue. The Kashmiris, Ogilvie, are Mohammedans—followers of the Prophet but ruled by a Hindu ruler and kept in subjugation by his Brahmin priests. Kashmir is a very beautiful land and physically the Happy Valley is well enough named. But the Kashmiris are not happy themselves."

"I understand Pertab Singh is well liked?"

"Oh, true—liked in himself! He's no more harsh a ruler, I suppose, than any other prince of India. But the vast majority of

185

his subjects—and believe me, they are *very* subject—do not love his religion or his Brahmins!" Butler waved his cigarette-holder at Ogilvie. "I am doing no more than pin-point for you what we have known all along: Srinagar is a good breeding-ground for dissension, an excellent place to start a rising, and we can take it that the Mullah has his ground excellently prepared in advance. Srinagar will not be found friendly to His Highness or His Excellency when the trouble starts. And, believe me, Ogilvie, a military solution is out of the question!"

"How's that?"

Butler said impatiently, "Think, man! Militarily, we shall be outnumbered, swamped even. And the Grand Duke Alexis is waiting with his army. We have no hope of reinforcements, of a relieving army, reaching us for very many days if at all. Of course—this goes without saying—if we're faced with it, we shall fight to the last man. But that won't save the Raj. When the Mullah gives the word, we may take it the whole subcontinent will rise against us. The whole of India will sink into the bloody morass of a religious war. And there is nothing more vicious, more appalling, and more damn downright *cruel* than a war fought in the names of rival gods, be they Christian or be they heathen. All this must be prevented. Humanity demands no less. I take it you agree."

"And the point, Major?"

Butler stared. "The point?"

"You promised no beating about bushes."

"Oh—yes, indeed. Yes. Very well: you've met the Mullah, you've some experience of our work as Political Officers in the past. I want you to meet him again...but in a rather special kind of way, and upon an unusual mission. A somewhat final one. You said you'd help."

"And you said I should hold my horses, Major. I'm holding them! What exactly is this mission?"

Butler said crisply, "I'm sorry, Ogilvie. I want your agreement, then I'll tell you. Once the scheme's put into words, there can be no backing down. From then on it becomes an order. And afterwards—total silence. I think you'll understand. Well?"

# 19

Out like a shadow through a side gate in the palace wall a little before midnight, Ogilvie, dressed as a native and with his skin once more darkened, made his way along a narrow and winding maple-lined path towards the maze that was the city of Srinagar. He felt naked, unprotected, utterly defenceless and filled with loathing for Butler's mission. Butler's tongue had been overly persuasive in its appeal to Ogilvie's sense of duty and patriotism. In consenting to help, Ogilvie had given Butler his blank cheque that could not afterwards be returned to any drawer. With that blank cheque safely in his pocket, Butler had coolly outlined the plan.

"There is one end to all this," the Political Officer had said. "If the Mullah dies, and if his body is exhibited to the mob, the mutiny is still-borne. Therefore he is to be killed—assassinated. In such a way that it will not appear to be a British act, but rather a Mohammedan one. A turning against him by his own side. Not Hindu, for that could start a religious war within a continuing Raj and we don't want *that*, thank you very much! You are to be the assassin, Ogilvie."

Ogilvie had been astounded, shocked: assassination had never been a weapon in the armoury of the British Crown and even now could never have the official sanction of Calcutta or Whitehall. Butler, however, had gone on to make valid points: the Mullah was himself a killer and a sadistic torturer who had held women and children under threat of death and worse, and he could never be permitted to count as a worthy life against the Raj and India's millions who, if he lived, would be plunged into the appalling horrors of civil war. The Pax Britannica was the Indians' one guarantee of peace and as such must at any cost be preserved intact. In spite of Butler's cogent reasoning and his smooth tongue—in spite of his positive order that he indicated would be backed by the weight and authority of certain highly-placed but unobtrusive persons in the Political Service—Ogilvie kept his word only with a heavy burden of misgiving and in the full knowledge that failure would bring anonymity in death, that his body would be mere debris of the holocaust; and equally that success would bring no honour or recognition. The deed, conceived in the darkness of Butler's brain without knowledge of or sanction from the military command, done in the darkness of the Srinagar alleys, must remain in darkness thereafter. Butler himself, knowing that he would get no kudos from it either, saw it as a simple act of duty on both their parts. For his own skin Ogilvie, brought up to the army's ideals, had no concern beyond the normal. He was going into no greater physical danger in fact than any officer or man who, in the long years of British rule and its story of high courage, had ever fought along the mountain passes of the North-West Frontier and, dying, left his bones to sow an alien land. As to the practicalities, Butler's plan was a devious and dangerous one: the Mullah, he said, would be only too anxious to get his hands on a British officer who had twice made a fool of him, and to contrive to be taken to the Mullah's hiding-place would be easy: all Ogilvie in his disguise had to do was to drop the word that he, a lowly native, had been in contact with the Captain Sahib in the many-coloured trousers, the son of the General Sahib in His Highness's palace, and the bush telegraph would speedily do the rest.

"But you'll have to insist," Butler had said, "on meeting the Mullah alone. That's your one safeguard."

"And the involvement of Muslims? If we're alone, and I get away afterwards, who's to say who the assassin was?"

Butler laughed. "Why, it'll quite obviously be you, won't it—*you* shall be the Muslim. You've acted the part before. You've only to act it again. The word will quickly spread that the Muslim who asked for the meeting was the assassin. As to a weapon, I leave that to you—something easily concealed. I'd avoid any standard weapon of the British Army, such as a revolver. I needn't tell you that the Pathans are accustomed to carry knives. I suggest you send for your armourer-sergeant and spin him a yarn—and in the meantime I shall let it be known to your colonel that you're leaving the palace on a plain mission to obtain information."

"And if I fail to get away, and my identity as a British officer becomes known? The last time I met the Mullah, he recognised me from my voice alone."

Butler brushed this aside. "You can be recognised by the Mullah for all I care—just so long as you strike the first blow! A knife can be very quickly drawn under cover of your proper obeisances, bowing and scraping and so on."

"But I repeat, if I'm captured and my identity becomes known to others afterwards—"

"That mustn't happen," Butler said crisply. "You mustn't reveal a damn thing, you know that."

"That's easier said than done, Major."

"It's been done before," Butler said off-handedly, and spoke no more than the simple truth. "Concentrate on killing the Mullah—that's the thing!"

Butler, cold-blooded as any fish, had said little more; Ogilvie was well aware that the Mullah's death of itself was the prime objective, that if his assassin was afterwards revealed as a British officer then Major Butler would somehow contrive to keep his own hands lilywhite. Down now into the city, Butler's final warning still in his ears: the General's son, whatever the Mullah might believe to the contrary, would have positively no hostage-value. Ogilvie moved into the criss-cross alleys, avoiding the canals that led from the river bank to carry the clusters of houseboats: here the smells were largely those of Peshawar and Nowshera rather than of the flower-scented night of the palace and the gardens of the English community, and were interlaced with the emanations from garbage-filled water. In the alleys were the inevitable running sores of the open drains, the flies and insects, the heaps of defecation, the occasional beggar's corpse that had been left to rot until the sweepers took it away and it would cease to offend the eyes and nostrils. Ogilvie walked along, huddled in his rags, keeping his head down, minding his own business, not appearing curious but remaining watchful. The alleys were crowded as he pushed through; there was a curious and unmistakable tension in the air as though all these people, men and women and even children, knew precisely what was about to happen. It was as though an upsurge of madness was being held down only with great difficulty, a feeling that liberation was at hand and never mind the slaughter that would come with it. There was singing at intervals, coming from the dark doorways of hovels with smoky yellow light inside; and there was laughter too, gusts of laughter that seemed to spring from a base of hysteria and high emotion, a crazy and frightening sound. It streamed after Ogilvie as he shambled past. Farther along he came upon a hovel with a well-lit doorway through which he could see a large crowd of men, a mostly silent and intent gathering until, as he stopped to watch, a loud shout came from them, a roar, apparently, of approval.

He joined the crowd that was overflowing into the narrow alley, became one with it and pushed his way through until he could see the whole room. It was not large: on a kind of stage at the far end a man was gesticulating, haranguing—a man dressed in a white gown, but it was not the Mullah. Ogilvie listened, able to pick up the drift of an impassioned monologue. Nothing specific was being said, but it was an incitement against Hinduism and His Highness the Maharajah Pertab Singh. There was as yet no mention of the British Raj as such, but it was plain enough that the speaker was one of the Mullah's disciples and that, if such talk could be made openly in Srinagar, there was little time left. Ogilvie waited, shouting with the rest when they shouted, waving a fist in the air when other fists were shaken. The place was airless inside, with a strong stench of human body and filthy garments, and already Ogilvie felt the creep of unpleasant animal life on his skin, a creep that grew to an overwhelming itch: but no-one else in the room scratched, and Ogilvie felt duty bound to suffer in silence and stoicism as his body was explored by vicious probosces. A few minutes later the ranting ceased. The white-clad speaker ducked down out of sight, and reappeared over the heads of the crowd with a large, square object in his hands—a picture frame. Lifting this above his head and turning it round to face the audience, the rabble-rousing native invited those present to spit at the picture. As gobs of saliva and phlegm sped across to impact stickily and revoltingly, Ogilvie recognised the portrait of Her Majesty the Queen-Empress, the white cap on the white hair, the bun behind, the ample breast with the blue ribbon of the Garter. A frothy spume obscured the imperious expression. To a rising sound of hate, a baying sound as though already blood had been smelled, and a forest of shaken fists, the speaker hurled the portrait against the wall: the glass broke in a shower of spikes and fragments, the Queen Victoria fell beneath the feet of the mob, to be trampled right royally into the grime and hard mud of the floor. Yet another symbol, and one that could not fail to be recognised. Hate came from the packed bodies like a miasma, almost tangible. Not joining in this demonstration, Ogilvie found himself confronted by a thick-set, bearded man who thrust his face close.

"Do you not show your feelings?" this man demanded, his eyes blazing into Ogilvie's. "Do you not also hate the British Queen?"

"I do," Ogilvie answered. "I wish only for the defeat of the British Raj." He let out a cry, and shook a fist in the air. The man seemed satisfied, and turned away; then turned back again.

"You are a stranger. How come you here, and where from, and why?"

Ogilvie smiled. "Do you know every man in Srinagar, friend?"

"I do not. But I know the way men speak in Srinagar. Your speech is not our speech."

"You are right," Ogilvie said. "I come from beyond Kashmir, from far away." He paused. "From Peshawar near the border with Afghanistan—"

"How?"

"With the British force that brought the Viceroy and His Highness the Maharajah of Mysore. I am but a camp follower, and feel no loyalty to the British Raj."

The man sucked in air, blew it out again in a stinking stream into Ogilvie's face. Ogilvie felt the beat of his heart, a strangling thump in his chest: he was walking a tight-rope, the whole point of his duty now approaching. "There must be more explanation," the native said. There was a sudden movement of his arm, and Ogilvie felt the prick of sharp steel through his garment. "Why come you here to this house?"

Ogilvie shrugged. "I have heard talk of a rising against the Raj. Had I remained in the palace as part of the British force, I would have been killed, for none would have known where my loyalties lay. Thus, you see, I escaped."

"I ask again, why do you come to this room?"

"I heard noise, and I was curious. I wish to help the rising. Also for another reason, a most important one."

"You shall tell me this reason."

"This I shall do," Ogilvie answered. "There was much talk on the march ... talk that said a British officer had been taken by the

191

leader and had made good his escape. That officer is named Ogilvie, a captain of a regiment whose soldiers wear brightly coloured skirts which they call kilts, and whose music is the bagpipes and the drums. He is the son of the all-important General who commands at Murree."

"So?"

"I wish our leader, the Mullah from Kashmir it is said, to know this, that I know how it will be possible for this Captain Ogilvie to be taken from the palace before the rising starts. I offer my humble help."

"For reward?"

"If the Mullah sees fit to offer reward, I shall be happy, but this I do for the good of all of us."

The man stared at him for a long time while the angry shouts and fist-waving continued and the busy feet ground the Queen-Empress to paper fragments. Then he said, "I cannot tell you where the Mullah is, for I do not know. Nobody knows his whereabouts other than his personal guards, who are with him in his sanctuary."

"Cannot the word be passed, friend, to the birds of the air?"

"It is possible," the man agreed after another pause. "You will come with me from this room—"

"Where will you take me?"

"You shall see. If you wish help, do not question." The steel pushed in harder and Ogilvie felt the slow trickle of blood down his side. "Tonight life is cheap in Srinagar. Do as I instruct, and do nothing else. Come!"

The man put an arm about his shoulders and, with the knife-tip still pressing, pushed him through the maddened, yelling crowd, through the doorway and out into the welcome fresher air of the alley.

\*     \*     \*

In the Maharajah's palace, safe so far behind well-guarded walls, the long ceremonies of Dasara had entered their last night before the climax. His Highness of Mysore, freed now of the confines of his howdah and the exigencies of the thunderbox ritual, was splendidy accommodated in Pertab Singh's guest apartments. Surrounded by his priests and well hidden from curious heathen eyes, he had been borne thither in state inside a closed palanquin on the first stroke of midnight. At the approach of the procession the duty companies of the Royal Strathspey, mounting the immediate guard upon the private apartments, were called to attention by the Adjutant in person, mounted upon his horse with its rump decently turned towards the invisible Maharajah whose approach had been discreetly signalled to him by a nod from Colour-Sergeant MacTrease.

"Guard will present arms," Black intoned. "Guard... present—*arms*! About—*turn*!"

The Scots crashed about: MacTrease was looking annoyed. Presenting arms in the dark hours went dead against any infantry training manual he had ever studied, and was bad enough; but when at the same time a row of kilted buttocks was presented to the person being honoured, it was time for a decent Scots NCO to draw a veil over his mind. MacTrease understood that the Maharajah, still unwashed until his nine-day period of purifying thought ended on the morrow, had been in process of a transformation towards godhead, contemplating the goddess Parvati, Siva's wife, and soaking up, as it were, her divinity. MacTrease wished him luck, even felt sympathy that, by order of the General Officer Commanding, Northern Army, His Highness's important ninth night had been ruined. Normally, had he been in his own capital of Mysore, he would have received the obeisances of the British population, with the British Resident sitting on his right as they passed bowing before His Highness with no Indians present at all and the princely form fully visible. This, Sir Iain had forbidden, over-riding, it was rumoured, the Viceroy himself: the Army Commander would not have the British population on the move through the tense streets of Srinagar this night. If and when they had to be brought to the palace, a strong guard would be provided along their assembly route; but until then, they were to remain indoors.

When the enclosed Maharajah had been borne up the great steps into the palace, Black called to MacTrease.

"Carry on, Colour MacTrease, if you please." Salutes were exchanged and the Adjutant rode away, vanishing around the angle of the building. MacTrease ordered arms and fell his men out, dispersing them to their makeshift guardroom where they would remain ready to answer any alarm from the posted sentries. Outside the guardroom stood the Regimental Sergeant-Major, twirling his moustache. He nodded at MacTrease. "You've put His Highness to bed, have you, MacTrease?"

"Aye, I have that, Sar'nt-Major." MacTrease loosened the neck-band of his tunic and gave a sigh. "All that thought and meditation, and ..."

"And what, MacTrease?"

MacTrease shrugged. "Oh, I don't know. When he dies, he dies. Just like the rest of us. He'll be no nearer to God than you or me, will he?"

"According to his lights, he will! Who's to say who is right? None of us know for sure."

"Aye. But all this thinking about Parvati and how good she is. What use is thinking and contemplating when all's said and done? Then there's the stone phallus."

Cunningham stared. "Stone phallus?"

"Siva, Sar'nt-Major. You see him everywhere. All those—"

"Yes, yes. I understand you, MacTrease." Cunningham rose and fell on the balls of his feet. "It's their way, and we must not criticize what we do not fully understand. For their part, they would find much to mystify them in the kirk!" The RSM pulled out his watch. "It's late, and I shall take myself off to my billet, but I shall not undress. You'll have me called instantly if there is any trouble, Colour MacTrease."

"Aye ..."

The Regimental Sergeant-Major marched away across the courtyard, deserted now but for the watchful sentries. The night was silent now, a heavy silence beneath a sky hung with stars of an amazing brilliance, clusters of white light against dark blue velvet, spreading their luminosity like so many heavenly lanterns. Moonlight slanted across the palace, throwing dark shadows and bringing up sharply the huddled dwellings of the sleeping city. Cunningham halted by the wall and looked out towards the mean alleys below the Kashmiri hills, at the bungalows of the English community with their proliferating gardens, at the native rooftops with their own growths, splendidly colourful by day and even now seeming to soak up and throw back the light of moon and stars. Cunningham stood in silence, thinking; blood was in the air tonight, blood that if and when the mutiny broke out and spread would redden the Indus, the Ganges, the Brahmaputra, the Krishna, the Cauvery in the south. No part of India would escape the flood-tide of mutiny, and all would be gone, the long years of work and endeavour, hope and pride, courage and endurance. Cunningham swore into the night: why were men so foolish, so wickedly foolish as to listen to the tongues of evil and self-aggrandisement, the tongues that promised all and in the end gave only death and famine? And why did all the gods in their collective wisdom permit it? With the strong barrage of prayer ascending, with Christians and Parsis, Mohammedans and Hindus, Buddhists and Sikhs and Jains, all seeking the same goals of peace and stability, surely the requests would register? Cunningham pulled thoughtfully at his moustache: possibly it was a case of too many Commanders-in-Chief, each god busy at a game of tug-of-war with the other instead of all of them manning the same rope in the common good. All at once Cunningham laughed: the simile had pleased him. God knew, the War Office was continually rending itself asunder with its intrigues and rivalries in the highest places, and much imagination would be needed to see, for instance, His Royal Highness the Duke of Cambridge hauling upon the same rope as Lord Wolseley!

Straightening his pace-stick to the regulation angle beneath his arm, the Regimental Sergeant-Major marched away towards the sentry-posts.

\* \* \*

From the crowded room Ogilvie had been guided to the left, along a narrow alley, a smelly progress as the open drain ran alongside, sluggish and horrible, damned now and again by solid matter that caused the liquid to overflow and ooze down the footway itself in dreadful pollution. He and his escort walked in silence: the man would not answer questions. They went on for some distance, then turned into another alley running across, an even narrower way than before, with the dwellings almost reaching out to their opposites across the foetid path. Half-way along this alley his escort stopped and banged upon a door. Without delay the door was opened by an old man: in the light of the moon Ogilvie saw matted grey hair and a face covered with the lasting ravages of smallpox, and running ulcers. The smell of the clothing was overpowering, rancid. Something was said that Ogilvie failed to catch, and he was pushed through the open door and down a flight of stone steps that led from immediately inside. He went out of the back of the hovel into a small courtyard. He looked in some surprise: the courtyard was paved with flat stones, and there were beds of flowers, and more flowers growing from the walls and hanging down in profusion, while the filthy smells were overlaid by the heady perfume of the garden. He was given little time in which to appreciate this, however. He was pushed across the paving stones to where a ringbolt was set into the ground, into the centre of a large square block of stone. Behind him came the old man, carrying a rope with a hook at its end, the rope itself running around the sheave of a pulley-block. This tackle was set up from another hook in the wall that abutted onto the stone segment, and with both men heaving, the stone rose, banging against the wall.

"Down," the Kashmiri said, gesturing towards the black hole in the ground.

"You mean to imprison me? I have told you, I come as a friend and helper." Ogilvie looked down into the hole: it was not deep—the moon was shining straight into it, and he could see the bottom. "I can be of much assistance to the leader—"

"Do as you are told." The man gave him a push towards the hole. "It shall not be for long."

"While I am there, you will pass the word?"

"This I have said, and it shall be done. Now go down."

Ogilvie obeyed: he sat on the lip of the hole, and eased his body through till he was lying at full stretch in what had all the emotive feel of a coffin, but a coffin occupied by unknown scurrying creatures beside himself. When the stone lid was settled back into its slot, the coffin-feel increased immensely: there was no chink of light and no sound beyond the dry crackling of his companions in captivity as they moved dead leaves and pieces of littering garden residue and began to explore the new inmate's body. There were squelching things also—slug-like, snail-like: Ogilvie tried not to dwell on serpents. The beat of his heart in that small space seemed like a drum. The atmosphere, such as it was, stifled him; he could not last very long in what was an almost airless place, a dungeon worse by far than the Black Hole of Calcutta. Hours seemed to pass: no-one came. The silence was intense, tangible. Even the creeping insects were making no sound, though he could feel their march upon his body, tickling him irresistibly towards insanity.

Sweat poured from him, the place became a bath, a bath in which the fearful beating of his heart filled his ears with sound.

His head began to burst, his lungs gasped and panted to be filled with life-giving air. So far as he could he moved legs and arms, thrashing, pounding in a useless attempt to breach his prison.

# 20

THE EARLY MORNING was fresh and bright before the sun got into
its stride across the heavens to lift high the smells, both foul and
pleasant, from Srinagar. Sir Iain was up and about soon after
the dawn, and before breakfasting with Their Excellencies sent for
Lord Dornoch.

"Today's the day," he said, "or anyway, I'm damn sure it'll
prove so. In the meantime, I propose taking a leaf out of
General Fettleworth's book, Dornoch."

"General Fettleworth, sir?"

Sir Iain laughed. "Oh, come, we all know Bloody Francis
and his set ideas! Most are terrible, but in this particular
situation, there's one that might help. D'you follow?"

Dornoch, returning the smile, nodded. "A show of strength, sir,
is his usual solution."

"Exactly! That's what I'm going to do. A parade in the
courtyard, with plenty of martial music! Then a march through
the city, or such of its alleys as are navigable by a body of
troops. I've mapped the route—I'll show you directly."

"Very good, sir. But you'll not reduce the palace too much,
I take it?"

"No. One battalion of infantry with a battery of mountain
guns and a squadron of The Guides. That should do."

"The infantry, I take it, being the 114th?"

"Correct, Dornoch. We have a reputation as hard fighters. It'll
do the Kashmiris a power of good to see the tartan! And the
pipes—they love 'em. Fear 'em, too! You'll mount a smart turn-
out, Dornoch, with fixed bayonets and every piper and drummer
on parade."

"I'll see to that with pleasure, sir."

"I knew you would!" The General laid a hand briefly on Dornoch's shoulder. "I'll talk to Lee about the parade itself. We'll get His Highness of Jammu and Kashmir to take the salute— poor young Mysore's not free of Dasara yet."

"And His Excellency?"

Sir Iain shook his head, waved a hand towards the higher points of the city. "We're within range of the jezails. I'll not risk His Excellency."

"But you'll risk His Highness?"

"Highness is more easily replaceable than Excellency, Dornoch. It's a case of the king is dead, long live the king. The appointment of a Viceroy is a political matter entailing a devil of a lot of talk and intrigue. In any event, His Excellency is the prime target, I believe. Have you breakfasted yet?"

"No, sir."

"Then go and get it. I'm ordering the garrison to parade at eight o'clock. At that time the Union Flag will be hoisted superior to His Highness's personal standard." Grimly, Sir Iain smiled again. "That damn Mullah hasn't any monopoly on symbols!"

\*     \*     \*

The parade was a brilliant affair. The regiments marched in column of fours behind the bands around the central palace building, past the marble steps where His Highness the Maharajah Pertab Singh, diminutive beneath the huge absurdity of his tea-cosy turban, took the salute flanked by his personal bodyguard and the British staff officers. The air trembled with the sounds of the fifes and drums, the tunes thundering out over the city. The Middlesex marched past the saluting base to the tune of their second battalion, 'Paddy's Resource'; the Border Regiment beat out 'John Peel', while the Connaught Rangers, for once not using their own march, chose 'The Wearing of the Green'. After the salute was taken, the regiments marched twice around the courtyard in quick time to the tunes of 'Trelawney', 'The Girl I Left Behind Me', 'Soldiers of the Queen', and 'A Hundred Pipers'; then they slow-marched to 'Daughter of the Regiment' and 'Let Erin Remember' before forming hollow square around the courtyard for a massed demonstration by the fifes and drums backed by the Maharajah's own brass. It was all, literally, a resounding success: Pertab Singh beamed his approval, and vigorously pumped the hand of Sir Iain Ogilvie, then of Sir Thomas Lee, then of the regimental colonels— nodding and smiling with simple pleasure in a great military spectacle, appearing even to enjoy the clouds of dust that still hung in the air after the thunderous passage of the cavalry and the guns, who had swept past him behind their limbers to the strains of 'Bonnie Dundee'.

Before dismissing the parade, Sir Thomas Lee gave the order for the outward movement of the Royal Strathspey. Standing at attention, he called, "The 114th Highlanders will detach in execution of their orders. Carry on, if you please, Lord Dornoch."

"Sir!" Dornoch saluted from horseback and nodded at Major Hay. To the skirl of the pipes and the beat of the drums the Royal Strathspey marched off parade to form column of route for the march through the city, passing once again before the marble steps of the palace. Sir Iain looked more than satisfied with their turn-out: the brass buttons and badges gleamed in the sunlight, pipeclayed belts and rifle slings shone white, the blue-green hackles in the glengarries worn by the pipers stood proudly out, the massed kilts swung as one as they marched past and away to the military strains of 'The Heroes of Vittoria'. As the naked blade of Lord Dornoch's broadsword had flashed in salute, Sir Iain Ogilvie's eyes had been a trifle moist: splendid men, men who had faced the long, hard slog of many days marching through wild country and who after little rest could turn-out for parade as though they were on the square at their depot in Invermore—there were, in the GOC's view, none like them. But there was someone missing: his son James.

\*      \*      \*

In the garden pit, cool air had come down, and a chink of light as the flat stone overhead was moved. Ogilvie could hardly believe it: he had begun almost to accept the fact of death. Now there was life returning and it was like a kind of re-birth. The stone went upwards on its pulley and the air was fresh and beautiful. Two men looked down, one of them the escorting native of the night before. It was the other man who spoke.

"The Mullah will talk with you. Come."

Ogilvie's voice was hoarse, cracked. "You must help me out. I am stiff and weak."

Hands reached down for him, and he was dragged upright to sit on the edge of the hole. He swayed, feeling dizzy; he put his head in his hands. He said, "You must give me time."

"Time is short, my friend. The Mullah is impatient."

"Then he must learn patience. In my limbs there is no strength."

"You shall be carried."

"I am unwell. You must leave me. The Mullah must come to me, if he wishes my help. I will stay with one of you under guard, and make no trouble. But when the Mullah comes, it is necessary that I speak to him alone."

"He will not speak to you alone. He speaks to no-one alone. Such a request cannot be granted."

"Then I cannot speak, and the matter is ended."

There was an angry laugh, and a hand came down on Ogilvie's shoulder, gripping hard. "When a matter is begun, it ends only on the word of the Mullah. Do you wish to die, like the British die tonight, also on the word of the Mullah?"

"I do not wish this," Ogilvie said. "It is tonight—you know this?"

"I know this. That is why time is short. Tonight the Raj and its Hindu support will crash to the ground. It is the will of the Prophet...to whom all praise and glory."

"To whom all praise and glory," Ogilvie echoed dutifully. His limbs were shivering now, a shake of reaction, but he was feeling less giddy and sick, and the stiffness was passing. He knew that somehow he had to get the Mullah to this place: if he was taken to the Mullah, he would have no chance. Playing for time he went on, "This is the time of Dasara, as the Mullah must know. Dasara ends tonight. Is it therefore intended that the Raj comes to an end at the same time?"

"That is so."

"And the Maharajahs, and the Viceroy?"

"They shall be the first to die. From a high place there shall come—" The man broke off sharply, standing up and looking away towards the palace. Into the hitherto still air had come a sound to shatter the peace, a sound of military music. As the two Kashmiris quickly climbed some steps leading to the top of the garden wall, Ogilvie stood up, swayed, fell, and got to his feet again. Excitement mounted in him, weakness fell away: the pipes and drums came loud and clear, the heartening sound of the

British military presence close at hand. He picked up the tune, was barely able to stop himself singing it out loud in concert with the Irish pipers of the Connaught Rangers, the 88th and 94th of the line:

"Oh, Paddy dear, and did ye hear
The news that's going round?
The shamrock is by law forbid
To grow on Irish ground..."

A song of revolution against English rule it might be, adopted for its own by the British Army with its curious ability to absorb all that seemed worth while from its enemies, yet it stirred Ogilvie's blood with its promise of action. Climbing the steps, he looked towards the palace with the two natives: above the high roof of the central building, the Union Flag crept to the truck of the flagstaff, with the Maharajah's standard below. The music played on, switching to the fifes and drums of an English battalion of the line. On the garden wall there was silence; after a minute or so one of the natives signed to Ogilvie to get down.

"The British make brave sounds," he said. "Tonight the sounds will be of weeping and wailing throughout the Raj. Come now. We shall go to the Mullah."

"I have told you, I am weak."

The eyes glittered. "Yet you had strength to climb when the music was heard. I think you make too much of this weakness. If you will not walk, then you shall be carried, as I have said."

Ogilvie looked at the man closely; to protest too much might well be fatal. So might be a confrontation with a well-guarded Mullah—yet there would be a chance, slim but possible, of using his concealed knife. Temporising still he asked, "Where is the Mullah?"

"A long way from here, friend."

"Within the city?"

The man nodded. "Within the city, and well hidden until the end of Dasara approaches."

"And after I have spoken to the Mullah, what then for me?"

"This will be decided by the Mullah himself, according to what you have spoken." The time for delay seemed over: the Kashmiri laid a hand on Ogilvie's right arm, holding it fast, while the other man took the left. Ogilvie was propelled back into the mean dwelling and up the steps into the alley and its rising smells brought out by the increasing heat of the sun. He stumbled, and his legs dragged: giddiness had returned. He protested; with an oath his original escort spoke to the second man, and Ogilvie was lifted, one man at his head and the other at his feet. They made fair speed to the end of the alley; when they met the main alley running across, progress became slower. The city was packed with men and women and though the bearers shouted and kicked and swore as they pushed their way through with their burden, they could move at no more than a snail's pace. From the manner of the two men, Ogilvie judged that such crowding was unexpected; he wondered at its cause, found a strong connection with the sounds of British military power from the palace. He grinned to himself: it could well be that the Kashmiris were having second thoughts about starting a mutiny from their own capital city when such power was at hand! Whatever the Mullah might say, however far the mutiny might, and indeed would, spread, there was one stark and inescapable fact: the British rifles and bayonets, and the limbered heavy guns, would cause much damage and many casualties in Srinagar before they were overwhelmed by the Czar's army waiting along the valley. There would be panic on the canals and in the alleys of Srinagar then, if it had not struck already: Ogilvie caught the glint of it in staring eyes, in high shouting voices, in the free use of fists as quarrels broke out around him and his bearers.

Slowly, they pressed on amid virtual bedlam, ears dinned at and deafened by the yelling voices of the crowd and by occasional bursts from drums and flutes and cymbals. After a long-drawn time of buffeting and sheer persistence, they were brought to a halt near the end of the alley, stopped by a massive inrush of Kashmiris yelling and shouting as they pressed through. There were more fights, fights in which the bearers became involved but by a miracle managed to hold onto Ogilvie. Then, as they fought through into a wider road leading from the direction of the Maharajah's palace, they found the whole area suddenly cleared of natives but filled instead with a different scene the sounds of which now rose loud above the dwindling shouts: to the splendour of the pipes and drums in full muster, with Pipe-Major Ross at their head, the Scots were advancing beneath a glittering forest of fixed bayonets.

The bearers, right out on their own now, naked and exposed,

stopped dead. With the pipers almost upon them, they dropped Ogilvie flat on the ground and turned and ran for it. Ogilvie heard an oath as someone all but tripped over him, then he was roughly seized and an astonished voice said, "Why, it's Captain Ogilvie!" In the split-second that followed he heard the Colonel's voice call an order, and then, from the leading files of A Company, four rifles crashed out.

# 21

"ARE YOU ALL right, Captain Ogilvie?"

"I'll manage, Colonel." Swaying on his feet, Ogilvie looked back along the roadway: two crumpled figures lay in the dust, spreading blood. A subaltern was bending over them; after a quick examination he straightened and ran back to report to Lord Dornoch that both were dead.

"Dead!" Dornoch looked down at Ogilvie. "I'm sorry. I intended only to wound them, and have them brought in for questioning."

"They would never have talked, Colonel—not once they were in captivity, I'm sure of that. As it is, I have a certain amount of information, though it's only confirmatory."

"Tell me."

Ogilvie did so. Dornoch asked, "But will it be of use now?" He stared towards the alley from which Ogilvie had come: the area around the troops was still deserted, but at any moment a mob might erupt from the alley. "This information—the Mullah will know, surely, and alter his plans accordingly?"

"Not necessarily, Colonel. I never made contact with him, and he'll not know what those men told me."

"But eyes will be watching at this moment! If we take you back to the palace, two and two will be put together."

"It's possible, Colonel, but I think we can deal with that. I suggest we give those eyes something to see!" He paused. "Suppose I break away in a few moments, before there's been too long a delay, and you open fire—"

"Shoot you down? Appear to kill you?"

"Yes, Colonel. You wouldn't kill an informer, someone you could use—I think the Mullah will take the point! You have my body dragged to the side, then you continue with the march."

"And you?"

"When you've gone on ahead, the mob will fill the empty space, Colonel. I'll come back to life and get away under their cover, back to the palace. We needn't worry about the disappearance of a dead body. The mob'll have other things on its collective mind!"

Lord Dornoch nodded, turned in the saddle and spoke directly to the leading company. Taking advantage, for the benefit of the prying eyes, of the Colonel's averted back, Ogilvie dodged aside and ran ahead along the road, fast, his tattered garments flying out behind him. A few seconds later he heard the crash of the rifles, and he went down realistically in the dust and lay as still as death. He heard running footsteps, felt the touch of hands, and was dragged through the dust and left in a huddle against a wall. Then the order was passed from the Colonel to march, and the pipes and drums crashed out, reverberating from the buildings. Ogilvie lay where he was as the battalion marched away, ready for an attack. But no attack came. As the pipes and drums faded away up the road, there was for a while silence. Then the rush began, and the shouting, as the Kashmiris crowded out in a mass from the alley, trampling the two corpses as they ran. Against the wall, thankful for the partial protection it gave against the running feet, Ogilvie quaked. He waited until the mob was all around him, dodging as best he could the bare legs of those close to the wall. Then, using the wall as a support, he stood upright and went with the mob, shouting and waving his fists. Edging gradually palace-wards in the growing heat of the day, he detached himself and dropped beneath the shelter of some tall green poplars until the mob had stormed on past; then he rose again and slid up the tree-lined pathway to the gate from which he had come the night before.

*    *    *

The General's voice was coldly formal. "I'm glad to see you back, at all events." Fury and passion took over. "You should never have damn well gone in the first place! I'll have Butler's guts over this, just see if I don't! He's already had his ears well and truly pinned back after I prised the truth out of him. Assassination! God give me strength!"

"It would have been effective, sir."

"So will a bullet fired from the front be effective." Sir Iain took a few turns up and down his apartment, simmering still. Coming to a halt, he faced his son again. "What's done is done and for now I'll say no more. As a matter of fact, this hasn't been all failure, since your information gives us a very precise time—that is, within say an hour or so, which is quite precise enough." Frowning, the General got on the move again, deep in thought, then stopped by his window and looked out. "From a very high point, you said."

"The exacts words, sir, were: from a high place there shall come—then the pipes and drums started, and no more was said."

"Yes—damn it! My fault, I suppose. A pity, that! However, what we have is useful. A high place—that must mean higher than the palace, obviously. There are not many such—you've only to look around. And there are only three within decent range of rifle-fire."

"You know this, sir?"

Sir Iain chuckled: his bad temper seemed to have been dissipated. "I do! I've not been sitting on my arse all the time! I've had words with the sappers and gunners, and some work's been done with their mathematical gadgets—measuring angles and so on. It always seemed to me that we were open to these high places of yours—the confirmation fails to surprise me. Come here, and look."

Ogilvie crossed the room to his father's side. Sir Iain pointed. "There, and there. And one more on the other side of the palace— not visible from here. Minarets, James. Hives of Mohammedans! Hives of damn Mullahs, tonight! He'll have his marksmen there, and for my money he'll not be far away himself. Well, I'll have my marksmen ready in position too. But they'll not be riflemen."

Ogilvie was puzzled. "Not, sir?"

"They'll be gunners," the General said energetically. "I'll have the batteries laid on all three targets, and God help anybody who sounds the *muezzin* when I open fire!"

"You actually intend to open on the minarets, sir?"

"Yes, I do, damn it. The moment the first hostile act occurs from one or any of those minarets, the batteries open. I repeat, I'm sure in my own mind I'll get the Mullah in person. It'll be from a nice, high tower he'll make his announcement of mutiny— they're all the same, these natives. They have to rouse the mob, they have to show themselves as widely and as *theatrically* as possible—and what better vantage point than a minaret?"

"He might not chose to be at the actual place his bandits fire from, sir—just in case he gets hit in the reprisal."

Once again Sir Iain chuckled. "God damn it, James, I know that! I have my brains in my head, not my damn bottom like poor Fettleworth. That's why I mean to open on *all three* simultaneously!" He checked something further he was about to say, and glared at his son. "What's the matter, hey?"

"The matter?"

"Your face. You have an expressive one. Don't you damn well dare to look censorious at *me*!"

Ogilvie flushed. "I'm sorry, sir. But I see dangers in opening on the mosques."

"I suppose you see a holy war?" Sir Iain asked sarcastically.

"And a martyr, sir."

"India's full of damn martyrs! What d'you expect me to do? Watch His Excellency and Their Highnesses killed by a sniper's bullet—and then have three cheers for the bugger's marksmanship? Are you mad, boy?"

"No, sir—"

"But I see you think I am!" Sir Iain's face had reddened dangerously, the blue eyes flashing steely fire. "You must learn to weigh things in the balance if ever you're to succeed to command of more than a company! The Raj is in mortal peril of disintegration in the face of mutiny and the Russian armies, and you stand there and talk to me of holy wars. A holy war can be contained within Srinagar, and immediately put down by the rifles and the guns and the sabres." He was clearly in some opposition to Butler's opinions as expressed earlier to his son.

Ogilvie asked, "And the Russians, sir?"

"My dear James, the Russians are waiting for mutiny on a sub-continental scale—not a conflagration inside Srinagar alone!"

"But—"

"There are no more buts! My mind's made up, I've weighed the balance. Unless the Mullah dies tonight—and there I have to agree with Major Butler—the Raj is at an end. That's it in a nutshell. We must act decisively, and afterwards we must cope with the lesser trouble as best we can."

"I see, sir. And—His Excellency?"

"His Excellency doesn't know, and *won't* know till it's too damn late for him to do anything about it. I've sworn the gunner and sapper officers to secrecy—when the batteries wheel into position it'll be seen as no more than a part of the normal and proper defensive manoeuvre." The General pulled out a turnip-shaped gold watch. "The day belongs to His Highness of Mysore until dusk. Let Dasara continue! At dusk the garrison will go to its war stations—and in the meantime, James, not a word to a soul about what's been said between us. Understood?"

"Yes, sir." Ogilvie hesitated. "Sir, the secrecy—does it not indicate that you realize His Excellency would refuse his authority, and that—"

"Get out of my sight!" the General roared, waving his arms in the air.

*     *     *

Within the high tension of the atmosphere there was, on the part of the Hindus from Mysore, much gaiety and joy: the long trek was over and into this, the last day of Dasara, was to be crammed as much as possible of the full ceremonial such as had not been feasible upon the march. His Highness the Maharajah, young and fresh-faced, now showed himself outside the great hall seated upon the tremendous throne that had been brought from Mysore in a heavily guarded wagon drawn by bullocks—a splendid affair of gold and silver figuration with a pearl canopy, resting upon steps of solid gold. Here, with some seventy priests, holy men from the temple of Chamundi, standing behind the throne, His Highness held durbar in the open air amid the most colourful scene in Ogilvie's experience of India. The priests alone were a spectacle: some in a bright blue-green, some in orange, others in crimson, with fumes of exotic burnt spices wreathing round them as they chanted the names and titles of His Highness. In the courtyard there was dancing and ceremonial wrestling, and a squadron of native cavalry performed a musical ride, the horses jostling the throngs of Indians from their path with magnificent abandon. Ballets special to the princely state of Mysore took place, and His Highness's white pony was led out to prance before a band. The air seemed to vibrate to the sound of music and every breath of the scented atmosphere was pleasure to the nostrils. Ogilvie, watching from the Royal Strathspeys' guardroom, shook his head in wonder: all this was typical enough of India, whose threats of war and bloodshed were ever intermingled with peaceful joys; yet it was still, to western eyes, incredible. There would be a very different scene when Dasara reached its climax and the heavy gun batteries opened on the minarets above the mosques: Ogilvie, desperately fearing the outcome of his father's proposed action, could only hope that something would occur to prevent the firing of the guns... he turned as Colour-Sergeant MacTrease came up: from somewhere MacTrease had obtained a freshly-starched tunic, and his kilt, too, looked freshly pressed. Ogilvie smiled. "Is this in honour of Dasara, Colour MacTrease?"

"It's only how I'll expect the men to be turned out, sir."

"We may be in action before tomorrow."

"Aye, sir. We still have our reputation to think about, sir."

"Quite right, Colour MacTrease."

MacTrease lifted a hand, shading his eyes against the sun as he looked towards the Maharajah at the top of the palace steps. "All that waste of effort," he said as if to himself.

"What d'you mean?"

"Turned backs, sir! And tarpaulins and thunderboxes. He's as visible now as if we'd never bothered." MacTrease frowned. "All that shriving of the poor bloody Middlesex! It's no wonder they call them the Diehards."

"It was necessary on the march, Colour MacTrease. Dasara hasn't gone according to plan this time, and no-one's to blame for that. His Highness is a good friend to the Raj, remember."

"Aye, sir. I have a feeling we're going to need all our friends before much longer. I believe—" He broke off as the Regimental Sergeant-Major marched up, right arm swinging from the shoulder, left hand clasped around his pace-stick beneath the arm-pit.

Cunningham halted. "Colour MacTrease, and you, Captain Ogilvie, sir. A runner's come from the Major-General. All officers and senior NCOs are required immediately in His Highness's durbar hall."

"Thank you, Mr Cunningham. Do you know what's in the wind?"

"A rumour, sir, no more than that. The Russian army is believed to be on the move. With your permission, Captain Ogilvie, I'll be on my way with Colour-Sar'nt MacTrease to chase up the NCOs."

"Of course, Sar'nt-Major."

"Sir!" Swinging his arm to the salute, the Regimental Sergeant-Major turned about with a slam of boot-leather and marched away with MacTrease. Ogilvie went round to the back of the palace, up a flight of steps as magnificent as those in the front, and into the great durbar hall of the Maharajahs of Jammu and Kashmir. Already a score of officers and NCOs had assembled, and were standing about in groups below a dais at the far end of the long apartment—infantrymen, cavalrymen booted and spurred, gunners, sappers, Supply and Transport, medical staff. The group swelled, half filling the durbar hall. The word was passed for gangway, and through the parting press of bodies Sir Thomas Lee came striding with his staff, his face set into hard lines. He jumped up onto the dais amid a sudden, tense silence, and stared around the assembly as though looking into the eyes of each and every man present. "I shall be brief," he said. "Word has come through from scouts of His Highness's army. There are signs that the Grand Duke Alexis is striking his camp. His Cossacks have already left their lines and are moving towards the city in company with some of the heavy gun-batteries. Now, we know what their objective is, but we can only guess at the strategy and tactics. In my opinion, they will still hold off until the sign comes from the Mullah. When that sign comes, they will attack with their artillery and at the same time mount a siege, encircling the city with their infantry. We can also expect some cavalry thrusts against weak points—which means virtually every part of the city itself. It is the palace, however, with which we are solely concerned—the palace and Their Excellencies. The Resident and all British and Europeans in the city will be escorted in shortly. We expect to be under attack not only from the Russian army but also from all the Muslim inhabitants of the city, who will at once throw in their lot with the Russians. We shall have our work cut out, gentlemen. The telegraph line has not yet been cut, and Sir Iain Ogilvie has passed a message to Rawalpindi, indicating that we shall hold the palace on our own until reinforcements are readily available. I have also made contact with the Government in Calcutta. You may be assured we shall not be forgotten, and that the British public will be solidly behind us and wishing us well." He paused. "Lord Dornoch?"

"Sir?"

"Your regiment remains the immediate palace guard. Your men will fight to the last in protection of Their Excellencies. That is an order, to be obeyed to the letter."

"It will be, sir."

"Thank you, Colonel. The same principle applies to us all, I need hardly say. The enemy must be held outside the walls and any breach contained. If there is a massive break-through, then the whole garrison falls back upon the palace itself to reinforce the Scots and hold the living apartments until relief arrives from Rawalpindi. All non-combatants will be armed to fight with the infantry. That is all, gentlemen."

Sir Thomas returned the salutes, stepped down from the dais, and stalked away, head high and back straight. There was a respectful silence in the durbar hall until the Major-General and the staff had disappeared, then a hubbub of talk broke out. Ogilvie left with the Adjutant and the Regimental Sergeant-Major.

"In regard to the non-combatants, Sar'nt-Major," Black said. "You'll see to an issue of rifles and ammunition at once, if you please, to all cooks, clerks and medical orderlies."

"Very good, sir."

"Some drilling would not come amiss."

"Yes, sir. And target practice, sir?"

Black shook his head. "I think not, Sar'nt-Major. The sound of firing might exacerbate the natives outside. When the time comes, the target will be big enough in all conscience!"

"That's true, sir—"

"Then see to a muster for drill, Mr Cunningham. And take care not to march the men through the ceremonies of Dasara."

Cunningham saluted and marched briskly away. Black and Ogilvie went down the steps and turned around the palace building towards the main courtyard. The sun was well up now and the day was hot, and a haze seemed to hang over the city and the surrounding hills, a light haze that met a clear, metallic sky above. The smell of flowers and spices was strong, and interlaced with the aroma of sandalwood coming from the continuing religious ceremonies, though in truth these were now more of the theatre and the show-ring than of the temple. Black swore as, rounding the angle of the building, he met a troop of Mysore cavalry who all but rode him down.

"I only hope they'll ride as well towards the enemy!" he

212

snapped, adjusting the chin-strap of his helmet. Walking to the outer wall, he stared down through an embrasure: the native population appeared to be massing below. They seemed orderly enough but a rising sound came up from them, a murmur of obvious disaffection that grew to a roar when the two British helmets were seen. Fists were shaken; the Adjutant dodged back in sudden alarm, as though he feared missiles, but none came. Ogilvie brought up his field-glasses and looked out to the northern and western hills: they were quiet, empty of men as was the track that led from the distant mountain pass, running alongside the waters of the Jhelum. So far at any rate, the Russian army was not moving close enough to show. From behind them came a tinkle of laughter, a joyous sound; Black swung round impatiently to confront a crowd of dancing girls and to have his unlikely neck hung with a garland of bright, sweet-smelling flowers. He changed his angry frown to a smirk of appreciation, looking highly surprised. As the troupe of young girls danced away, Ogilvie had difficulty in restraining his own laughter.

"Someone loves us, Andrew," he said. "Or anyway, you."

"The devil take it!" Black fumed. "Upon my word, I must look most ridiculous!"

"Take it off, then."

Black hesitated, scowling. "That might be foolish. They are not to be upset—that is the order."

"It would help if you looked happier, Andrew."

"Oh, shut your mouth!" Black marched away rapidly towards the guardroom, his garland swaying from side to side in harmony with his step. When Ogilvie met him again just before luncheon, in the apartment set aside as an anteroom, the Adjutant was without his decoration and morosely drinking a *chota peg* with Major Hay. The anteroom was crowded with officers from the various regiments and there was a somewhat feverish air of jollity that only increased the feeling of the edge of the abyss. The downing of the *chota pegs* was hearty enough, but at luncheon, more than amply provided by His Highness's kitchens, the appetites were small. Ogilvie's was no exception: in his mind's eye he was seeing once again the bloodied trunk of the headless major, the terrible symbol of what was about to happen.

# 22

AFTER LUNCHEON, IN the main heat of the day, the Border Regiment was paraded with a squadron of cavalry and marched out through the gates to act as escort to the British and other European nationals in the city. These had been mustered, minus their possessions, in the Residency compound; the march back to the palace was accomplished without casualties but under a rain of shaken fists and angry cries and occasionally a flung stone. In the palace, all through the afternoon, Dasara continued towards its climax: Ogilvie, advised by Lord Dornoch via the Adjutant to turn in and catch up on lost sleep, tossed and turned and then gave up the attempt. The air was filled with sound, and that, together with the scent of flowers and spices and incense, tended towards heaviness and headache. Ogilvie made the rounds of his company, currently one of the duty companies on palace guard, and then from the top of the steps fronting the main courtyard watched the ceremonies and worried again about his father's plan for dealing with the situation: there was considerable danger in it. If the artillery bombardment failed to kill the Mullah—who might or might not be present whatever Sir Iain's views might be—then the whole thing would serve only to explode the situation irrevocably. The fighting would be even more bitter. And even should the Mullah be killed, Sir Iain himself would at the very least stand accused of acting independently and without prior consultation and Viceregal approval. However, he had appeared perfectly willing to accept the risk and Ogilvie knew very well the truth of the hypothesis that in the army virtually anything was forgiven provided it ended in success...

The afternoon wore away, slowly: men became even more tense. The regimental officers, all of them on parade now though not with overt formality, stood ready to react instantly to anything that might happen. At four o'clock the ceremonial seemed to quieten and the priests and their attendants and performers melted away, leaving the courtyard to the British. In Ogilvie's ears the footfalls of the sentries sounded out like knells in the otherwise still air. Walking around the perimeter, he studied the minarets rising slender and straight from the mosques. There, all was peace; no-one was visible, nor would be until the sounding of the next *muezzin* when all good Muslims would crouch upon their knees, touching their foreheads upon the ground and uttering prayers to the Prophet. They would be in a bitter mood; all this day their feelings would have been affronted by the sounds of Hinduism coming from the palace: in India two things were true as between Muslim and Hindu: trouble mostly arose over the Muslims' uncaring slaughter of the sacred cows, and over rival noises outside mosques to disturb prayer. Today, such had been the noises of Dasara, that up here in the palace at all events it had not been possible to hear the *muezzin* calling out to the faithful, and tempers would be high accordingly. They would be in frenzy when the British guns sent the minarets crashing in clouds of dust.

As the sun, moving down the western sky, threw long, weird fingers of shadow across the courtyard, Sir Iain Ogilvie emerged from the palace and stood for a moment at the top of the steps. He returned the salutes of the sentries, then called to Lord Dornoch who was standing outside the guardroom with a group of his officers. Dornoch moved across to meet the Northern Army Commander as he came down the steps.

"You know the official drill, Dornoch."

"I do, sir. In a few moments, the Maharajah of Mysore will appear—" Dornoch broke off. Round the corner of the main building a procession was advancing, a string of camels ahead of a lumbering elephant, hung with gold and jewels, and armoured. "His transport's coming for him now, sir."

Sir Iain turned to look. "As you say. Well, now's the beginning of the end—though not, I trust, for the Raj! His Highness is now due for final purification. Once purified, I understand, many truths will be revealed to him, but don't ask me what, or how either—it normally emanates from some sacred tree, and he hasn't

215

got his sacred tree with him this time. It's all something of a balls-up really," he added. "I don't know how he intends to square it with his gods, but no doubt he'll find a way."

"It's obviously been considered worth the risk!"

Sir Iain blew through his moustache. "We hope so, Dornoch, we hope so. The vital talks won't take place, of course, until we've cleared the air of the damn Mullah." The general pulled out his watch. "We have three hours, Dornoch. I expect the trouble to start round about eight p.m. Here comes His Highness now."

The two officers watched, coming to the salute, as the Maharajah of Mysore appeared at the top of the steps. At the foot the elephant halted and went down upon its knees, and His Highness, attended by Brahmin priests, embarked in the howdah. The elephant swayed upright and moved slowly away behind the camels. In rear of the elephant marched a body of His Highness's infantry in uniforms of red and green, followed by the cavalry wearing blue, gold and silver. The procession ambled off, His Highness surrounded by his personal standard-bearers carrying furled silk banners, umbrellas, yaks' tails, huge fans of peacocks' feathers and poles with golden discs that flashed fire from the sun. Trumpets sounded out and drums beat, making the air reverberate with sound that rolled back from the palace walls.

"Into the last act now," Sir Iain said, and wiped sweat from his face. "Poor little bugger, it must be the very devil of a strain, especially since he's so far from home. At this moment, he should be heading for Chamundi Hill. As it is, he's just going to ride round in circles. If he's not careful, he'll ride up his own fundamental orifice, like the cock-yolly bird! And no damn shrine."

"I beg your pardon, sir?"

"The sacred tree, Dornoch, the missing sacred tree!"

"Ah yes, sir. No revelations, amounting really to a waste of time?"

"Precisely. I trust the Government in Calcutta will appreciate his sacrifice. I suppose it's like the Archbishop of Canterbury finding no ruddy door to knock three times on with his crook—isn't it?" The General looked round as an ADC approached and saluted. "Yes, Captain Baines?"

"Sir, His Excellency presents his compliments and wishes to speak to you at once."

"All right." Sir Iain nodded, and the ADC marched back to the palace. "See your men are constantly alert, Dornoch, and remember, the moment of danger will come, or I believe it will, at full dark, when in theory His Highness reaches Chamundi Hill and shifts to horseback for the actual end of Dasara."

"I have the drill, sir. But what about His Excellency?"

The General gave a hard smile. "His Excellency will not appear, as I've said before. The thing will reach its climax at the top of the steps, which shall act as Chamundi Hill, and the two Maharajahs will meet there—plus myself, in the place of His Excellency."

*     *     *

As the sky grew darkly into its brief purple twilight, the gun-batteries moved with a rumble of their limber wheels into the appointed positions and were laid and trained upon the three targets of the minarets, their crews ready behind the breeches. The men of all the brigades that had formed the column of march were now standing-to, watchful before and around the living apartments and along the outer walls. The native guards on the gates had been reinforced with men of the Middlesex Regiment. The Regimental Sergeant-Majors of all the infantry units, with their colour-sergeants, made their rounds constantly. As close a watch as possible was kept on the natives from Mysore and upon those domestic to the palace, a precautionary measure in case of any infiltration of elements loyal to the Mullah. As the interminable circular procession went into its last lap, two squadrons each of The Guides and the Bengal Lancers rode towards the gold-encrusted elephant and its princely howdah, and wheeled to come up on either flank as extra protection for His Highness of Mysore, a small, solemn figure who, when he reached the end of this final circuit, would descend and be surrounded by his priests who would wash him and bring him offerings of food. At the top of the steps stood the Maharajah of Jammu and Kashmir with a turban that appeared bigger than ever before in the luminous darkness; with him was Sir Iain Ogilvie. Without staff or attendants the two stood alone and vulnerable to the assassin's bullet; though they were currently shrouded by the dark, their anonymity would vanish under the light of flares when the Maharajah of Mysore, after washing and feeding, started out from the bottom of the steps on horseback for the

217

centre of the courtyard and the last act of Dasara. Already his black charger was being brought across by a *syce*: standing in front of his company of Scots, James Ogilvie heard the 'clop' of its hooves. A strange silence now hung over the palace as the ceremonial washing and feeding took place; for some while there had been quiet among the Muslim crowd outside, the shouting and murmurs held in check as though the mob waited with bated breath for the sign of mutiny. Slowly, as the ceremony ended, the horse was brought up to the ring of busy priests, and held in disciplined patience. Still under cover of the darkness, the Brahmin circle opened and Sir Krishnaraja Wadyar Bahadur IV, Maharajah of Mysore, stepped out to be assisted onto his horse.

He moved away: tonight, in his makeshift Dasara, there would be no Chamundi to glide in her boat on the dark waters below her temple to signify the long-awaited ending. Dasara would end when the Maharajah rode back to the steps and, mounting them on his charger under a deluge of light from the many flaring torches, ceremonially met his brother in religion.

Ogilvie held his breath as the dark shadow of His Highness moved past the ranks of Scots, out into the centre of the courtyard. The hoofbeats stopped, there was a momentary pause, an intense silence, then the first of the flares was lit. On its heels, more and more burst into life until the whole courtyard seemed ablaze and the uniforms of the native troops in their review order sparkled like jewelled ghosts in the night. More flares came up along the front of the palace, lighting the steps and the important personages at their top.

Once again there was a silence: it did not last. It was shattered by a series of rifle-shots that seemed to reverberate round the courtyard. There was a gasp, a kind of concerted sigh. No-one had seen where the shots had come from, but Ogilvie, staring towards the palace steps, saw his father clap a hand to his shoulder and stagger a little, then fall to the ground. A voice—Sir Thomas Lee's, Ogilvie fancied—roared out: "*Extinguish those damn flares!*"

As the flares died and the courtyard darkened, Ogilvie saw the moon reflected dully from the metal of the guns and limbers, ready laid and trained on the three minarets: so far no order had come for them to open. His father was possibly badly wounded, but now the flares were out and he had no view of the top of the palace steps. Looking anxiously through the comparative dark, his eye was caught by the closer of the minarets: there was a curious glow at its top, a glow of white—a figure, outlined in the light of torches, a figure dressed in white with arms uplifted. In the same moment that Ogilvie saw this vision-like figure, a shouted order came from the palace steps— Sir Iain, recovering from whatever wound he had sustained:

"Major Bellamy!"

The answer came from the left of the courtyard: "Sir?"

"Open with your guns, man!"

In the next split-second, James Ogilvie's voice rang out, loud and clear, though he scarcely recognised it as his own: "Hold your fire! You open at peril of the Raj." As he spoke he turned swiftly, and grabbed a rifle from one of the Scots behind him. He ran fast for the parapet, at a point near the minaret where the Mullah stood. As he halted and took aim, he was aware of Colour-Sergeant MacTrease at his side. The moment his sights came on, he fired: in the same instant, MacTrease also opened with his rifle. A cry rang out and the figure in white slewed sideways: below him, the city was bright and silver beneath the moon and the clustered stars. Behind Ogilvie the palace courtyard was in uproar, the natives running hither and thither, and Dasara lay in ruins. Ogilvie saw the young Maharajah, a shadow in the night, riding for the steps, where Sir Iain was now standing, supported by an ADC and shouting imprecations at the unfortunate Major Bellamy of the gunners, who had not as yet opened fire, not knowing who had countermanded the General's order. His Highness Pertab Singh had vanished, no doubt despatched inside his palace by Sir Iain. Behind Sir Iain, just inside the great doorway of the reception hall, Sir Thomas Lee could be seen with the Viceroy, with whom he appeared to be arguing. There was a rising sound from beyond the walls, a sound of mob anger and violence as the white-clad Mullah swayed above their heads; but so far there was no attack. The Mullah was almost bent in two now, clearly visible in the light of the torches, with his acolytes about him. He seemed to be resisting them. Ogilvie ran back towards his company with MacTrease, and moved his Scots closer to the steps, falling them back in a tight guard upon the palace entrance. Then Lord Dornoch was seen, dismounted and running up the steps with Andrew Black. At the top he turned, nodding at Black, who passed

219

the order:

"Up the steps at once! The 114th will enter the palace and hold it as a fortress. Company Commanders take over independently."

One by one the companies were marched in, their heavy boots clumping on the marble. Ogilvie saw his father, pale-faced but apparently not seriously hurt, with a medical officer attending to his shoulder. For an instant their eyes met: Sir Iain's look was murderous. The time for opening with the gun batteries had long gone now. From the distance, clear to the west above the noise from the courtyard, came the warlike sound of military movement —the thump and clash of brass, the beating of drums, the voices of bugles and trumpets: the Grand Duke Alexis was marching upon the city at the last with his ravening Cossack cavalry, his massed infantry and his guns. Halting his company inside the great doors, Ogilvie reported formally to Black: and just as he did so a sergeant of the Middlesex Regiment came up the steps at the run, saw Lord Dornoch, and halted in front of him.

"Sir! The minaret where the Mullah was hit, sir. It's taken fire, sir!"

"Fire! How the devil—"

Black interrupted. "Colonel, like so much else in Srinagar, the minarets are largely of wood." He turned to the sergeant. "How did the fire catch, do you know?"

"From the natives' flares at the top, sir, I think. Some of our men have opened without orders, and the flares were struck out of the natives' hands. The wood is bone dry, sir."

Black glanced at Dornoch. The Colonel said, "I'll go along at once. Captain Ogilvie?"

"Sir?"

"Come with us." Dornoch dashed for the steps with Ogilvie behind him and the sergeant running ahead. They went to the western wall and looked out over the city. There was flame rising from a red glow over the Mullah's minaret, flame that licked around the half-upright figure in white who appeared to have been deserted now by his acolytes, whether by his own wish or by their own fear of staying could not be said. Ogilvie stared through his field-glasses, brought the Mullah up close, the staring eyes, the shapeless white garment, the stick-like legs, the scar from temple to mouth, the hairless head.

"It's the Mullah, is it not, James?"

Ogilvie turned: his father stood behind him, his tunic bloodied and torn away from the bandaged shoulder. "It is, sir," he answered.

"Poor bugger," Sir Iain said quietly. "He's burning himself now—look! Like a torch, James. A torch that will flame for a while, and then go out, and be seen clearly to go out."

They watched the flames curl around the white garment: it appeared as though the Mullah was already dead. Dornoch turned to address the General. "Yes, his torch will go out! And the mutiny, sir?"

"That, too, will go out—you shall see!" Sir Iain gave a short laugh. "We of the Staff, Dornoch—we're not *always* wrong, you know!"

"Perhaps. The Mullah...I think he's dead. But would it not be an act of mercy to make sure, sir?"

"An act of mercy, yes, but we, as well as he, have a strong need of symbols tonight." Sir Iain put a hand on his son's shoulder. "You were right, James, about the guns. They were not needed."

Nothing further was said; the group of officers, and all the men along the western wall, now joined by the hordes of natives from Mysore, stared down at the burning Mullah and the crowd below him, the crowd that was no longer a mob, but a strangely silent and cowed audience to the end of a dream. Crackles came across, and faintly the stench of burning flesh. Then, as the bent body seemed to shrivel, it lurched a little, leaning towards the palace, and toppling towards the edge of the high platform of the minaret. Suddenly it plummeted. The body took the ground in a shower of flying sparks, and continued burning, first in yellow flame, then in a low blue light as around a cinder, flickering to extinction, visible through the archways into the quadrangle of the mosque. Sir Iain Ogilvie called for flares to be brought along the parapet of the palace wall. As he waited, a low keening came from the crowd below, a rising sound of sorrow and fear. One by one the flares came up on the outer wall, flickering over the massed soldiers, striking fire from rifles and bayonets. In a strong, carrying voice Sir Iain spoke to the multitude below, using English and apparently hoping for the best.

"Your Mullah is dead, a flame has gone out forever. The British Raj lives on and is not weakened. There are armies upon the march from Rawalpindi. Inside these walls the garrison is strong, and will open fire upon my word, and you will die in the mouths of my gun batteries. I call upon you to disperse peacefully, without shedding your blood, in the name of Her Imperial Majesty the Queen-Empress." He turned and spoke over his shoulder to Lord Dornoch. "I fancy His Excellency may now hold his conference with the Maharajahs at his leisure, and settle the Russians' hash for good! But one more thing first, to set the seal. The pipes and drums, upon the walls, if you please."

The word was passed: without delay, the pipers and drummers were doubled up to be spread out along the parapet. The flares lit upon the kilts and tunics, upon the tartan of the Royal Strathspey on the pipe banners, upon the bonnets and hackles; air was blown into the bags and as the dummers beat out a tattoo the full muster of pipes sent the stirring strains of 'The Badge of Scotland' winging out over the city.